I0764626

IMAGES *of* *Silence*

D.S. Kirchen

This book is a work of fiction. Names, characters, places and incidents are either products of the author's imagination or used fictitiously. Any resemblance to actual events or locales or persons, living or dead, is entirely coincidental.

IMAGES OF SILENCE

Story edited by John Schroeder
Author photo by Cecillio Murillo

WGA Registration No. 66417

Library of Congress Cataloging-in-Publication Data available.

Printed in the United States of America

ISBN 978-0578086385
10 9 8 7 6 5 4 3 2 1
Second Edition (Hard Cover)

Creative EnDEBers
Publishing
www.CreativeEnDEBers.com

for Jack

Thank you, Christian, for remembering my abilities when I did not and for your loving help and guidance with this book.
Thank you, Mom, for coming through for me so many times, and thank you, Jeanne, for sharing my belief in magic.

IMAGES

Tormented survival resides here,
created by secrets
kept silent.

Distorted by boundaries set in fear,
life is stagnant
and violent.

And a spirit of youth endures the
pain and darkness
we see.

In the calm before the storm,
what is unacknowledged is
the key.

Picture an existence that illustrates
stifled
confinement,

With a door shut firmly on the
hope to secure
alignment.

And beyond,
is a child who can no longer be
innocent.

PROLOGUE

Dark, swirling clouds moved swiftly overhead. Against his instincts, the boy ran along the narrow lane in the cold night air, his bare feet making no sound as they pounded toward the dreaded place.

He had been there before.

Blurs of gray scenery whizzed by as he frantically rushed forward. His breath formed humid puffs in the chilly air. Shadows became discernable forms as he moved toward them, unable to restrain his steps. A light, noiseless snow began to fall and the air grew much colder.

Panic took over and he began to run even faster, rapidly closing the distance, wide-eyed with terror. One shape was completely visible now. It was a savagely crushed and damaged car. Desperation screamed soundlessly through his brain. He was almost there.

Everything stopped when he stumbled on something very cold, very wet, and very slippery. He recognized her as he fell into the mess. Rachel. Lying on the ground in a twisted and distorted mound of purple flesh. Her small angelic face was swollen and split open. Her hair was clotted with blood and brain tissue and clumped grotesquely to the sides of her head as her sightless eyes cast beseechingly upward, as if asking, "Why?"

Shocked, the boy tried to scream in horror, but all he could manage was a thin moan of anguish. He scrambled away from her and jumped to his feet to run away, but now he was heading toward the car.

He stumbled at the driver's side, catching himself roughly against the opened door. A woman's lifeless body toppled toward him. There was a black electrical cord wrapped around her neck, the flesh beneath it puffy and bruised. Her empty arms extended and he could see the perfect, parallel slashes that had drained her blood while the noose had cut off all oxygen.

The boy jumped away in terror. The woman's head flopped backwards, dangling over the edge of the car seat. Her blank, dead eyes stared up at her son, detached. Departed. Gone.

Slowly the sky grew light and the snow evaporated.

He was alone. The world was quiet and blank. Breathing became increasingly difficult until he was gasping, crying out for help. But no one could hear him. No one was there. Only he. Alone.

Silent...

BOOK ONE

THE SILENT ALONE

"...Sometimes you can see the quiet..."
– Dean Wilde

CHAPTER ONE
Trinity, California

I'd been driving a while – days, actually. After that much time alone in the tiny interior of my Scion *Xa*, it was quite a challenge to stay coherent. I was blasting Pink's most recent CD so that I could scream–sing along. At least when I was singing, I wasn't thinking about how lost and afraid I felt.

***

So much fear in the world.

There is something about the fear of wasting time and living a lost life. It's the ultimate tragedy. It comes from feeling too much pain, and the suspicion that more of it is just down the road. Your senses shut down to never be closely analyzed again. With practice, a behavior model emerges that is incredibly effective in destroying familial bonds, minimizing instances of personal joy, and equating to a lot of wasted time.

I snapped my mind back to the present. Typically, when I get philosophical, it's a bad sign.

"Save it for the manuscript, Amy," I advised myself. "You need to get out of the car and take a break, maybe settle in for the night." It was eleven a.m.

I was southbound on the narrow section of Highway 101, somewhere between Oregon and Northern California, and saw a sign for Trinity. I'd never heard of this town, but the junction would take me west and I wanted to get to the coast.

I zoned out again. When I returned to earth, I was staring glumly through the windshield, only peripherally aware of the ominous gray clouds overhead that were ready to burst into late September rain. My eyes indifferently surveyed the long wheat colored grass that bent in drifting waves with the cool autumn breeze. Something about the scene reminded me of childhood.

When I was young, I used to yearn to be a bird soaring above sights like this. Such a free and innocent spirit, and yet I'd refrained from taking risks at an early age. Even as a child I chose to be a spectator, not a partaker.

Even then, I had lived in fear.

"Fuck!" I griped, trying to distract myself from my inner voice with my outer one.

Well, I did live in fear then. I argued defensively from within. *And I still do. Back then, I was afraid of physical pain. Now, I fear emotional pain. But so what? We're all afraid of loss. Some of us are so afraid of losing someone we love to tragedy we simply shut everyone else out. And we live our lives as a shell... alone.*

"Oh Christ!"

Nice words for a young woman – no wonder I was single. But I was so sick of hearing this crap in my head. It seemed that fear had overpowered every aspect of my life. I couldn't get past it.

I looked down at my gas tank and my stomach clenched in, well yes, fear, again. I've always been afraid of running out of gas in an unfamiliar place such as this.

"Wherever it is."

***

I talk to myself a lot. That's what happens when you spend too much time alone.

When the sign for Trinity, California appeared, I was driving too fast to read the population, but it was a small number. I began to descend into a cove that contained a little fishing community. There were lots of houses dotting the hillsides, many with long unpaved driveways winding out of sight but eventually leading to the front door. The business area became visible as I turned off onto a road that led into town. I came to a gas station first. It was old and full–service only.

As the attendant approached, wearing a filthy blue coverall with Norman inscribed in red stitching over his left pec, my first impression of Trinity became rather uncomplimentary. It wasn't so much his looks that sent a chill down my spine, but the *look* in his eye as he leered at me. He was a couple of inches taller than I and had a solid build with broad shoulders. His otherwise plain face was distorted as much by the lusty gleam he directed at me as by the acne scars and permanent grimace etched in the lines around his mouth. I guessed his age to be in the late–thirties.

"Can I pump it?" he asked in the heaviest, backwoods Southern accent I can ever remember hearing. I thought of places where your brother could be your father *and* your uncle. But this was California. Did we have a backwoods?

I chose to reveal my disgust in my tone as I told him to fill the tank and stood aside watching him "pump it." I studied him, his movements. The fumes of gasoline intermingled with his stale body odor as he slowly and purposefully inserted the nozzle. I wondered if he had ever wanted to do anything else with his life. Did he have any dreams? Had he been a victim sometime in his life, causing a profound change in his thirst for adventure? Was he ever afraid, and now living a safe but worthless existence, the way I'd been trying to live for years? Or was he the town creep that everyone avoided, probably because he needed to bathe? Or... was he just plain evil, capable of violent murder and destruction.

With an involuntary shudder, I stopped myself from looking over my shoulder.

"There I go again!" I muttered to myself. Death. Life lost. Fear. They had become an obsession with me.

***

I fancy myself to be a writer and consider my habit of analyzing people to be part of the role. There are some defensive behaviors in people that I can see right through. Phony personalities really irritate me and tend to trigger a ruthless desire to find out what the person is hiding. I also am a true connoisseur of sarcasm and can easily anticipate a cutting remark long before it forms in a person's mind. Add this to all of my inner fears, and the result is the one–dimensional characters in my stories who are all a bunch of bitterly sarcastic goody–goodies, like me.

I'm not sure how I got this way. My childhood had been typical: I grew up in a decent neighborhood in a non–violent household, and like all of my friends, my parents went through a bitter divorce while I was in junior high. In my world, that had made me normal. Outside of the divorce, I'd had no experience with human malice, or irrational minds. But then I'd hit adulthood, and I'd been dodging some pretty awful characters ever since. My fear of my own gullibility had finally driven me away from my home in Los Angeles three weeks ago.

That, and grief.

***

"That'll be fifteen dollars 'n' fifty cent," the attendant told me. I handed him the money.

"Is there a store around here?" I asked him then squirmed as he made direct eye contact with me. "Someplace where I can get something to eat and maybe buy a souvenir?"

He moved his eyes to my breasts as he pointed a large grimy finger down the road in the direction I had already been traveling. I nodded my less than sincere thanks and got back into my car, aware of him watching me go as I drove slowly along the newly paved road. Moving on, I pushed my thoughts away from Mr. Creepy, instead rolling down the window to smell the fragrant ocean breeze. The air was crisp, and the darkened sky combined with the casual, seaside imagery of this little town suddenly had a definite appeal.

Maybe this is the place I've been searching for, after all, I thought.

***

It had been exactly three weeks ago today that I had taken flight from my home in Los Angeles. *I didn't even say good–bye to people,* I thought to myself. Not that I had a long list of friends. When you choose a life of security, you forfeit a social circle. My family knew I wanted to travel and would eventually nest in a quiet place for a few months to write. And, truthfully, they were far enough away to be unaware of what I was doing, or feeling, anyway.

They knew I'd seen my share of tragedy and drama and believed that time would heal the wounds. Yeah, time is great. It paves the way for the development of dysfunctional coping mechanisms. Mine manifested themselves in fantasies of adventure and heroic acts that lead to satisfying resolution, and also in the mass consumption of chocolate chip cookies. At the point that I'd decided to leave L.A., I'd pretty much had two choices:

suicide or radical and immediate change. I chose the latter. And who knew? Maybe I would find adventure, the good kind, here.

Or maybe I'd find another mess for myself.

"God damn it!" I complained out loud. I cuss a lot too, emphatically, and mostly in my head.

Drop it! I commanded myself. *That's your past now, and it can't be changed. The future is what's important. It's the only thing you* can *change. Get a grip. Your life depends on it!*

CHAPTER TWO
Transition

The general store had a ghost town appearance to it from the outside, but once I stepped inside, it was transformed into a very quaint all–purpose establishment. I could fill prescriptions, rent movies, sample locally grown organic fruits and vegetables, sign up for volunteer services, or buy a pack of gum. The diner style counter in the front section beckoned, so I immediately took a seat and opened the menu. Fish and chips, chowders, burgers, fries, shakes and malts. Perfect. I was hungry enough for one of each, but refrained, and settled for a burger, fries and soda.

The proprietor, a withered old man who winked kindly at me as he took my order, made me feel welcome. He brought my beverage, complete with a flexible straw, and set it with a shaking hand on the counter in front of me. I thanked him with one of my winning smiles and sipped it slowly, not wanting to finish it before my meal arrived. I watched the old man fry my hamburger on the griddle while my fries were sizzling in oil on the stovetop beside him.

"Do you have a restroom here?" I asked him, at once aware of how long I had been driving with a full bladder.

"It's just around that corner, dear," he said, shakily pointing the spatula in the general direction of the restroom.

***

By the time I returned, the food was ready. The old man was serving it up very carefully when another man approached the counter. I was crossing toward the second man, listening to his clipped words, spoken louder than necessary, as if he thought the old man was hard of hearing.

"I'm taking this bloody advert down from your notice board," the second man said with an obvious British accent. His tone suggested that there had been a failure to produce on the part of the old man.

"All right, Mr. Wilde, do as you please," the old man said patiently. "Where else will you advertise? This is the only place in Trinity that attracts both the locals and the ones passing through, except Lucky's Pub, and I'm pretty sure you don't want to advertise to *that* crowd."

"I'll be advertising in the San Francisco and Oakland local papers," Mr. Wilde answered with an exasperated sigh. Then he ran his hand through his long dark hair, drawing my attention to his features. He was very handsome. Perfect, actually.

He looked to be pushing forty, his thick dark hair only slightly peppered with gray as it lay naturally back upon his head, the way most people have to try to mousse and gel their own to do. The angular line of his jaw gave him a rugged strength, but the fineness of his nose and cheekbones added an almost aristocratic air to his appearance. He was a couple of inches over six feet, and had a lean, wiry body. His clothes were way too expensive and well tailored for this anonymous little town, and yet he obviously was a resident here. If not for his openly uptight quality, he could have been a model.

My writer's curiosity overpowered my reservation to interrupt their conversation, something I rarely do to uptight people.

"I couldn't help overhearing you," I said in my least intrusive, but friendliest voice, "but may I ask what it is you were advertising?"

Mr. Wilde turned a cursory glance my way, probably intending to make me shrivel, but I just steadily returned his look. He inclined his head and nodded once, saying condescendingly, "Excuse me, but we are having a private conversation–"

"I realize that," I deliberately interrupted him again, proud of my confidence. "The only reason I asked was because I am looking for a job." *I am?* I asked myself. Obviously, my mind had come to that conclusion without me. That would mean I'd be settling in this little California fish town.

The man called Mr. Wilde sighed rudely. "If you must know, I'm looking for someone to care for my son," he said tersely.

"Interesting choice of words," I muttered so that he could hear me. Then, "Oh? In what capacity?"

"As a governess, so to speak," Mr. Wilde informed me, his eyes narrowing suspiciously. "He doesn't need much supervision, but rather someone to take him to and from school, and to be responsible while I'm away."

"Oh?" I asked again, my curiosity slightly peaked. I needed some form of employment that allotted me plenty of time for my writing. "Is this a live–in situation, or an hourly?"

He was giving me his full attention now, as if suddenly aware that I might be a prospect. "It's a live–in position, six or seven days a week, depending upon my schedule," he answered me with a slightly more appropriate tone. "Do you have the credentials for such a position?"

"I have a teaching credential, if that's what you mean," I volunteered, deliberately obtuse.

He seemed aware that he was being toyed with. But he again inclined his head as he addressed me. "Perhaps we should have an interview," he said. "Would you care to meet me at my home after you've had your meal?"

I blinked to cover my trepidation. Interview? I looked at my burger and fries, waiting for my attention. "Sure, I think that can be arranged," I said, this time with more confidence than I felt. I wasn't certain what the source of my fear was at the moment, whether it was the thought of being interviewed, or being alone with this stranger. After the hell I'd been experiencing most recently in my life, I knew I had better make damn sure that I wasn't placing myself in danger. "Will I be meeting your son?" I asked.

His eyes had narrowed again, as if he had been reading my thoughts and was affronted by them.

"No, he won't be through with school yet," Mr. Wilde told me. "But you will have an opportunity to see first hand what your accommodations would be and I will have the opportunity to screen you for undesirable qualities."

My eyes widened at his last words, then I burst out laughing. "Me? Undesirable qualities? Unheard of!" I returned. I've often been told I have a beguiling charm.

He gave me a look of grim tolerance, then handed me a business card. "Take Trinity Road northbound to Brookshadow and head east. When you reach Wilde Lane, take it to my home. It's about a two mile stretch."

I took the card and said, "Okay, I'll head out that way in about thirty minutes." I looked down at my watch. It was 12:30 now. "Oh, and by the way, my name is Amy Stuart," I added, thinking he'd want to know. Mr. Wilde ignored me, as if my name was inconsequential, and left.

Hmm, I think I just found yet another one of the world's many pricks.

***

"What kind of person is this Mr. Wilde?" I asked the old man, who had put my food back on the grill to keep it warm.

"Oh, he fancy's himself to be a gentleman," the proprietor told me. "But no one here gives a damn." We both laughed as he put my plate on the counter for me. Already, I had the idea that if I did work for Mr. Wilde, I'd be required to keep an aloof perspective and not be looking for him to give an inch.

I turned the business card over in my hand and read aloud, "*Bryson Wilde, One Wilde Lane, Trinity, California, 1(800)–JK5–6566.*"

"Does he do much besides attempt to be a gentleman and name streets after himself?" I asked the old man.

"Oh, yes, dear. He's apparently been very successful at writing. Rumor has it he got his reputation early on as a reporter for one of the tabloids. Most of the people around here think he uses a pen name. No one I know has any idea what he writes."

"Does his wife work?" I asked.

"Oh, there's no wife in that house," he said in hushed tones. "A fellow I know made the mistake of asking about her and that Wilde character nearly bit poor Joe's head off! Said people ought to mind their own business."

"What does that mean?" I asked. Was he divorced? Widowed? Neither?

"Heck if I know, missy. He's not one to take up a conversation with, that's for sure."

"Hmm, I wonder what kind of employer he'd make?" I pondered out loud.

"One that doesn't want to be asked any questions," the old man replied.

***

After I ate, I headed back to my car and started to get in, then paused. I gave my appearance a cursory appraisal in the reflection of the driver's window. My height and dimpled grin were my most attractive features, I thought. At five feet eleven inches, one hundred sixty pounds (on a good day), I was satisfied, overall, with my build. My body image was fairly good, although I will admit that it could falter at times of insecurity. The light humidity in the air gave my brown hair more curl than usual, making it somewhat unruly, somewhat sexy. Not that I expected to use my sex appeal on this Mr. Wilde. He had given off no vibes of interest whatsoever.

I then glanced down at my attire and wondered if I might be better off changing into something else. After all, the low–riding stretch Levi's and thick black belt with my well–worn white T–shirt weren't exactly interview proper. Then I sneered in self–annoyance. *No, Amy, you don't need to impress him with better attire. You haven't got anything that's much better with you, anyway.*

That decided, I got in and hit the road.

CHAPTER THREE
Subtle Indicators

Mr. Wilde's directions were simple enough, and I found both Brookshadow and Wilde Lane without a problem. When the house appeared at the end of the lane, however, I started to feel strange. The building before me held a measure of some negative force, which left me feeling overwhelmed.

Besides, it was huge!

A two story gray brick building that looked more like a beautifully landscaped hotel, it resembled something out of *Architectural Digest.* I was intimidated, to say the least, by the obvious wealth of its owner. I pulled the car up into the immense circular drive that was paved with smooth gray and buff colored cobblestones, and parked.

***

He emerged from the front door, descending the steps to greet me. There was no welcome in the greeting, however. If anything, there was suspicion. Well, the feeling was mutual. I handed him my resume. He took it, eyeing my attire, as if speculating.

"Is this your typical mode of dress?" he asked pointedly.

"It is at the moment," I returned noncommittally. I let my direct stare into his blue eyes tell him that I would not be told how to dress. *His eyes are very blue, indeed, like sapphires,* I noticed. (One would have to have been color blind not to.)

"Will you follow me inside please?" he requested, unimpressed. I did.

We entered through the large front door into the vast entrance hall. I looked around. The entrance floor was tiled in brick red ceramic hexagons, with dark gray grouting. A broad staircase that wound with a flourish down from the second floor greeted us. It was carpeted in thick, tight gray shag, the kind that inspired a child to slide bumpily down it on her behind.

"This is lovely," I commented. *But cold.*

Mr. Wilde didn't acknowledge again, but led me through a smaller hallway that introduced a huge dining room, a breakfast room, sunroom, and kitchen. I fell behind, taking a moment to look in at each room. Each was decorated in a completely different motif. One would not know how to label Mr. Wilde's eclectic taste, except expensive.

He waited impatiently for me to follow him through the kitchen to the service porch area, and finally beyond, to a suite of rooms. "These would be your quarters," he stated, a bored look on his face.

I felt a smile curl the corner of my mouth. He was so God damned arrogant!

"Wow," I said sarcastically, as if I was not impressed. I was of course ready to take the job if only for the sake of these rooms. They were stark white; a bedroom and a sitting room. The walls were bare except for a selection of black and white prints, mostly photos of Paris.

"You're disappointed?" he challenged me unexpectedly.

My humble nature got the better of me. "No, actually, this would be a perfect set–up," I told him honestly.

"Set–up?" he queried.

"I'd hoped to secure a small space for myself that would enable me to write undisturbed," I informed him.

"You're a writer?" he asked in a tone of disbelief. Or was it disapproval?

My insecure nod prompted him to ask warily, "Ever been published?"

"Uh, a couple of short stories in small publications," I said unwillingly. This was not completely true. I'd had a novel out as well.

"What do you write?"

"Fiction," I said noncommittally again.

He laughed harshly, his lack of mirth intimidating me somewhat. "That's a rather broad territory," he said.

I already knew that my lack of confidence in my work was my worst enemy, but somehow men, simply by their nature, were never impressed to hear that I liked to write romance stories.

"I've written a couple of books," I admitted. "They were rejected by several publishers, but I'm currently working on a project that will either begin, or end, a career for me." There, I'd admitted it out loud to a snob.

"Well, good luck," he said insincerely, as if he thought me to be too green to be successful. Unfortunately, that was what I'd thought as well.

Refusing to be intimidated any further, I pressed on. "So, what about that interview? I thought you'd–"

"This is essentially what I had in mind," he informed me. "I wanted to see your reaction to this environment, and to know what you would be doing with the numerous free hours you will find that you have."

"Oh," I said, surprised. "So, what exactly will you require of me?"

"Essentially, you will be a presence in the household to provide supervision for my son while I am working, which is most of the time," Mr. Wilde said. "My son is very self–contained and keeps mostly to himself. You will be responsible for driving him to and from school, and getting him up in the mornings. I have strict rules about his bedtime and homework."

"How old is he?" it suddenly dawned on me to ask. I had been picturing a pre–schooler.

"He is nine years old."

"And you require a nanny for him?" I was careful to phrase my question with a tone of simple curiosity. At his frown I quickly tried to justify my asking. "I mean, he sounds so independent. Is he given to bouts of mischief?" I realized I was imitating his speech patterns, a terribly embarrassing habit, unfortunately.

"Dean is never openly defiant to me. He is much more subtle, Miss Stuart. You should be alert to his deceptively docile demeanor," Mr. Wilde warned. "My son takes great pleasure in deceiving those who are not keen enough to catch him at his game."

"But you catch him, I take it?" I asked, intrigued.

"Usually his victims bring things to my attention," he told me.

"Victims?" I repeated. How capable could a nine year old be?

"Most of his trouble occurs at school, Miss Stuart," he said. "His teacher is too compassionate for her own good. She would do better to apply strict discipline, rather than try to bond with Dean."

That comment sounded reminiscent of what the father of one of my own students had said to me. That particular child had been used to sell and deliver crack on the streets during school hours, I'd later found out. *After* he had died.

***

As usual, my gut wasn't telling me what to do. So, I let my curious side make my decision. "How much will you pay me?" I finally thought to ask.

"I'm offering six hundred a week, cash."

I felt my smile light up my face. Six hundred dollars a week, on top of free food and rent, was quite attractive to me. "Well, Mr. Wilde, I'm interested in the position," I declared.

"Then we'll move on to the next step," he said with reserved satisfaction.

He motioned for me to follow him. We retraced our path as far as the entrance hall. From there we took another, shorter hallway that had two doors. We entered through the first, which was apparently his office, or would that be called his study?

"Please have a seat," he said.

I took the chair he had indicated, which had been set in front of an enormous mahogany desk. He sat opposite me and fished through a drawer for some papers. He found the ones he needed and placed them on the surface of the desk, then folded his hands on them and looked over at me very sternly.

"As my employee," he said, "you will be expected to honor a certain ethic about your own personal life. I strongly discourage you from bringing it into my home."

"You mean my sex life?" I asked deliberately not using his chaste phrase. "I wouldn't dream of it!"

He gave me a withering look of barely controlled tolerance as he continued, "You will have some access to privileged information." He paused to make sure he had my attention. He did. "My work is very well known, but my life is completely private. The people in this community know very little about my writing, only that I am successful."

"I see," I said. He had to know I was dying to know what that pseudonym was. But I didn't ask.

"I have no intention of jeopardizing my security and privacy," he went on to say, "by employing anyone with any sort of questionable history. Further, I will expect that if your employment is terminated at any point, that you will continue to honor your commitment to protecting my privacy, and that of my family."

"I understand," I said in my most cooperative tone. Oh, the intrigue!

"I hope that you do, Miss Stuart, because before I officially hire you, you must sign this sworn statement, which attests that you will maintain the highest standards of propriety and authority with my son. In addition, you are to protect the integrity of this family by refusing to divulge information that could result in a compromise to my privacy. I will run a background check on you to confirm your resume and legal record." He glanced at his watch. "I have some standardized forms for you to fill out, with some personal information about yourself. Once you've completed them, you'll have about an hour to begin getting settled before you'll have to leave to get Dean." He rose to escort me out of the room.

"Wait!" I sputtered in amazement. "You want a complete stranger, whom your son has never met, to go pick him up?"

"That is correct," Mr. Wilde informed me with his impatient tone again, "and it is unacceptable to be late."

***

The "standardized" forms were more like an FBI investigation, for Christ's sake. He asked for my last four places of residence, my mother's maiden name, five references, and my credit history, my criminal history, my next of kin, marital status, and any addictions that I might have.

I admitted to shopping and chocolate.

***

An hour later I encountered Mr. Wilde in the entrance hall. He handed me a scrawled set of directions to Dean's school. "I still can't believe you'd send a stranger to pick up your son from school," I couldn't help persisting.

"Miss Stuart," he sighed with exasperation, "do you want this position or do you not?"

I shook my head and walked outside of the house to my car. This guy was so full of himself.

"Dean knows I am seeking a new governess for him, Miss Stuart," he called after me. "He'll be waiting for you."

"Whatever," I quipped under my breath, unimpressed. I got into my car and popped a new CD into the stereo. It was a compilation of recent pop hits. I deliberately rolled down my window and let the volume blare loudly as I shifted into gear and sped off. I don't know why I had agreed to try the job, since I obviously felt all–too–compelled to annoy my employer. But something about the feeling in the air told me that this was where I was supposed to be right now.

***

The tall trees lining Wilde Lane made a nice backdrop to my distracted imagination. I began to paint a picture in my mind of this young Dean Wilde as I drove along. He would probably be unpleasant and uptight, like his dad. Probably dark haired, and probably chubby and inactive. I then surmised that he would be tall for his age, and overindulged in all of the amenities available to man. He would be fashionably dressed and be carrying a cellular phone or one of those PDA's, with an attitude that I was an intruder in his space. A typical little rich kid, right?

***

The sky was still dark and ominous overhead when I reached Silverside Elementary. It was beautiful, for a public school. There was grass! A lot of it! Not a typical sight for anyone from most of the metropolitan areas of California. Clearly, this school district knew how to take care of school grounds.

The bell was just ringing, signifying the end of the school day. There was a wide circular drive that several cars were crowding into to pick up students. Boys and girls emerged almost instantaneously, an obvious dress code of collared shirts and slacks or skirts defining their attire. I scanned the crowd of children, looking for the ones that seemed to be about nine years old. There were several boys of that age group, but I knew that none was Dean. I looked for a boy with an attitude on his face. After another couple of moments, I spotted him.

I couldn't have been more off on my estimate of his appearance. He looked almost waif–like. He had huge eyes and long black lashes. His face was in similar character to his father's, equally shut down to an outsider's analysis, but those eyes told a thousand tales of pain. His brown hair grew thickly on his head, cut conservatively, with no particular emphasis on style. He was unbearably overdressed in gray slacks, crisp white shirt, sweater vest, blazer, *and* a bowtie. He had a small, lean body and broad shoulders that had an arrogant set to them. There was defiance in his demeanor, which suggested the confidence was a facade. I knew just from looking at him that it would be a challenge to be his caretaker. And probably one big pain in the ass.

Dean was scanning the crowd warily and spotted me shortly after I had completed my assessment of him. He seemed to know who I was as well, because he jumped down from the five–foot high wall that he had been perched on and started toward me, seemingly uncomfortable by my studying gaze.

I waited until he was within earshot. "Are you Dean Wilde?" I asked him.

"Yes," he said in a dull, unenthusiastic voice.

"I'm Amy Stuart," I told him, "I guess I'm here on approval to be your new governess." I held out my hand to him, but he didn't take it. I let my hand fall to my side. "Not impressed, huh?" I asked him with a raised eyebrow.

Dean's eyes shot up at me, his face taking on a pinched, annoyed appearance. "It doesn't matter if I'm impressed or not," he said coldly, "only that Father is."

"Well," I said without hiding my surprise at his arrogance, "I'm not sure that 'Father' is impressed either, but for the moment anyway, I'm the new governess." I put my hands on my hips and eyed him up and down.

Dean frowned up at me disdainfully, as if I was uncultured and ignorant. "Is there a problem?"

I could feel the amused smirk making its way to my face as I looked at this little shit. "So, tell me something, Master Wilde," I said, "which type of person would you like to have as a governess?"

Dean squinted his eyes as he regarded me warily, then said in his cold tone again, "I'd like someone who'd just mind their own bloody business and leave me the hell alone."

Strong words from such a babe. Glib, too.

"Oh?" I asked, as if he had just said something that I found delightfully interesting. Then I told him, "Hey, that sounds good to me, because I really don't feel like being a babysitter to an arrogant little brat." I paused for effect, giving him a challenging look. I silently marked a point scored for me as he took a step backwards. "On the other hand, I really like most children. If there's a nice person somewhere inside you, we just might become friends."

"I doubt it," Dean mumbled as I walked away from him and headed toward the passenger door of my car. I chirped the alarm before opening the door for him. Then I got in on my side. He sat silently next to me as I drove the car and sang along to the songs on the stereo.

"So your school is pretty nice," I said during the silence between songs. "I noticed everyone was dressed pretty conservatively. I used to wish the school I taught at would make the kids dress better."

I glanced over at Dean. He was staring straight ahead, but was aware he was being watched. He rolled his eyes in bored disdain. He was lucky I'd decided not to comment on the way *he* was dressed.

***

I pulled the car into the cobblestone drive and parked. Dean got out and slammed the door, making a hasty path toward the front steps. I was following at a more leisurely pace when the front door opened and Mr. Wilde emerged. Dean stopped short, his body stiff and his eyes cast downward, waiting for his father to address him.

But Bryson Wilde was eyeing me speculatively. "Well, Miss Stuart, you've met my son, what was your first impression of him?" he asked.

I regarded him carefully for a moment then looked at Dean, who continued to hang his head. Something told me that there was a cruel streak in the father that he was likely to vent on his son. I inclined my head, imitating the way he had done to me earlier in the day, as I informed him, "He's quite the little communicator, actually."

"Oh?" Mr. Wilde asked, clearly looking for a more explicit response from me.

"I find him to be delightfully independent, Mr. Wilde," I said, emphasizing the word delightfully. "Other than that, we will need some time to get to know each other."

"Are you indicating that you have no reservations about working with my son?"

"That is what I'm indicating," I said, mimicking his speech again. I glanced over at Dean, but he had averted his face completely so that I had no view of him whatsoever. He still stood in his tracks halfway up the wide stairway. He was very tense, silently waiting for the two adults to finish their discussion about him. "Are you indicating that I'm hired?" I asked Mr. Wilde.

"Unless the inquiry turns up something dreadful," Mr. Wilde replied. "You are free to finish settling into your quarters. Dean will go up to begin his studies. Dinner will be served at six o'clock."

I chuckled to myself as I headed back toward my car to get the last of my belongings. What a character this guy was, referring to my room as "quarters". He was living in a coastal fish town for Christ's sake, who the hell cared about propriety? And his kid was just like him, an arrogant little turd. I was going to enjoy breaking down that boy's defenses.

But not as much as I was going to enjoy my new freedom to write.

***

I made no detours in my escape from the tension I felt between those two, and headed back to my "quarters" with the last of my things. I had brought some of my stuff in after I'd finished Mr. Wilde's standardized inquiry. The extent of my personal belongings came to 2 duffle bags, 2 cardboard boxes, and my favorite knapsack that doubled as a purse. I opened up a box to begin unpacking. The box contained an assortment of CD's and cassettes to accompany the compact stereo unit buried beneath. Remembering my thoughts as I had sorted through the belongings I had taken with me when I left Los Angeles, I smiled. My rationale for taking every component of my music collection was quite simply that *music was more important than food.* I've always felt that way.

So, while the average person setting out to start a new life might have brought cookware or small pieces of furniture, I had brought my music, and every T–shirt and pair of jeans I had ever owned. I had held an impromptu "sidewalk sale" in front of my apartment building and sold all of my furniture, dishes, cookware, cutlery, knick–knacks, and a lot of my nicer clothing. To me, those items had represented an image that no longer worked for me, an image that had sputtered and passed out at my time of greatest need. I didn't want to be that powerless person any longer.

Looking around the room, I decided that the accommodations of this job were perfect. I was in the bedroom at the moment, which was a good size with three large windows. A queen–sized bed was set against onc wall, folded white sheets and an off–white down comforter sat on top of it for my use. I walked over to the window that overlooked the side of the estate. There was a wide paved driveway that led to the rear of the property, extending out of my line of vision. A twelve–foot hedge closed in the lot, obstructing my view of what lay beyond.

Curious, I went into the sitting room and took a look out of that window. Now I could see the backyard, which looked more like a resort. It was quite expansive, sectioned off with a gorgeous stone deck and pool on my left. There was a landscape lush with flowers and green grass flowing around the deck and a footpath which led further back to a guest house that looked to be as large as the house I'd grown up in. The right side of this "yard" had the rest of the paved drive that I had seen from the other window, which lead to a porte–cochère and large, six car garage. Over the garage were two separate apartments. I wondered if any of these guest facilities was occupied.

I stepped back from the window and admired the sitting room again. There was a long couch, television, and a computer set upon a good size desk. I wondered who the PC belonged to, and hoped I would be allowed to use it. My laptop was dying a slow death at present. The bathroom was just outside the sitting room, fully equipped with tub and shower, and towels already set out. Even the bathroom was stark white except for the black marbled toilet seat and sink basin.

The service porch had two other doors that I had wanted to investigate. One, I found led outside to the drive, the other to a staircase, which I assumed was a back way to the second floor. Satisfied that I had a sufficient image of at least this portion of the estate, I returned to my bedroom and proceeded to add my own personal touches to my new living space.

CHAPTER FOUR
Subtle Warnings

I left the dining room shaking my head, wondering if I should have agreed to work for this man. He was so arrogant and cold, basically a major dickhead. I was not used to being spoken to as if I was some form of lower class, peasant–like nobody who deserved little more than one's disdain.

Admittedly, I was somewhat intimidated by Mr. Wilde. Intellect is a very impressive quality, after all. And yet in spite of this, I suspected that like his son, his attitude was a front, at least to a certain extent. His was harder to see through though, because of his worldly and intelligent ways, the likes of which I had only thus far encountered in books. Oddly though, he lived here, in Trinity, hiding from the rest of the world. I was doubtful that he was happy; his son's demeanor was an obvious reflection of the untold reality. But what was the reality? And how hard should I try to find out?

Truthfully, I had little desire to find out.

I recounted the conversation that had taken place over dinner as I approached my rooms. "Most importantly," Mr. Wilde had very strongly emphasized, "my son is never to be left unattended." I was to know Dean's whereabouts at all times.

I sat down with a pad of paper and listed my duties: at six o'clock every morning I was to get Dean up. He was to shower and dress then be down in the kitchen by six–thirty. By this time, I should have prepared his breakfast and would then supervise his meal. He was to eat everything served to him and be ready to leave by seven o'clock. I would then drive him to school so that we would arrive by seven thirty. Dean would spend the hour that remained before school began studying his lessons in the school library.

I sighed, remembering Dean's unexpressive face at dinner. The boy had seemed to retreat into another world, shutting out as much of his surroundings as he could get away with. But, as I contemplated his profile, I could see etchings of unspoken grief and pain. His father had his life so programmed that he had to budget time to go to the bathroom. But when did he have any of his father's attention or time to spend with him?

Mr. Wilde had summed up the list of my duties by saying that I should pick Dean up at three o'clock sharp each day and bring him home to do his homework. The rest of the time I would be free to do as I pleased, as long as I knew where he was at all times. Dean, in the meantime, would complete his homework and then find something to occupy his time until dinner, which was once again always served at six o'clock sharp. Dean's bedtime was eight–thirty.

The household ran on a steady routine, which Mr. Wilde strongly discouraged any attempt to disrupt. He frequently left town for a variety of reasons, all apparently related to his writing. In his absence, the evening meal was to be prepared by the housekeeper, whom I had yet to meet. Weekends were likely to be open for me to take some free time, except again, when Mr. Wilde left town.

When he was home, apparently Mr. Wilde did the cooking. I did reflect, reluctantly, that our dinner had been incredible. There had been a delicate green salad, tender lamb chops with a peach chutney sauce that melted in my mouth, and linguini pasta with a pink salmon cream sauce that had taken my breath away. I was definitely a connoisseur of fine cooking and this man was a genius. When I had said as much to him, Bryson Wilde had been unreceptive to my compliments. But I refused to accept that he was not pleased that I had enjoyed the food.

I also managed to find out that there were other employees around on a daily basis. One was the *groundskeeper*. I prefer *gardener*, but once again this was a whole new world for me. Anyway, this guy tended to the yard work, and apparently was available for any assistance I might need around the house. The other regular employee was the housekeeper, who happened to be married to the groundskeeper, and was supposedly around on a daily basis as well. They lived in one of the apartments over the garage. I had yet to meet either her.

***

I had asked Mr. Wilde's permission to use the PC in my sitting room. Now I was free to use my time in the way I liked best. Needing a taste of the past, I fished out my old *Chicago's Greatest Hits* CD, put it on at a moderate volume, and sat down in front of the computer. The hard drive had both word processing programs that I frequently used. I had my notes for my story on disk and I was all set to work. I opened a new file to write a scene that had come to mind while I had been driving earlier today. Don't ask what had stimulated the thought, maybe the vibrations from the road. And don't laugh. With my sex life, anything is a form of stimulation. Anyway, I wrote.

He positioned himself above her, lowering his hips slowly until the tip of his organ found her opening...

I stopped writing and reread. *The tip of his organ?* I laughed out loud. Believe it or not, I have this need to avoid graphic language in my writing, which makes sexual description somewhat limited. Somehow the tip of his organ finding her opening did nothing for my lonely heart. If *I* was not impressed, my audience sure as hell wouldn't be! I tried again...

He moved over her, using his legs to open hers, to ready her to receive him. The hard thrust of his arousal met her welcoming body and he entered her quickly, grinding deeper within her–

What was that? My creative process was interrupted by a rustling sound outside my window. My heartbeat quickened as I turned wide eyes to the source of the noise, but beyond the glass I could only see darkness. I had the eerie sensation that I was being observed, and a familiar surge of hysteria threatened to overtake me.

Not again!

"Not fucking again!" I seethed through gritted teeth, using my stronger sense of fear to feed my struggling sense of anger.

I bolted out of the room to the service porch and threw open the side door. "Who the hell is out there?" I rasped, controlling my hysteria, just barely. I stepped down the three steep steps and turned toward the area in which I expected to find an intruder.

When I saw him I jumped, more from the anticipation of danger than the actual reality of it. I met the soft eyes of the biggest black hound dog I'd ever seen. He stood watching me, as if he could see the blush of embarrassment rise up my cheeks. He must be the watchdog, or maybe he belonged to the couple that worked for Mr. Wilde. I held out my hand, but he did not approach. He just stared at me.

***

After one full day of the Wilde household with its tightly run scheduling, I felt even more reluctant to continue working here, but was ironically too intrigued to leave. I had probably exchanged no more than a dozen words with Dean during the course of the daily routine. The same could be said for Mr. Wilde and me. I didn't like the idea of being part of a group of such withdrawn, shut down people! Of course, I tended to be withdrawn and shut down, as well. But I had a valid reason to be. Besides, I'm normal. What a hypocrite, eh?

I found myself waiting for an opportunity to interfere a little bit, to test the boundaries, so to speak. The most obvious target would be Dean. So far, he had been glum and silent in my presence, and there had not been much of an opening to strike up casual conversation with him, save for the drive to and from school. I had tried again to make conversation with him by asking about his class, but he had responded with such an unpleasant, disdainful tone, that I had cut him off in disgust, telling him to forget I'd asked.

***

Thursday night, I was walking in the upstairs hallway that led to Dean's small wing of a bedroom, study, and bathroom. I was contemplating checking on him, thinking maybe if I approached him when he was sleepy, he'd be more malleable, maybe even sweet. Right. He'd probably be whiney and crabby. Mr. Wilde found me pausing in thought outside Dean's door.

"Miss Stuart, I need to leave town tomorrow to see my publisher in London," he announced. "I'll be gone for several days. I'll leave some cash in an envelope for your use on the kitchen counter. I should return by next weekend. Goodnight, Miss Stuart." He turned to leave me.

"Goodnight," I responded quietly. I watched him go, still wondering if I should check on Dean. His door was closed and no light shone in the space beneath it. I decided to leave well enough alone.

***

Friday morning, I rose at six o'clock, dressed in shorts and sweatshirt before I went up to wake Dean. I tapped on the door and asked if he was awake. He responded coldly that he was. I refrained from telling him to change his tone with me, and instead went back downstairs and put on my jogging shoes. I made my way outdoors and began to run down the private lane to get my daily exercise. When I reached the end of the two–mile road, I turned around and headed back at a fast paced walk.

By the time I arrived back at the house, it was six forty–five and Dean was already waiting for me in the kitchen. I made no excuses for running late, as he greeted me with a hostile look. I just ignored the little shit and his arrogant attitude and pricey geek clothes and walked over to the pantry and removed a box of Cheerios. I got milk and juice from the refrigerator and set them on the booth table where Dean sat watching me with marked impatience. Pretending to be unaware that I was putting food before him that he was unaccustomed to eating before school, I deliberately did not speak to him as I went to a cabinet to get down bowls and glasses, then to a drawer for spoons.

Finally, I sat across from him on the opposite bench. He glared at me with cold eyes when he realized I was daring him to challenge me. "What's the matter?" I asked nonchalantly. "Have you got something against Cheerios?"

Dean's eyes narrowed in disdain. "Miss Stuart, I'm used to having a prepared breakfast."

I smiled tolerantly at him, despite the impulse to snap his little spine, and said, "My name is Amy, so cut that arrogant formality. And for your information, this *is* a prepared breakfast. I just went through the preparations while you sat on your spoiled butt watching me." I challenged him again with a deliberately raised eyebrow, but didn't give him time to respond. "Anyway, what's the point of stocking the pantry with cereal if no one's going to eat it?"

Obviously Mr. Wilde wanted to have every convenience at hand, including everything edible that one could think of, but was not inclined to make use of it. I watched Dean direct a sullen look to the bowl before him.

"Father wouldn't approve of this," he said as if I should be worried.

"Well, Father won't know what you don't tell him," I said sarcastically. That wasn't really fair of me to do, I know, but I had no intention of fixing something over the stove this morning. I watched Dean's unhappy face as he glowered at nothing in particular.

CHAPTER FIVE
Warnings

"Dean, do you have any friends?" I asked him during the drive to school. Silence.

"I'm not trying to insult you, I just wondered if you ever had anyone over to the house." I tried to explain.

"I prefer to be alone. Can't you get that into your stupid brain?" his snotty little mouth replied condescendingly.

That pissed me off. I pulled the car over with a screech, which surprised him. "Listen, mister," I said with real warning in my voice, "You'd better show me some respect starting right now!" I leaned closer, glaring threateningly into his pinched little face. "I am in charge of you whether you like it or not–"

"I don't," he declared gustily.

"Too bad! That's a shame," I said sarcastically. I wanted to smack his arrogant mouth. That was my upbringing getting the better of me. "I can teach a child to show respect the same way your father does. Is that what you want?" I held my breath, waiting.

"No."

"Then we should understand each other much better from now on."

I took a couple of calming breaths, keeping my eye on Dean as I warned myself not to make threats that I wouldn't follow through with.

***

I sat alone in the house for a while that morning, wondering where the housekeeper was. Then it occurred to me to look out the window at the garage apartments and I saw both her and her husband busily gardening in a little plot at the foot of their stairwell.

Snoop time. I wasn't going to do anything but take a stroll through the house, mind you. I have a very defined sense of personal boundaries that I never violate. But Mr. Wilde hadn't indicated that there were any rooms that were not to be disturbed, so I started with his office. I was mainly looking for photographs. There weren't any. In fact, there weren't any photographs in any of the rooms on the first floor. What the *hell?*

Didn't Dean even take a school portrait? There must be some pictures somewhere. I went upstairs and went over to the west wing, where there were some other bedrooms and sitting rooms. On one wall at the far end of the hallway were a series of photographs.

I walked over and stood before the display, wondering who was who here. There were several older photos of a young boy and then of a teenager. I assumed they were all of Mr. Wilde, although the hair color was lighter, more the shade of Dean's. Maybe Mr. Wilde was a Grecian Formula kind of guy.

There was one of a girl. She must be Mr. Wilde's sister, or something. There was a striking resemblance in her features to both him and Dean. The photograph was a black and white head shot, and difficult to assess for a date.

There was a picture of Mr. Wilde with a woman who was probably Dean's mother. They looked to be a very tense and distant couple. *They must be divorced,* I concluded.

And finally, there was a school portrait of darling Dean Wilde. The kid had the most morose look of displeasure on his face I've ever seen. What a happy household this was.

***

I pulled up to the front of the school that afternoon and saw Dean standing with a small woman. She was holding his hand, as if she expected him to flee. I watched as the woman shaded her eyes and looked out amongst the cars that gathered to collect the children. *I guess she's waiting to talk to his father,* I thought, and got out of the car.

"Hi, Dean," I called, letting my voice carry the expectation that I was about to hear he'd been in trouble again today.

The other woman looked at me in dismay. "Oh," she said, "are you Dean's governess?" I nodded, she sighed. "I'm sorry, I was hoping to speak with Mr. Wilde."

"He's left town for a week or so," I informed her. I happened to glance down at Dean and caught an expression of disbelief surface briefly, then disappear from his face. Obviously his father had not informed him that he'd be gone. *Cold hearted bastard!* "I'm Amy Stuart, I'll be staying on for a while. So, if there's a problem, I'm the one to inform," I said.

The woman introduced herself as Edna Carter and said that she was concerned about Dean. "He's so unpredictable," she told me. "Sometimes he's silent and sullen, and other times he's alert and interested, and still other times he looks like he's ready to burst into tears. He won't tell me what's bothering him, but clearly something is." She shook her head and smiled in reluctant amusement. "He certainly surprised me today with his new class clown image. He had the class is hysterics. I was speechless."

I allowed myself a smile in return, knowing that it had been my anger and parting comments to Dean this morning that had likely triggered the inappropriate behavior. But I also know what it's like to be a teacher who has a problem child in her classroom, and how frustrating the constant disruption can be. I had vowed to myself long ago that no child of mine would be that kind of a pain in anyone's ass. Dean wasn't my son, fortunately, but he was my responsibility.

"That would have surprised me too, Miss Carter," I said. I knelt down on one knee in front of Dean and took his chin in my hand. Looking at him in reproach, I told both boy and teacher, "I don't like the thought of you disrupting the class." Dean surprised me by looking down. He did not display the defiant disregard I was expecting.

Edna Carter hesitated then sighed. She lowered her voice as she said, "Frankly, Miss Stuart, I'm concerned that something's very wrong at home. That he's being mistreated."

"I can certainly understand your suspicion," I told her. "I also know that Mr. Wilde is concerned that you are too lenient with his son." She bristled defensively at that, but I continued as I stood back up, "I personally believe that children who act out are reacting to circumstances they can't control. Something is definitely unbalanced in his home environment, but at the moment, I'm not sure what it is." I held out my hand to her. As she took it I said, "Please continue to let me know when problems arise."

She thanked me in measured relief as I took Dean's hand and escorted him to my car. We drove in silence for a while before Dean quietly asked me if he was going to be punished. I kept my eyes on the road, wickedly letting my silence torture him for a few delicious moments before I finally answered.

"Well, that's certainly a consideration," I told him firmly. "But I'm more interested in finding out some things. How about a bargain?" I suggested. "I'll trade you the punishment for a little information."

"I'll take the punishment." That made me laugh. I was starting to feel sorry for him, and since I was not really angry with him, I had an urge to let him off the hook. I reached over and patted his knee. He jerked away, rigid with tension.

"Listen, turkey," I said, "I'm not like your dad. I think school should be fun sometimes. I just don't want you to be a brat to your teacher. She seems pretty nice." I glanced over at him and found him listening intently. I softened my tone, hoping to strike a chord of need in him. "But I'd like to understand why you are so unhappy. I haven't seen you smile once. You refuse to talk about anything. It's hard for me to punish a kid without making sure that he really deserves it. Something tells me you don't."

Dean was not swayed by my nice voice. Now I was even more determined to make a breakthrough with him. "Look, you take some time to think about all of those secrets you have."

"I don't have secrets!" his voice was shrill.

That silenced me for a second. "Baloney," I challenged him, deciding to push harder, "I can see them in your eyes. There must be something you can tell me that won't kill you."

"Or else?" he asked in a tightened voice.

I shrugged as if I hadn't a care in the world. Dean didn't answer back. He looked frightened, as if I had proposed something dreadful. I had a sudden, if only momentary, yearning to give him a hug, but refrained, for the sake of sanity.

***

"Dean!" I called up the back staircase, "come down for dinner!" My stomach growled impatiently for food. I hadn't eaten since noon and it was pushing seven o'clock. *Another rule broken,* I thought with glee.

There was no response, so I climbed the stairs and headed down the hall to Dean's rooms. I opened the door to his bedroom and entered uninvited. Dean was asleep on the bed, sprawled on his back, with arms outstretched as if in defeat. Well, at least that was my first impression. I tiptoed quietly over to him and looked down at his sleeping form. *Whoa! Are those real tears dampening his cheeks?* I stared in surprise for a moment, not sure what I wanted to do about this. My stomach clenched a little bit, as I realized my motives to find out information had actually been a form of some kind of torture to this strange little guy. On the other hand, now I knew Dean was fallible, and I knew how to take him down.

His eyes flew open, and the sudden cringe that brought his hands protectively to cover his face made me jump with a start. He let out a whining moan and then turned away, curling onto his side in the fetal position. I watched in bewilderment as he rocked himself back and forth, moaning in fright...and dread?

"Dean?" I said softly, "Have I really given you a reason to fear me like this?"

He stopped rocking and lay still. Then he demanded in an affronted shriek: "What are you doing up here? Get out! Get out!"

What in the hell is his problem? "It's way past dinner time, Dean," I said levelly. "I came to tell you to come down to eat."

I sat down on the bed beside him. He squirmed away. "Don't!" he shrieked.

"Don't what?" I asked, now really beginning to be affected by his behavior. Something was definitely wrong with this picture.

"Don't!" He yelled again.

I leaned across his side and braced my hand against the mattress. The movement must have made him think I meant to trap him. He kept cringing and moaning, jerking away from the touch of my hand on his arm. I moved my hand to his head and tried to stroke his hair.

"Don't! I'm not going to tell you anything!" he bawled out, losing control of the resurging tears he had been fighting.

"Okay," I said calmly, "you don't have to tell me anything."

"I don't want you to punish me," he said through his tears. He wrenched away from my touch again.

"I don't have any plans to, Dean," I told him honestly. "I had no idea that asking you to talk to me would be so hard for you." He didn't respond, but just lay tensely waiting to see what I'd do next. *Okay, now what the hell should I do?* This was one disturbed little kid. Common sense suggested bringing an end to the scene.

"Dean, you need to calm down," I advised. "Why don't you go splash some water on your face and wash your hands. Then we'll go eat dinner."

"I'm not hungry," he said flatly. Then, as if by Karma, his stomach growled loudly.

I chuckled. "Yeah, right," I said. "Come on, do as I say." I got up and stood aside waiting for him. "You'll feel better."

"I'm not allowed to eat dinner if I'm late to the table," he said, not moving.

"I'm late too, my dear," I told him. "Now come on, get your butt up and into the bathroom." Surprisingly, he did finally get up. I waited for him and then we went downstairs.

***

I thought a lot about Dean that night as I lay in bed. He had not wanted to watch TV with me and said good night after dinner. There was something creepy about the way he had acted earlier. God only knew what he had experienced in his life. He had obviously been attacked in bed in the past, probably by an irate Mr. Wilde. He must have been told not to talk about family problems as well. His parents must have had an ugly divorce. Still, I was very curious about the mother and where she might be just now.

***

The weekend passed. After two days at home with Master Dean, the recluse, I was getting philosophical again. He'd stayed hidden in his rooms both days. I'd taken another opportunity to write. I looked at the segment I had just written on the computer:

It's always fear. Always.

We fear consequences of risk, so we stay safe by not risking. But we're not really safe, and are silently grieving and yearning for more in life. Or, we do risk, but the consequences are far more severe than we had hoped, so we have regrets that taint us indefinitely.

Life...fear... What's the difference? Fear is everywhere, in every aspect of living. To live is to fear. Every decision we make is based on some level of fear. Fear of God. Fear of purgatory. Fear of consequence. Fear of pain. Fear of loneliness. Fear of failure. Fear of loss. Fear of dying. Fear of intimacy. Fear of heights.

Quite the happy camper, aren't I?

***

I did manage to get past the sex scene in my story. Suffice it to say that the guy did successfully get his organ into her opening and they both got off on it. But then what? It was too soon for them to fall in love. What about his fear of intimacy and her fear of infidelity?

CHAPTER SIX
Subliminal Warnings

I don't tend to be paranoid, but something about this house and the family that dwelled within it was just *off* (obviously). I mean, I'm not exactly the model specimen of a stable human being myself. I'm as dysfunctional as the next person. But the Wildes, now they were a different story altogether. I knew there was a multitude of twisted, unfathomable secrets stored in Dean's mind, as well as his father's. What I didn't know was how to find out what they were.

Dean was so shutdown and unapproachable. I'd thought he'd be the easy one to get information from, but no. Not that I was that curious. I certainly had enough of my own stuff to deal with. I had simply lumped the past several months before my flight from Los Angeles together in my brain and labeled them the "fear factor", not to be disturbed until further notice.

***

I saw that black dog again. He was watching me through my window, in the dark again, and scared the hell out of me again. This time I didn't go outside, instead making a mental note to ask Dean what his name was and who had taught him to peer through windows at single chicks working at their computers.

***

Mr. Wilde hadn't called at all while he was away, not even to let me know how to get hold of him.

What a devoted dad.

By the following Friday, I was ready for him to come home so that I could drill him with questions about his strange son. He had said he'd be back by this weekend, although he hadn't indicated which day.

On Friday night, I insisted that Dean and I drive into town and pick up a pizza for dinner. He didn't argue with me, but was not happy that we were doing this. I will give him some credit: his attitude had improved toward me significantly. Not that he was friendly, but just that he wasn't so rude.

We drove up to Lucci's Pizza Parlor, which was the last business on the short downtown strip, and parked in front. There was a parking lot on the far side of the building with a sign for Lucky's Pub parking. Apparently, there was an Irish pub adjacent to the pizza place. I tucked that little mental tidbit away for later as I led Dean inside the restaurant. About half of the tables were filled with customers. (I'd guessed this was the big Friday night crowd). I looked around at the pizzas set on pedestals on each of the nearby tables. They looked authentically prepared and smelled marvelous, the way I used to get them as a kid before Dominoes and Pizza Hut had changed the definition of good pizza. I ordered us a large pepperoni to go and guided Dean over to a table to wait for it.

"We shouldn't be here," he grumbled quietly, keeping his eyes down on the tabletop.

"Why not?" I asked.

"We just shouldn't."

"Would your father disapprove?" I asked, wondering why in the hell everything in this kid's life had to be a problem.

"He just doesn't like to give the town anything to gossip about," Dean admitted.

I smiled at him. "What are they going to say?" I asked naively. "That Mr. Wilde hired a new governess for his son? That they had the audacity to go out for pizza? Big deal!"

Dean just shook his head. "I get in trouble a lot," he said.

"Oh?" I asked. "You mean you're about to do something naughty that will embarrass him?"

Again he shook his head. I got the feeling he might actually admit something. *Something!* "I think he gets mad that people will see me and say, 'There's Dean Wilde. He's in my son's class and he's always in trouble'."

"Have you ever heard anyone say that?" I asked.

"No."

"Then how do you know they do?"

"I don't care what they say," he said firmly, a slight remnant of that attitude returning to his voice. "It's Father that cares."

A boy approached from behind Dean's seat. "Hey, Dean," he said.

Dean looked at me bug–eyed, seeming literally shocked that someone had spoken to him. He turned to face the boy. "Hi, Bill, uh what're you doing here?"

"I'm getting pizza to go with my mom. We're going to watch some old movie called *Close Encounters.* I think it's going to be boring because she let me pick whatever pizza I wanted." Bill suddenly looked uncomfortable, as if he'd just realized he'd compromised his reputation by talking to Dean. "Uh, well, I better go back to wait with her," he said nervously.

Dean stared after Bill's retreating figure for a minute before he turned back to me.

"He's in your class?" I asked.

"Yeah."

"Do you want to set up a play date?" I jumped at the chance to try to get some excitement into this kid's life.

"No!"

"Why not?"

He wouldn't answer me.

***

Saturday was unusually hot, about seventy–five degrees. I couldn't convince Dean to go for a swim with me, so I went alone. I stood on the deck, staring into the crystal blue heated water like I always do, waiting to work up the nerve to dive in without checking the temperature. My mind was a blank, and I was almost trance–like.

"So, you *don't* spend all of your time writing, I see," Mr. Wilde's voice startled the crap out of me.

"Ahh!" I yelped. Then I realized I was wearing my bikini in front of The King of Propriety, and could feel myself turning red. My figure had improved recently with my regular running, but I still felt self–conscious. "It was hot," I explained lamely. "I tried to get Dean to come in with me, but he refused."

Mr. Wilde, as usual, was disinterested. He also spared me the need to feel self–conscious by not even glancing at my body. He was impeccably dressed in a linen suit the color of which reminded me of the tall wheat grass that lined the roads I'd recently traveled. "Well," he said abruptly, "I'll leave you to it, then." He started to leave.

I trotted over to him, grabbing my T–shirt off the lawn chair and pulling it quickly on. "Mr. Wilde?" I called after him.

He turned back toward me. "Miss Stuart?"

"I'd like to ask you a question," I said.

"Then ask it."

I stepped another step closer to him and looked him calmly in the eye. "Why didn't you call to check up on your son this past week?" I asked directly.

He stared at me with a blank expression, not responding.

"What if something had happened to him?" I reasoned. "Wouldn't you have wanted to know? I didn't even have a number to reach you."

"There were ways to have gotten hold of me, Miss Stuart," he said icily, as if I had no right to want to know.

"What? Did I miss something?" I asked sarcastically, my irritation with his callous disregard of his son uncontrollable now. "You left no itinerary or phone number, Mr. Wilde."

"Perhaps not with you, Miss Stuart."

"What do you mean?" I was frowning at him now.

"I don't want just anyone to have access to me, Miss Stuart," he bit out between teeth gritted in impatience.

I blinked. So, in other words, the woman who cared for his son was not anyone. "You don't have a whole lot of regard for your son, do you?" I asked him in a low voice.

"Let me give you some advice, Miss Stuart, that you'd do well to follow," he said acidly. "Don't trouble yourself with details that do not pertain to your responsibilities."

Then he walked away.

***

"Mr. Wilde is very peculiar about privacy Miss Amy," Riba Regan, the housekeeper told me. I had finally tracked her down and asked her to explain the way things were around here. She had an accent, that I know was

English, but I had no idea from which region.

"But he trusts me enough to leave his son in my care."

Riba looked up at me sharply and interrupted. "Mr. Wilde trusts no one, not even my Simon or me," she said firmly, referring to her husband, the groundskeeper.

"But you said he always leaves his travel itinerary with you," I said in confusion.

"He leaves the itinerary, not the phone numbers, dear," she explained. "He travels under an assumed identity, you see."

"Then how would you get in touch with him in an emergency?" I demanded in exasperation.

"I have his friend Mr. Ryan's direct telephone number. He's never too far away, you see." I didn't see, but had heard enough. I began to wonder if I was working for a drug dealer or something.

***

Later in the afternoon, I trekked upstairs to see what Dean was doing. I found him in his playroom, seated at his desk.

"Hi," I interrupted his deep concentration. "What're you doing?"

Dean moved a notebook over his work, covering it from my view. He looked up at me resentfully. "I like to draw in private," he said icily.

Private. There was that word again. "Oh," I responded without reacting to his tone. "Is that what you're doing? Can I see?"

"No."

"Why not?" I demanded, somewhat hurt. "Is it something nasty?" I chuckled teasingly. I couldn't even imagine Dean drawing for pleasure, let alone creating something improper.

"No," his tone was cold and dangerous sounding (to the extent that a nine year old can sound dangerous).

"Please? Don't forget, I was a teacher. I've seen some pretty pathetic stuff, you know," I tried again.

"Mine's not pathetic," he informed me.

"Oh really?"

Dean sat staring at me for a moment, as if measuring my trustworthiness.

Then he moved the notebook aside so that I could look over his shoulder. He reached up and pulled down one of several leather bound books from a shelf over his desk and opened it. The pages were of plain white paper that contained his work. I couldn't believe what I saw. There were sketches of images, some inanimate and some of people. All of them were far more sophisticated than a nine–year–old should be capable of doing.

"My God, Dean," I breathed, looking up to find his face had softened with pleasure at my reaction. "You are one heck of an artist. Who taught you to draw?"

"My mother liked to draw," he said, a strange look coming over his face.

Opportunity! I jumped at it. "Dean," I said as carefully as I could, "I've been wanting to ask you about your mother–"

"She's dead," he interrupted me in sudden agitation. "We don't discuss it."

"Okay," I said easily. I had found out the answer to my main question, anyway.

I continued to look carefully at each page. One was of a tree; a perfect climbing tree. "Is this a real tree?" I asked.

"They all are real," he told me proudly. "I only draw what I've seen."

"You are truly gifted," I praised. "Who's this?"

"That's Albert Campbell," he answered, referring to my inquiry about a drawing of a boy. The detail was remarkable, from the creases in the boy's jeans to the dimple in his cheek as he grinned. Furthermore, the child was looking downward, casting his head to an angle, and Dean had been quite capable of creating appropriate dimension and perspective within the image.

"He looks like a fun guy," I said carefully. "Is he your friend?" Dean's face suddenly shut back down to its usual unapproachable self. He took the book from my hands.

CHAPTER SEVEN
Silent Interpretations

I had resolutely accepted the fact that my employer was an uptight asshole, and during the days that followed, avoided him at all costs. We encountered each other only during meals, which was fine with me. Monday and Tuesday passed without notable incident and I began to see a pattern in the routine while Mr. Wilde was at home. For example, I saw an awful lot of the Regans. They suddenly seemed to have an abundance of chores, and were present from dawn till dusk. They really did live in the "quarters" over the garage, I found out. I even saw them come and go a couple of times.

Another thing I noticed was that when Mr. Wilde was not locked up in his study, he made use of the many rooms on the first floor. There was a game room that was furnished in high tech black leather and chrome, fully equipped with large screen TV, stereo, VCR, DVD player, all with surround sound, an amazing assortment of movies and CD's, and a pool table. There was a sliding glass door that lead out to the deck by the pool, and I had spotted him through it on more than one occasion when I had gone out to swim again. The weather was cooling off, but the pool was still heated, so I was swimming every day.

And finally, Dean was even more morose and withdrawn with his father home than before. The way he dressed was the best indication of his mood. He wore no necktie with his school garb when his father was out of town, or keeping his distance from Dean. But when the tension got higher, simply by nature of proximity, Dean seemed to prefer the bowtie. He looked like such a poindexter in it. A true class nerd. I had started to secretly refer to the bowtie ensemble as his dork clothes.

And he was such a recluse. He rarely left his room, except to eat and go to school. I noticed that he didn't seem to snack on anything, only eating at mealtime.

***

On Wednesday afternoon, as I returned to the house with Dean after school, I asked him if he'd like to play catch with me. He just shook his head slowly.

"Why not?" I demanded. "It's a beautiful day! You might even have fun."

"I don't like to play."

"Do you know how?" I asked intuitively. Why should I assume anyone had bothered to teach him?

"Not really," he admitted. "I'm always the last one picked for teams at school."

"Maybe all you need is a little practice," I suggested. Then before he could argue, I threw in, "Wouldn't it be pretty cool if you caught the fly ball that saved the game?"

"I'll think about it," he said reluctantly.

"That's good enough," I agreed. I could tell I had made an impression. I looked over at him. He was so small for his age, and could stand to gain some muscle. He literally could almost qualify for the "failure to thrive" label, in my mind, as if his growth had been stunted by trauma.

Dean went up to his room and I went into the kitchen. I had spotted a bag of chocolate chips in the pantry several days ago and could no longer deny the temptation to bake. I made half of a batch of chocolate chip cookies, to be on the safe side. (I had no idea whether I'd be breaking some cardinal rule by doing this.) The cookie sheets were large enough for all of the dough, so I was finished within thirty minutes.

I put a few cookies on a plate and poured a glass of milk and took them upstairs to Dean. He was startled by my appearance, and looked at me as if I had lost my mind. "I thought you'd like a snack," I said. I handed the plate and glass to him and looked over his shoulder at his homework.

Dean sat holding the dishes as if he didn't know what to do with them. I ignored his reaction and started reading through the grammar worksheet he had been working on. All of his answers were correct and his writing was neat. "Good job," I told him. Then I backed away a few paces and folded my arms. "Why don't you try one? They're not poisoned, I promise," I said, referring to the cookies.

"No, they most certainly are not," Mr. Wilde said from behind me.

I spun around in surprise. I hadn't expected him to appear or to eat the cookies. But he was standing there with a stack of them in one hand while the other hand fed his mouth another bite. He was clearly enjoying them, although I couldn't tell you how I knew this. His face certainly still had his distant expression as usual, but somewhere in his eyes there was a glimmer of pleasure.

"This is a very unhealthy indulgence, Miss Stuart," he said, standing in the doorway in his expensively tailored gray slacks and black sweater. "I don't usually allow such atrocities in the house."

I looked at him in exasperation. "Then why do you have the ingredients on hand?" I asked somewhat defensively.

"Because I can resist the temptation to make them," he returned.

"They're pretty good aren't they?" I goaded, not taking offense at his comment. I don't think he'd intended for me to.

"Hmmm," he said, then gave a wave and left us. I noticed he had directed his comments to me only, as if Dean had not even been present. I looked at Dean. He still sat there, holding the plate and glass. Sighing, I took them from him and put them on his desk. "Eat," I ordered. "Enjoy." Then I reached out and ruffled his hair. Big mistake.

"Don't." he growled quietly.

"Sorry," I said quickly. Christ, he didn't seem to like any form of contact.

***

"Mr. Wilde?" I called softly through the door to the game room where he was sitting alone.

He glanced my way. "Yes, what is it?" he said, letting me know I was disturbing his solitude. Like father, like son.

"I'd like to ask you something about Dean," I began hesitantly. He looked at me with a warning, but I didn't heed it. "Is there something wrong with his health?" I asked.

"No, there is not." He said in his usual matter–of–fact way.

"I'm concerned that maybe there is," I tried again. "You see, he often has dark circles under his eyes, and he's never interested in eating. I've tried to encourage him to get some exercise, but the way he adamantly refuses has left me wondering if–"

"Miss Stuart, if the boy refuses to join in your activities, it is because he doesn't want to participate. I suggest you respect that."

"I'm wondering if perhaps he worries that you'll disapprove." I tried to explain.

He interrupted me again. "He might, and he might have a legitimate concern."

"Mr. Wilde," I let my anger come into my voice, "perhaps you will tell me, if there is anything that you *do* approve of him doing?"

"I approve of activities that do not disrupt the household or his schoolwork," he declared. "Now, if you'll excuse me, please?"

***

Thursday morning after I dropped Dean off at school, I went into town and bought a baseball and two gloves. My car needed gas, so I headed down the road to the station. The freaky attendant was there again, but this time he wasn't as obnoxious.

"Fill 'er up?" Norman asked, with the hick accent again. At my nod, he suggested, "Why don't you pop the hood for me so I can check yer oil?" He cleaned my windshields, inspected my wiper blades, and replaced the wiper fluid. And, he never leered inappropriately once. Maybe I had been a little hasty in judging him.

"Word has it that yer the new gal out at the Wilde place," he said conversationally.

"I'm the governess, yes," I agreed carefully.

"What's it like, working for Wilde?" he asked. "The last coupla gals left after a few days because he's so uptight."

"Did they?" I responded. I hadn't known that I had been hired to replace anyone.

"Yes indeedy, that's what I heard, anyway," he said. Then he looked over at me, as if expecting me to either confirm or deny Mr. Wilde's alleged nature.

"Well, I'm happy with the job," I said.

"They say yer from L.A.," he commented.

"That's true," I confirmed, wondering who "they" were.

"Why'd ya leave?" he asked. "I mean, ain't it a pretty happenin' place to live? Much more excitin' than here, I'll bet."

"That depends on what you'd consider to be exciting," I told him. "I wanted a break. Something more quiet."

***

I tried to get Dean to play catch with me both that afternoon and the following, but he refused. I tried to find Mr. Wilde to ask him if he'd disapprove of a game of catch between Dean and myself, but I couldn't find him. He also didn't appear for dinner on either night. I began to wonder if he was even home.

"Dean!" I called into the bedroom on Friday afternoon. "What kind of car does your dad drive?" I asked, thinking I would check the garage to see if the car was missing.

"He has a Jaguar and a Range Rover," Dean told me reluctantly, as if he was divulging confidential information. "Why?"

"Let's go see if one of them is missing. Maybe your dad left town again."

"No, he hasn't gone anywhere. He's probably locked himself in his study to make a deadline," Dean said, disinterested.

"Well, if he doesn't show up for dinner tonight, we're going for pizza again," I told Dean. He just gave me a look of dread.

***

We went for pizza, unbeknownst to Mr. Wilde. He apparently couldn't tear himself away from his work to notice. I guess the rules about meals only applied when he wanted them to. That did not mean that there was no dinner, of course. I chose not to notice the whole roasted chicken and vegetables that Mrs. Regan had prepared for dinner, just wrapping them in cellophane and depositing them in the fridge.

***

It was late. There was nothing on TV, I was having a writer's block, and I was restless. I decided to go peer into the pantry for a distraction. The kitchen lights were out, as I'd left them, but another light was on somewhere, because it was casting a low glow down the hallway. I padded on stocking feet over to the doorway and looked down the hall. The light in the game room was on. *Who left that on?* I wondered.

I started to trot on the polished wood floor and felt the soles of my socks slide over the sleek surface. Temptation overtook caution as I ran a few paces and then slipped precariously over the final stretch of floor, only to come to an embarrassed and abrupt halt in the doorway.

Mr. Wilde sat, facing away from me, seemingly unaware of my appearance. His profile looked uncharacteristically bleak and bleary–eyed. I walked into the room and saw the silver flask clasped in his hand – just too classy of a guy to drink straight from the bottle. He still didn't acknowledge me, probably wasn't yet aware of my presence.

So, I looked at him for a bit longer. His face was pale beneath a growth of beard that must have been a couple of days old. His body was slumped on the couch, and he looked exhausted. That's about the time I noticed that he was wearing jeans and was barefoot. This was too much to take in without comment, I'm afraid.

"Wow," I said.

He jumped then turned his gaze slowly toward me, not really focusing on me. *He must be drunk,* I thought. "I've never seen you in such casual attire," I continued with deliberate lightness. "You look almost approachable."

"Well, don't let appearances deceive you, Miss Stuart," his crisp voice responded. He wasn't drunk.

I stood there looking down at him for a moment, while he ignored me. The man was truly handsome. The whiskers gave him some very real appeal, I realized. Dangerous. *No, Amy, he's not your type.* I acknowledged my thoughts, but even they could not deny the fact that at the moment, something was obviously wrong in this man's life. Maybe he needed someone to talk to. I glanced around and spotted an ottoman. I slid it over toward him and sat down on it.

"You look like you've been through the ringer," I commented, hoping he wouldn't bite my head off just yet. He didn't say anything, but his look did not reveal any appreciation for my efforts to make contact.

"Mr. Wilde," I tried again, "I know you're a very private person, and I am a mere employee–"

"Miss Stuart," he interrupted me, then closed his eyes. He ran long fingers through his dark hair and sighed in exasperation. Then he opened his eyes and stared heavily at me. "I've received some bad news," he revealed. "I'm afraid I'll need to leave town again immediately, and I'll be gone at least two weeks."

I just looked back at him with raised eyebrows. I wished I could say something to encourage him to trust me with his thoughts, but I couldn't. Truthfully, I didn't want to endure anymore of his belittling ridicule. He must have read my mind.

"There is a sense of stability about you that is reassuring," he admitted in a tone that was almost kind. "And that quality is one that a person should want in a friend..." his words drifted off. Then he seemed to give himself a mental shake and met my eyes with his crisp blue ones. "It will ease my burden significantly knowing that my son is safe in your care."

I smiled, surprised and warmed by his honesty. "I'm glad, and if there is any other way I can help, I want to," I said. He nodded to acknowledge my offer, but clearly had no intention of taking me up on it. "When will you leave?" I asked.

He looked at his watch. "In about an hour."

CHAPTER EIGHT
Measured Façade

Things began to change subtly during those two weeks that Mr. Wilde was gone. I began to let the diligent adherence to the routine weaken just a little bit, but only on the weekends. The very slight relief that this seemed to bring for Dean was encouragement enough to risk the patriarch's wrath upon his return. I got him to come out in the mornings and run with me. We'd slow to a walk when he was out of breath then start up again. I explained that this was how he could gain stamina, and get his body stronger. The idea seemed to appeal to Dean, and he visibly pushed himself. I was impressed.

As usual, I had little idea when Mr. Wilde would return or where he'd gone. And, as usual, he had left an envelope of cash on the kitchen counter with "Miss Stuart" scrawled arrogantly across the front. I couldn't think of anything to spend it on, so I left it where it was.

***

On Wednesday afternoon of the first week, I arrived at Dean's school and found him talking to Bill and another boy their age. I got out of the car and approached them, fascinated at the sight of Dean socializing. He introduced me to the other boy, whose name was Todd. Both were in his class and both were on the school's junior league baseball team. Perfect.

"Why don't we plan for you boys to come over this weekend and hang out at the house?" I offered. Dean grew measurably tense.

I watched Bill and Todd exchange a look, then kind of shrug. Hmmm.

"I think I can come over," Bill answered me.

"I know I can," Todd said. "My sister is planning her wedding. They don't want me around because I keep complaining about all the fluffy bride stuff she brings home.

"Then I'll set things up with your mothers," I said, totally proud of myself.

***

Overall, we had a great weekend. I wanted to monitor the vibe between

Dean and his new friends closely, to make sure they weren't going to be cruel to him ...or vice versa. I lead a team effort to get Dean started with learning the motor skills required for playing baseball. He didn't know how to throw *or* catch. Fortunately, with some strong encouragement from me, Bill and Todd were not openly inclined to make fun of him. Thank God.

I suggested a challenge to them to make it their goal to turn Dean into their star infielder. They accepted. They spent all of Saturday in the front yard, working with him, and every time I checked on them, they were actively playing together. And Dean looked happy.

I made spaghetti and garlic bread for dinner, and a big chocolate cake for dessert. Dean seemed to be in his element with these other kids. He held his own, and the three of them had a blast. Like normal children should. So far so good.

***

I took Mr. Wilde's Range Rover and drove the boys home late Sunday morning, in time for their AYSO soccer game.

"Thank you," Dean said to me on the way back. "We had so much fun." He was smiling. I think that was the first smile I'd ever seen from that kid. It transformed him.

***

I turned on the stereo and flipped to the local classic rock station. Don Henley's *End of the Innocence* was playing. Dean reached over and turned the volume up. I looked over at him, impressed that he liked the song. He was sitting with his head against the seat, eyes cast longingly out the window, watching the passing scenery. My favorite artist's voice sang on, his words touching this young boy at my side in ways of which I had no comprehension.

"...Offer up your best defense. This is the end of the innocence..."

I had no doubts that Dean's innocence had been tampered with, but I had not yet determined to what extent.

***

"Let's not go back home yet," I said spontaneously to Dean as we drove.

He looked over at me. "What will we do?" he asked. He was game for anything.

"Let's go down to the ocean and watch the water for a while, and then get some chowder," I suggested.

***

The chill wind blew through our hair. We sat on big boulders, well out of reach of the raging waves.

"I like the sounds here," Dean said. "It's like quiet noise."

"I know what you mean," I told him.

***

"Amy?" he asked me as we drove home. "What's the scariest thing, to you?"

That's an odd question, rather out of the blue. Maybe the boys had been talking about it late last night, after the lights had been turned out. I came out of my reverie and answered him.

"When I'm alone and someone's there, watching me, maybe waiting to hurt me," I told him in all honesty.

I glanced over at him. He gave me the strangest look.

***

Monday night, late, I finally gave up on accomplishing anything at the computer. Anyway, I'd been having that feeling that there were eyes watching me through the window again. Knowing it was that big black dog, I decided to beat him at his own game. I darted out of my room and out the service porch door, stomping bare feet down the three steps and landing in a warm, slimy puddle of something I couldn't identify by foot sensory alone. I looked down at my feet. I was standing in a pile of cat intestines. I knew they were cat intestines because the cat they belonged to lay curled around them.

How can I describe my reaction? I freaked! I'm not a screamer, but I did let out some kind of primal moan of disgust and despair. Then I stepped out of the gut pile and walked the few feet to the area below my window. The light cast from the ceiling fixture indoors revealed that no one (or thing) was there anymore. But I knew something *had* been.

I was gasping and mumbling to myself, not knowing what to do. I moved back toward the cat carcass, and bent down to peer closely at it. There were no wounds, other than the slit in its belly. It hadn't been killed by another animal then! It had been murdered in cold blood. *Uh oh... Who the hell did this?*

Feeling shaky with fear, I walked slowly over to the hose and sprayed the gunk off of my feet, then tiptoed carefully around the carcass to get back inside. I grabbed a couple of plastic garbage bags and a ratty looking broom and went back out to clean up. This time I switched on the floodlight. I placed the cat's remains in a double plastic bag and then into a trashcan nearby. Then I scrubbed the pavement with the broom and water from the hose. As I finished, I looked up at the second floor and saw Dean, watching me through the window. His expression was unmoved. For the slightest moment I had the sensation that I was looking at Damien Thorn. An omen?

***

"It was Dean! He's got a cruel streak in him, he does!" Mrs. Regan balled to me when I told her about the cat. It had been her pet.

I was appalled. How could she accuse a nine-year-old of such brutality? I scared myself, though, as I momentarily contemplated the likelihood of Dean having done the killing. He *had* been watching me clean up the remains.

No way. My gut kicked in its conviction. Dean had definite emotional problems, but he wouldn't have done this. "Mrs. Regan," I said calmly, reasonably. "Please calm down, I think you're getting a bit carried away."

"Then who else?" she wailed. "I have no enemies! My Penelope was an angel."

"Maybe it wasn't an enemy of *yours,*" I said unexpectedly. Where had *that* come from? I certainly was not the type to look for evil where it did not exist.

***

"Miss Stuart!"

Yes Master? "Mr. Wilde?" I turned to face him in the kitchen, leaving the things I had placed on the counter for a moment.

"What is this about the Regans' Penelope?"

"All I can tell you is that I stepped in its remains." I said sarcastically. Then I suddenly had the urge to burst into tears. I averted my face and blinked quickly.

"Miss Stuart? Are you all right?" His voice was almost gentle, but not quite, as if he didn't really want an answer.

I cleared my throat. "I'm fine, Mr. Wilde. I simply hope that you are not giving Mrs. Regan's accusation any real consideration."

"Her accusation?" he asked. He apparently didn't know what I meant.

"That Dean was responsible," I said carefully.

He sighed. "Why would she think that, do you suppose?"

"He's a weird kid," I said dismissively, not acknowledging the way my employer's posture went tense at my words. "But he's very gentle. He's not capable of such cruelty."

"I'm not sure I can agree."

"Why not?" I was getting pissed on Dean's behalf.

He gave me a warning look through squinted eyes. Then he seemed to reconsider whatever he was about to suggest. "You've become protective of the lad, haven't you?"

"I have," I agreed, a smile of realization spreading across my face.

"That's both reassuring and disturbing."

CHAPTER NINE
The Fear Factor

It was Tuesday night when I looked out the window at the crisp twilight sky. I could see stars, and I felt at ease and very much in the mood for socializing. And for some reason, I had the yearning for a cold beer in a sports bar setting.

What the hell.

I waited until Dean was in bed, told Mr. Wilde I'd be back in a couple of hours then I went for it.

***

Sometime around nine o'clock, I sat at the bar in Lucky's Pub sipping a cold beer. It was immediately obvious that I was a spectacle of some sort as the manly men shifted around in their seats and tried to surreptitiously glance my way. I guessed my status as the governess at the Wilde house gave me some stretch of dignity, which prohibited their approach. Good. I suddenly didn't want any of their attention, just the change of scene.

Some dude walked in about twenty minutes into my first and only drink and took the stool that was next to mine. I eavesdropped on his conversation with the guy on the other side as he talked about a fight he'd had in this same bar the previous night. He was slurring his words, already drunk.

What a loser, I thought sarcastically to myself. *Get a life.*

The guy he was talking to must have thought the same thing. I heard him say something about not letting his friend's ass get kicked without retaliation. Then the next thing I knew, both men were flying my way, literally airborne, arms flailing, and spit spraying.

I felt the rush of air from their bodies as they whipped past me, falling against a table and then onto the floor. Two guys ran over and grabbed them, pulling them apart and then escorted them out of the bar.

Another man, with dark skin and eyes came over to me, and asked politely, "Are you okay?"

"Yeah," I said, letting my disgust sound loudly in my response.

He chuckled good naturedly. "Where I'm from, this is quite common," he said.

"And where is that?" I asked, although I could already guess.

"The island of Maui," he told me.

One of my very favorite places. His name was Chester, and he had come over to the mainland to surf and fish, and to try to make a living at either. He told me to stop by and see him at the docks in the late mornings, and he'd sell me some of his fresh catch of the day. I got good vibes from him, like he'd be a good connection to the community for me.

***

I've found that the best remedy for an unexpected upsurge of adrenaline is a snack. So when I got home, I headed out to the kitchen. Mr. Wilde was there, fiddling with something. I started to address him, then stopped. He had his back to me while he faced the butcher block section of the counter top, where the knife sets were.

He was counting them.

I stood, in silent observation, thinking that he was unaware of my presence. He wasn't.

"Why do you stand there, staring?" he asked abruptly, keeping his back to me.

Oh!

"I'm just wondering what you're doing," I told him. "Why are you counting the knives?"

"I like everything to be in order, Miss Stuart," he said testily.

Okay...

***

Something just didn't jive about his response, though, and it bugged me before I went to sleep, and when I woke up the next morning. I was getting a bit sick of the elusive way that nothing I asked was ever given a direct response. I needed a resource of information. I thought perhaps the townspeople could offer some guidance here.

***

I dropped Dean off at school and then decided to go look for Chester at the dock. I found him cleaning the day's catch of fish. I kept my eyes focused on him, ignoring the piles of fish heads and guts surrounding his work area.

"Hey, Amy," he said, giving a nod of greeting. "Seen any good bar fights lately?"

"Not today," I told him.

"So you're working for the recluse, yeah? That one, Mr. Wilde?" Chester asked. "I heard he was one weirdo."

"He is," I agreed, chuckling. It felt good to say that out loud. I hadn't shared my feelings about the Wilde's with anyone, except Dean's teacher that first time I'd met her. I remembered the confidentiality agreement and had a moment of panic that voicing such an opinion about Mr. Wilde had been a breach. I was going to have to watch my loose tongue if I wanted to stay employed.

"What's that all about?" Chester asked me.

I liked the way he talked. Sort of *da–kine,* island style. I had lived in Hawaii for a time, in my past.

"I haven't the slightest," I told him as I sat down on a crate that looked fairly fish–free. I knew there had to be a reason for Mr. Wilde's behavior but so far, I had gotten nowhere with my quest for explanations.

"You know, in Hawaii, people make the *hei'au.* They are little towers of lava rocks made as a spiritual demonstration of faith and prayer; an offering to the gods for guidance, you know? Some of the more bitter locals call it a bunch of *waha nui.* You know, bullshit. But I believe sometimes the answer comes from within. You may already know the truth, or at least how to find it," Chester told me wisely.

Hmmm. Helpful.

***

I picked Dean up from school. By now he knew where I kept my CD's for my stereo, and he pulled out the Don Henley one. We'd been listening to this album while we drove all week. He put it into the player and forwarded it to *The Heart of the Matter.* I loved that song most of all, so I sang along as we drove. Dean kept his eyes closed, listening intently. When it was over he advanced to *End of the Innocence.* I let my own thoughts drift off for a moment, remembering my own loss of innocence. I had at least been in love, but as with so many of us it hadn't been what I'd hoped.

I looked over at Dean, wondering what his life would bring to him in the love department. Poor thing, he wasn't exactly on a road to happiness. I watched him listen to the music. He had a frown of intense concentration for the duration of the song. I refrained from singing, not wanting to disrupt his thoughts– or break any sound barriers.

"What does *innocence* mean?" he asked.

"It means you've done nothing wrong, and that you don't know better," I said, not sure if that would make sense to him.

"What's *your best defense?*" he asked next.

I thought. "Well, I think the song is about a lot of different ways to lose your innocence, like when two people who are going to make love. The best defense for them is protecting themselves from the consequences..." *like a broken heart...* I drifted off. I had no idea how much Dean knew about sex, and I wasn't about to give him an explanation without his father's consent.

"What can happen?" he asked, fortunately not asking the question about mechanics that I didn't want to answer. But we weren't out of the woods yet.

"Well," I said, slowly, "you can make a baby."

"Not homo's," he surprised me by saying. "Homo's can't make babies."

"That's true," I said, careful to keep my expression and tone casual.

"I think I'm a homo," Dean said suddenly.

"Really?" I asked, as if he'd just told me he preferred vanilla to chocolate. "Why do you think that?"

"I just do," he told me.

"Do you have special feelings for a boy you know?" I asked evenly.

"Sometimes," he revealed.

There were a million things that I wanted to say. I wanted to say something about the normalcy of *any* feelings he may have for *anyone*, especially another boy. I wanted say something to reassure him that he was special no matter what sexual identification he had. I wanted to say something to tell him that I suspected he might simply envied this other boy, probably because the boy seemed to have something that Dean didn't, something that he longed for. But then, what if he really *knew* this about himself already? I wanted to say something to tell him that he was still innocent. But I really didn't know what Dean knew. And I also didn't want him to take any negative connotation from my words. So I said nothing, and hoped that I had not overlooked a need for reassurance.

***

I thought a lot about my young charge over the next several days. He needed so much, but he was so guarded. I knew I could help him, but I had my own reasons for not wanting to get too involved with him. His father was a weirdo, just like Chester had said, and I didn't know how long I'd be willing to work for him.

But Dean was a special case.

Still, I'd given up on working with children when I'd given up teaching, and for good reasons. At thirty–one, I was frequently worrying about the fact that I'd not found someone to settle down with, and that I'd failed at a career at which I thought I'd excel. I loved children. But when they aren't your own, the frustration of watching them suffer because of their circumstances at home was too damned much. As a teacher, I'd been in that position so frequently. At least with the inner city kids, I was able to make myself available to them to fill in the gaps that their parents left. But the neighborhood violence and gang problems overrode any progress I'd made.

And so one day, one particularly horrible day, I'd faced the truth: I'd lost.

I'd lost, big time, with that job. I'd lost a piece of my heart, and a piece of my soul. I'd almost lost my will to live, as well. And it had been the catapult that had sent me on my way. And now I had managed to get back into a situation where my heart was on the line again with a little kid! I knew my maternal instincts were trying to surge through, and if I let them, I'd be hooked, and then I'd find myself giving everything I could to Dean, and not giving anything to myself. No matter what, I couldn't let Dean come to matter so much to me that he could destroy me by impeding my progress toward a better place in this world.

***

We all have our secrets. Some are very much in our conscious mind and they torture us regularly. And some secrets chose to hide out in the unconscious, and some of those come out in self–destructive ways. I was well aware of my burdens. They were right in the forefront of my mind, and they tortured me daily. I kept them to myself and I tried to hide my fear. Truly, I hoped that this removed location that I'd found for myself would keep me safe from the pain of those secrets and the fear they aroused in me.

And I didn't even let myself wonder if anything else could happen to me, to add to my burden.

CHAPTER TEN
Conflict

The next afternoon, when I arrived at Dean's school, he wasn't out in front waiting for me.

Great. He must have gotten in trouble, I immediately decided.

I saw Bill and waved at him. He came up to me with a skeptical look. "Is Dean in big trouble at home or something?" he asked. "He didn't want to play today. He said he didn't know how."

"He did?" I asked. That sounded strange. But then, Dean was.

Bill told me Dean was sitting by himself on the benches beside the baseball diamond. I made my way over to him and sat beside him. The sky overhead was full of low clouds. An evening fog was setting in a little too early for my taste.

"Did you have a bad day?" I asked.

He jumped, as if he'd not even been aware of my approach. He gave me a startled look. "What?" he asked defensively, as if I'd just accused him of something.

"That's what I want to know, turkey," I answered. "What? What's up inside that brain of yours?"

He frowned at me, not answering.

"Why are you over here, instead of out in front?" I asked him.

"I don't know," he said sullenly.

Something was wrong here, but I was clueless. "Maybe I should have a chat with your teacher," I suggested, not really meaning for that to sound like a threat, but he took it that way.

"I didn't do anything!" Dean bawled out. Then he sat very erect, his face pinched, glaring off in the distance.

***

"He was off on another planet today," Miss Carter told me as she wearily gathered her things to leave. I remembered that kind of exhaustion from teaching and it hadn't been worth the payoff, unfortunately. We could see Dean where he still sat, through his classroom window. He seemed to be in a daze.

"Did he get in trouble, or do poorly on his assignments?" I asked, wishing someone would give me a straight answer here.

"No, I don't know what was bugging him today. He's been doing a little better overall since you've been with him, though. I haven't seen him like this in a while," she told me.

That sounded nice, but it still didn't answer my question.

***

I went out and took Dean by the hand, gently drawing him toward the car. I decided careful indulgence was my best approach here, and proceeded accordingly.

To cover the silence while we were driving, I put on a CD of old top forty hits from about a year ago. I looked up at the sky through the windshield. Above the fog, new storm clouds were moving in and were ominous and gray. Dean's dull funk mirrored the mood the sky bespoke.

***

When we reached the kitchen, I asked Dean if he wanted some cocoa. He said he didn't.

"I think you should stay downstairs with me for a bit," I told him. "I want your company, and I want to make sure you're all right."

He gave me a withering look. The first in quite a while. I responded by taking a dramatic step back, as if he'd struck me. He was unmoved. I pointed to the booth and said, "Sit."

He did. I made us some tea and found some butter cookies in the pantry and made a little plate of them. Then I sliced an apple and some cheese. Dean waited in the booth, oblivious.

I sat across the table from him and stared at him, trying to think about what he'd confided in the past that I could associate with his mood.... *Think, Amy...what might have happened today to set him off like this?* I remembered his comment about his suspicions of being a homosexual.

"Was somebody mean to you today?" I asked.

He raised angry eyes to meet mine. "I didn't do anything. He said that, but he thought it all by himself. I never said or did anything."

Okay.

"Who said what?" I asked casually.

Dean covered his ears and scrunched up his angry little face, as if he was trying not to hear whatever was going on in his head. I lay a finger on his arm. He jerked it away, and sat stiffly back against the backrest, and looked at me in something oddly akin to fear.

"You can tell me anything, Dean," I said meaningfully. "I promise I won't turn on you."

His breathing took on a very agitated quality. His little heart must have been battling a coronary episode. "He knows I'm a homo," he said, finally.

"Who?" I asked gently. I felt a surge of sympathetic emotion for him. I had to fight the urge to touch him again.

"Albert Campbell," he said.

"He's the one you drew in your book," I remembered. Dean nodded. "Tell me about him," I suggested.

"He's really lucky," Dean said, after a brief hesitation. "He has fun, and his family is nice, and he gets to go places, and he can play baseball really good."

"Is he your friend?" I asked.

"Not any more," Dean said softly. "He said he hates homo's."

"And you're feeling pretty certain that you are a homosexual?" I asked carefully.

He didn't answer.

"What's making you think that about yourself Dean?" I asked. Then I hurriedly added, "I'm just curious, sweetheart, I don't have much to say about it either way. You're still my special boy, no matter what."

That got to him. He shot a look of wonderment at me then quickly looked away, blinking in a struggle not to cry. "I don't know what I am," he said in a tight, frightened voice. "I just wish I was him sometimes."

"I can understand that," I told him. "It sounds like he has a nice life. There are lots of things missing in your life, Dean. Some things we can make up for, but others we can't," I paused to let that reality sink in. Then, not wanting him to lose hope, I added, "It's that way for everybody, believe me.

Even Albert. Albert is missing things in his life too. We all are. But you won't see how true that is until you're grown up."

"He has a mother," Dean said. He looked up at me in time to catch my sympathetic tears welling up in my eyes. "Can I please go upstairs?" he begged.

I nodded, letting him go. I figured I had at least got him to admit to what was bothering him. As to helping him resolve it, I was at a loss.

***

Alone in my room I struggled with my conscience. What could I do for Dean? He was in very real pain. How could I help him without becoming his foster mother? If I did that, I'd be tied to the Wilde's forever. That was not likely to be a good thing.

Then I heard the rustling sound.

Damn that dog!

***

"Dean?" I knocked on his door and opened it. He looked at me, startled.

His bedroom window was open. Huh?

"It's freezing, turkey," I said, moving over to the window and closing it. Then I turned to him. He was staring into space with wide, disturbed eyes.

Now what?

"Whose dog is that?" I asked. "You know, the black one?"

"It's the guard," he said, not looking at me, but continuing to have that pained look on his face.

It's the guard... I guessed in Deanspeak that meant he was a *guard dog.* Well, considering how strange everything else was around this joint, I supposed it made a little bit of twisted sense. But whom was the dog guarding, anyway, if he was always watching me?

***

It's the guard.

***

I had a little time before the meal would be ready, so I went to my computer and typed out the phrase. *It's the guard.* Why was I fixating on this?

I opened the file containing the most recent work on my new book. The focus on romance was just not happening here. I didn't know why. All I knew was that I wanted some drama, and intrigue in the story. Or, maybe just some downright human reality. My heroine was too high strung anyway, always such a victim. In the real world she'd probably be due for a breakdown... why not?

I wrote:

Sally Jo listened to her messages, and once again, Larry hadn't called. Damn him! she thought miserably. All at once her worst insecurities flooded through her mind, leaving her defenseless and feeling broken. She gave in to the urge to pour a drink, and downed the bitter tequila quickly. Then she had another, and then another, and then she slept.

Saturday and Sunday passed, and Sally Jo didn't get out of bed. She barely ate or drank; she just slept. When Monday rolled around and she didn't wake up for work–

I stopped writing. Jesus, this woman was really a loser. I didn't want to write about her. *She just wants it too damned much,* I thought, *that's the best way for a woman to leave herself open to disaster.*

Shit. Now my book sounded stupid and dull. I turned off the computer without even saving what I'd written.

***

At the table, Dean ate like a robot. He put food in his mouth and chewed reflexively as if he wasn't even tasting it. I looked over to see if Mr. Wilde was aware. He was.

***

I checked on Dean at about ten o'clock. I cracked his bedroom door open and peaked inside. The bedside lamp was on, the window was open, and Dean was thrashing around on his bed emitting tortured, smothered moans.

Jesus.

I opened the door completely and he woke up. He rose to his knees and stared at me as if he didn't recognize me.

"Did you smoke something funny at school today?" I asked him. "And why do you keep opening the window? It's freezing in here."

"I don't know," he said. There were traces of his normal self in his voice now.

"Are you okay?" I asked. I didn't say anything about the way he had been moaning in his sleep.

"Yes," he said agreeably. "I guess I got hot and it woke me up. Then I didn't like the dark so I opened the window and turned on the light."

An acceptable answer for the moment.

I walked over and tucked the blankets around him. He turned onto his side and closed his eyes. "Goodnight, Amy," he said.

Goodnight, strange one, I said inwardly. But to him I said a sincere, "Sweet dreams, Dean."

CHAPTER ELEVEN
Strange Danger

The smell of smoke woke me several hours into the night. I heard frantic, accented voices calling for help and a call to 911. I jumped out of bed and pulled on sweats and sweatshirt and tore out through the side door. There was a cloud of smoke emerging from the Regans' apartment over the garage. They were standing in indecision at the base of the stairs, wringing their hands in the moonlight, and clearly incapable of acting.

I raced back inside and dialed 911 on the portable phone, calling loudly up the front stairwell for Mr. Wilde to wake up. I saw him emerge from his room as I trotted back into the kitchen, yelling into the phone that there was a fire at the Wilde residence. I guessed it would take about twenty minutes for the volunteer firefighters to arrive, which meant that we needed to try to put it out ourselves.

Mr. Wilde was ahead of me as I headed outside again. We both went for the garden hoses. I ran for a second one that I new was hooked up to a faucet near the pool. We connected them together and then took them over to the Regans' garden and connected them to the third hose there. I followed Mr. Wilde up the stairs with a second grip on the hose and we headed toward the smoke. I could tell that the fire was still contained in one room, judging by the amount of smoke wafting out the front door. We sprayed water on the fire, which was burning on the couch and drapes in the living room, and managed to extinguish most of it.

The fire department arrived and took over, and I followed my boss back down to where the Regans waited.

"We can't figure out how that happened, sir," Simon told Mr. Wilde hurriedly. "We've been asleep since about nine–thirty, you know."

I looked at Mr. Wilde. He was frowning, but not in a way that I interpreted as disbelief. His face was sooty, and so were his clothes– jeans again. I almost laughed, but then I realized I was probably a similar sight. So I stifled it.

"Mr. Wilde, say something!" Riba implored. "It's the last thing in the world that we'd want, is to destroy your property!"

"Of course it is, don't give it another thought," he said. And I think he meant it. But he was disturbed, nonetheless.

For a moment, I wondered if he suspected the fire had been deliberately set. For a moment, I guess, I did.

***

Dean stood off in the distance, watching quietly. I approached him and saw how morose his expression was. "What do you think of all of this?" I asked him.

"Someone was playing with fire," he said.

Good call.

***

"Miss Stuart, will you see that Dean gets back to bed? He has to get up for school in a short while," it was an order, as usual.

"What are the firemen going to do?" Dean asked over his shoulder as I followed him up the back stairwell.

"They go through and chop up everything that burned, to make sure it's really out," I said. I had never been on the premises where a fire had occurred before. But I was pretty sure I had answered him correctly.

"Are the Regans in trouble?" he asked as he climbed back into bed.

"It doesn't seem like it," I told him. "If the fire was their fault, it was an accident. But they don't know how it could have happened."

***

The following morning, after I'd taken Dean to school, Mr. Wilde told me that the fire department had been unable to determine the cause of the fire.

"Do they smoke cigarettes?" I suggested.

He shook his head. "No, they don't, nor do they spend much time in that room..." he drifted off in thought for a moment, then cleared his throat. "It must have been an electrical short."

I wouldn't know about such things, so I let the explanation suffice.

BOOK TWO

INTERPRETATIONS OF SILENCE

"What I didn't see, I couldn't hear..."
–Amy Stuart

CHAPTER TWELVE
Silent Scream

Not too long after that, the Regans suddenly rushed off to England, for some family emergency, or something. Mr. Wilde hired a crew to make repairs on their apartment, and an agency to send out a team to come clean the house twice a week, and yet another to tend to the yard work. He asked me to pay special attention that they all attended to their duties and stayed out of his business.

Then he told me he was leaving town for about three days.

These changes meant that there were going to be a lot more bodies around than usual and I would either have to find something to do while they were at the house, or be in the position of being in their way.

I guessed those were going to be the days when I ventured into town to talk to the locals, like some of the mothers of Dean's friends and classmates. Or my new friend Chester.

***

I heard a scuttling sound in the kitchen and assumed it was the new cleaning crew. I went out to introduce myself and to give a few instructions about things that should not be touched in my quarters, but when I reached the kitchen, there was no one there. I heard footsteps in the hallway beyond, so I headed that way. Again, as I passed through the doorway, I found that I'd missed the cleaning person once again.

Jesus!

This time, I trotted after what seemed to be the sound of retreating footsteps, rounding through the living room archway, in time to catch the tail wind of the illusive cleaning person. Now I ran, through the living room to the gallery, and thought I saw the swish of fabric, probably a skirt, snatch through the far doorway of that room.

I started to laugh. Whoever I was chasing was either playing with me, or, was bound and determined not to have to be given any additional instructions.

Or maybe I was only imagining that I'd heard someone, and was chasing nothing? And if this was the case, what in the hell was my problem?

I decided to let well enough alone. It wasn't my house, anyway.

***

But later, as I was leaving the house to get Dean from school, I caught a glimpse of one of the cleaners. I saw the back of her as she made her way into the sunroom. She had fuzzy blond hair, and her pearly pink party dress looked like something out of a thrift shop. Hardly the typical attire for a cleaning woman. But then, who was I to judge? She probably got bored wearing ratty old sweats to work in all of the time.

***

Mr. Wilde actually called after dinner to see if things were going all right in his absence. I attempted to ride him a little on the fact that he had actually called.

"Shouldn't you be more careful? I mean, maybe the phone lines are tapped," I suggested.

"I'm not amused," he snapped.

I backed off. "What is it that has urged you to call and check on us?" I asked with a more appropriate demeanor.

"Simply that you are now the only one in the house who has any business being there, other than for specific duties," he said.

"Oh." That made sense.

"I'm requesting that you keep yourself alert to anything suspicious, all right?" he asked.

"Certainly," I agreed. "I don't suppose you'd be willing to indulge me on what it is that leads you to think this is required at this time?"

"I thought I'd already made that clear," he responded with impatience. "The Regans are no longer present to keep that sort of surveillance, so I'm asking you to. And Miss Stuart, this is likely to be one of my last trips out of town for a time now."

"I'm glad to hear that," I told him. *I am?*

***

I awoke with a start, feeling frightened.

What woke me?

I waited, listening. The sound came again, a muted, animal cry. I remembered the cat and a slow chill spread across my neck as I struggled to identify the noise I was hearing. Where was it coming from? I got out of bed quietly, leaving the lights off, and padded lightly across the floor to the window. The eyes were there again. What was it with that damned dog? Then I heard the sound again, but it wasn't coming from outside. I heard it more clearly now, a wounded, agonized moan. It was coming from Dean's wing up the stairs.

I took the stairs three at a time, tripping twice in my agitated haste. Images came to mind of an intruder, as the cry came yet again, more urgently. I was convinced Dean was being tortured, just by the hideousness of his ululations. I braced myself for physical combat as I burst into his room with my fists balled and raised to strike.

But there was no intruder, only Dean.

The room was cold and still. I shivered away the feeling of violation about the room. *You're reading into the situation, Amy. The kid is dreaming. That's it.*

The lamp beside his bed illuminated his body. He was on his hands and knees, the sheets and blankets long since wrestled from the bed as Dean fought some terrible, invisible force that entrapped him in his nightmare. His lips were tightly clamped together, denying any emission in the form of words. I watched him, trying to calmly assess the situation.

I wasn't certain whether I should wake him from his dream state, having been told once that it was best to let the dreamer endure the sequence of events, hopefully long enough to find a resolution to the terror before waking.

Suddenly, Dean sat up on his haunches atop his bed, his eyes wide, his mouth open. He was sucking in air in irregular panting breaths. He seemed unaware of my presence, as if hypnotized. His body began to quake and he broke into a cold sweat. Not wanting to startle him, I turned on the overhead light and waited.

Dean looked at me with glassy, unfocused eyes. Now he was aware of my presence, but could not yet separate himself from the tableau in which his nightmare had been set. He was shaking uncontrollably.

I walked over to him and held out my hand, but he moved out of my reach. His brows were knitted in a frown of confusion, and anger.

"Hey Dean," I started.

"What did you hear?" he demanded in a cold, emotionless voice.

"I heard you having a nightmare," I told him levelly.

"What was I saying?" his tone was harsh, as if *he* were the adult addressing a child.

"You didn't say anything–"

"Good, then you can leave me alone now." It was an order.

"Excuse me," I said in my sharpest tone of voice. "I don't intend to go anywhere until I know that you're okay." Perhaps my revealing my concern would get through his defiance.

Uh, no.

"I said go away!" he blared at me. An icy, cruel voice from such a babe.

"As you wish," I said, leaving quickly before I could give in to the reflexive urge to rebuff him. Whatever his problem was, challenging him on it, at this stage, was not the route to successful communication. But, *Jesus*, how he could push my buttons with his disrespect.

***

When Dean appeared the next morning, he had dressed carefully in his usual fashion, wearing a sweater and blazer, and the darling bowtie, and brought his overcoat for protection from the cold over his arm as he came down the back staircase to the kitchen for breakfast. I was waiting for him, letting my eyes assess him for signs of attitude carry–over from the previous night.

There was no attitude, only tension. He met my eyes briefly, then darted his glance away as he sat down in the booth. I put a bowl of Cream of Wheat in front of him and handed him a spoon. He took it but kept his eyes downcast.

"I'm sorry I woke you up last night," he said, to my surprise.

I sighed and frowned at him. "Dean, please don't apologize for something you cannot control," I said as gently as I could. But I was still angry enough with him to give him a tongue lashing for the way he had spoken to me. He should know by now that I was not the enemy.

He raised his eyes and looked at me. His face was unreadable, except for a hint of apprehension. I sat across from him.

"Let me fill you in on something that you don't seem to know about me," I said in a low, controlled voice. He kept his dismal eyes on mine as I spoke. "I'm not the enemy. In fact, I'd like to be someone you can trust. But if there's one sure way to push me over the line, it's to be disrespectful."

"You want to hit me," he said with petulance.

"No, Dean, I *don't* want to," I corrected him, not being completely honest, but deciding to protect him from my wrath nonetheless. "That's why I'm telling you this. Give me a chance before you decide that I'm the bad guy."

I'm not certain, but I think he smirked at my suggestion. What did *that* mean?

***

"I was embarrassed." Dean told me before he got out of the car in front of his school.

"What?" I wasn't getting it.

"I don't want anyone to know about the dream. PLEASE don't tell Father." He was struggling to keep his voice level.

"Okay, I won't. But dreams aren't anything to be ashamed of, Dean," I said, wanting to reassure him.

"This one is." He slammed the door shut and stalked off.

It struck me then just how much intensity this kid carried around with him. What did he do with it? Obviously nothing, hence the hostility he was capable of. I was beginning to wonder if I wanted to be around when he finally blew a fuse.

Then I thought of Penelope, and the fire. *Oh God, what if he already had blown a fuse, and I'm just being blind?*

***

Friday after school Dean asked when his father was due back.

"Any day now, I guess," I told him.

"Do you think I shouldn't have invited the guys over again?" he asked, indicating the plans we'd cooked up for the next day with Bill and Todd.

"I think it'll be okay," I said, but I wasn't so sure.

We'll sure as hell find out if it isn't okay, I silently acknowledged.

***

We had a calm Friday night, watching music videos and playing Clue. Dean won every round, which was somewhat eerie.

Then came Saturday. The father returned late that morning.

***

"Mr. Wilde, you're back. I wasn't certain when you'd be returning, welcome home," I was saying to him, intending that the extent of my sincerity be unclear.

"I said I'd be a couple of days, did I not?" he said back, probably intending to sound precisely as rude as he did.

My eyebrows shot up as I looked off to the side, sighing, "So you did."

We stood in the entrance hall. Mr. Wilde removed his overcoat and tossed it over a hand carved armchair a few feet away. Then he removed his black suit coat and tossed it aside as well. I had rarely seen him in his shirt sleeves. He had a powerful set of shoulders. I wondered how he stayed fit.

He caught me assessing him, but did not acknowledge it. Instead, he commented on the boys outside.

"Dean's entertaining friends, I see."

"Yes," I agreed. I could tell he was irritated, and became defensive on Dean's behalf. "You're angry, aren't you?" I demanded to know. What was the big deal?

"I'm not angry," Mr. Wilde replied, not convincing me.

I watched him saunter off. *You know, he's really a pain in the ass,* I thought to myself in my usual Amy fashion. *I'm getting a bit tired of that attitude.*

He continued on his testy way, and I went over to watch the kids through the front glass. They seemed to be having a heated debate. As I stood there assessing the potential for volatility, it broke into a fistfight between Dean and Todd. I tore outside, calling for them to separate. Todd tried to pull back, his face pinched in indignation. Dean jumped on him, knocking him down. I arrived in time to catch Dean's fist before he delivered a powerful blow to his playmate's face.

"Stop!" I ordered Dean, wrapping an arm around his shoulders from behind and pulling him against my legs.

"Don't tell me when it's my turn!" he yelled in something akin to raging hysteria.

"But it is!" Todd said, his face suddenly crumbling in confusion. "Why are you so mad?"

Dean stopped struggling and stood still. His chest was heaving and his limbs were trembling violently.

"Yes, Dean, why are you so mad?" I asked, truly wanting to know.

"I don't need you to tell me it's my turn!" he said, forcefully.

"What's the big deal, Dean?" The silent Bill finally dared to ask. He was looking at Dean as if he considered him to be insane.

"I don't know," Dean said, suddenly deflated. "I just get mad when..." he drifted off.

We all stood there in silence for a time. "What do you boys want to do?" I asked.

"I want to play," Todd said. He looked at Dean expectantly.

"Me too," Bill added.

"So do I," Dean said, at once calm and in control of himself. "I'm sorry you guys, I guess I just got pissed off at nothing."

I smiled at his explanation. That was an understatement.

"Yeah, no kidding, bro," Bill agreed.

I left them to go back to their game, but kept a close vigil just in case.

CHAPTER THIRTEEN
The Noose

The boys left later in the day, this time Bill's mother came to pick them up.

"You've got a carpool going?" Mr. Wilde asked me, entering as I closed the front door after them. Dean sat on the foot of the entrance hall stairway watching us morosely.

"We're taking turns driving the boys for their excursions," I answered him.

"Excursions?" he asked testily.

"Yes, to go play ball at the park, for some ice cream–" I started to explain, but was interrupted.

"I don't want Dean left unattended for even a moment!" he snapped.

I frowned at him, my patience thinning. "At what point have I indicated he's been left unattended?" I asked with exaggerated patience. "Are you trying to tell me not to take him anywhere away from school or home?"

"I pay you to be responsible for him!"

How does he keep answering me without giving an answer! I stared at him. He was regarding me with a smug superiority that just egged me on. I raised my hand to my brow in a salute. "Yes, sir!" I said emphatically.

Whew! That really pissed him off. He looked like he wanted to strike me. "Miss Stuart–"

"Mr. Wilde," I said tolerantly, "I can assure you that Dean has not, and will not, be left under anyone else's supervision but my own. I am well aware of what you pay me to do."

***

There was a sharp rap on my door after dinner that evening.

"Miss Stuart," he called through the door. "A sudden engagement has come up. I'm leaving for Los Angeles in the morning."

So much for the last trip actually being the last.

I opened the door. He seemed to be in a better frame of mind than he had been earlier. "What do you *do* on these trips you take?" I asked, expecting to be told to mind my own business.

He looked at me for a moment then said, "This particular occasion is a book signing tour with a major bookstore chain, as a matter of fact." He paused before adding, "Something that published authors are expected to do, I'm afraid."

Nice jab to the gut, there, boss.

"I guess I left myself open for that one," I said with self–deprecation.

"Well, one can always dream, Miss Stuart," he returned with that smug arrogance.

I flipped him off as he retreated.

***

Three days later, Mr. Wilde was home again. Dean and I were returning from a midweek scrimmage soccer game in the late afternoon, when we saw his car in front of the house.

"Your dad's back," I observed to Dean. "He's returned much sooner than I would have expected."

Dean sat, immobilized. Was that dread in his eyes? Why was he so fearful of his father? I mean, yes the man was cold and full of disdain, but whether or not he was home shouldn't really make a difference to Dean. It's not as though they spent any time together. But, no doubt Mr. Wilde would want an explanation and justification of yet another disruption to his carefully developed routine. What could Dean say in his own defense? He had followed my lead, knowing that Mr. Wilde would not necessarily approve.

"Yo, turkey, are you still with us?" I said, jabbing him in the ribs gently.

Dean looked at me warily at first, not liking the fact that I'd touched him. "Have you ever tried to scream really loud, but no sound comes out?" he asked mysteriously.

"You mean like in a dream?" I asked, wondering what he was trying to tell me.

"Yeah, like in a dream."

"Is that what you feel like right now?" I pried.

"Kind of," he admitted. "Then I think about it and figure I'm just mixed up about stuff." He shot me a defensive look and then got out of the car and hurried inside, not bothering to wait for me.

***

I had already begun preparing tortilla soup that morning and had planned on making a taco salad to go with it, so I told Mr. Wilde that I would fix dinner tonight. (I called through the door of his study, so that I wouldn't have to see his condescending expression.) I also asked Dean to come down to help me make the salad. Dean reluctantly agreed to help, probably because he feared condemnation from his father. I conned him into it by telling him to put whatever music he wanted to hear on my stereo downstairs, and we'd listen while we prepared. He retaliated by putting on some Muppet soundtrack that was annoying as hell. Maybe I was being unfair, using Dean to goad Mr. Wilde, but, what can I say, I wanted to see how much I could get away with these days.

Mr. Wilde entered the kitchen at one point and found us, side by side at the counter, cutting vegetables. "Have you already finished your studies?" he asked Dean, frowning at him.

I took that as my cue, cutting in before Dean could answer. "Of course he's done, how much homework can a third grader have?" I said, letting my tone indicate that I considered Mr. Wilde's expectations of Dean's study habits to be a bit unreal. I looked at Dean. He'd closed his eyes, apparently wishing madly that I'd not interfered.

"It was merely a question, Miss Stuart," Mr. Wilde told me tersely.

"Oh?" I asked innocently.

He left the room, and we continued our task in silence. When dinner was ready, I served it, in silence, in the dining room. We also ate in silence, except for the one comment that Mr. Wilde made.

"This is an interesting version of tortilla soup," he said.

I deliberately did not infer a negative connotation in his comment. "You think so?" I asked, "It's authentic. A good friend of mine is Mexican, and he taught me how to make it. Sometimes he purees it in a blender before he serves it. I chose not to."

"Ah, that must make the difference." Mr. Wilde said, frowning down at the bowl in front of him.

Asshole.

***

He requested that we linger at the table when the meal was over, because he wanted to discuss something with both Dean and me. My ego was still smarting from his earlier jab at my cooking, despite my resolution to remain unaffected, and the expression on my face must have been as morose as Dean's. I was ready to pick a fight.

He looked at me challengingly. "Is there something on your mind, Miss Stuart?" he asked mildly.

I sighed in exasperation. "Don't get me started," I muttered between gritted teeth. Dean shot me a look of alarm. "Has anyone ever told you that you are very arrogant?" I asked, going ahead and starting in anyway. I did manage to refrain from using the expletive that was coming to mind.

"Why, of course, Miss Stuart," he responded airily, as if it were a compliment that he richly deserved. "Why do you ask?"

I shook my head, feeling my frustration rise to a boiling point. I guess I shouldn't have held my tongue for so long about all the things regarding Dean that I'd not shared with him, or all of the other odd things about this house, this job. I was quite close to explosive rage.

"Hmm?" he urged condescendingly.

"What is it that you wanted to discuss, Mr. Wilde? I have other things to do," I asked from between gritted teeth. I decided to avoid the overdue confrontation in Dean's presence. He was looking quite disturbed just now.

Mr. Wilde stared at me for a long moment, as if measuring the consequences of pushing the subject with me. Fortunately, he backed off too. "I wanted to let you know that in a short time, a friend of mine will be coming for an extended stay on the premises." He turned to Dean. "You know him, Dean," he said.

"Mr. Ryan." Dean did not look pleased.

Mr. Wilde turned back to me and began telling me that his friend was a frequent guest, and that I was to consider him as such, but that on occasions when I needed some time off, that I could leave Dean in his care.

During this conversation, I kept my eyes on my employer's, but in my peripheral vision, I could see Dean's body wiggling in agitation as he swung his feet beneath the chair. I didn't look directly at him, so as not to distract Mr. Wilde, but I had that sudden feeling of the calm before the storm again. A front of control coming to an abrupt, explosive finale.

"I doubt that will be necessary," I said, watching to see if that would put Dean at ease. It didn't seem to. I surmised he was agitated by the tension between his father and me. It wasn't as though he had a high threshold for tolerance.

"Nonetheless, Miss Stuart, I am not unaware of how little free time you've had in the last several weeks," he went on. "Surely, you'd probably benefit from some time away from your duties?"

I looked at him questioningly. "Are we talking vacation time here?" I asked. I didn't remember benefits as part of my employment package.

"I wouldn't go that far, no," he said. "I was thinking about a full weekend, perhaps."

I thought for a moment. He must be a very intuitive man indeed. How was it that he had decided to propose this idea to me just as I was ready to go off on him so ferociously that I'd probably end up being fired?

"I suppose that would be beneficial, yes," I relented. "But, perhaps there're some bigger issues here that ought to be brought out in the open, before I agree to your suggestion."

Mr. Wilde looked at me with deliberate warning, his whole demeanor changing, and becoming almost hostile, almost immediately. "Don't–" he started to say.

It was right about then that Dean bolted out of the room and I jumped up to follow.

***

The noise of the sash window being slid frantically upward penetrated my consciousness, as I raced after Dean. He'd climbed outside by the time I'd gotten to his room.

"Dean!" Mr. Wilde bellowed out to him, startling me. I hadn't realized he'd matched my pace to the second floor. "Get your bloody little backside back in here now! Stop this uncalled for behavior!"

The lights from the upstairs rooms cast a glow outside to the tall tree that stood beside the house. There were numerous branches extending over the roof at varying degrees of height. It was the perfect climbing tree, except that the lowest branch was a good twelve feet above the ground.

I could see that Dean had reached the edge of the roof and was grabbing at a noose that hung from one of the branches over his head. He couldn't reach it.

How in the hell did that get there?

It was obvious what he had in mind. He stood as if in indecision for a moment, staring at the rope that was swinging in the wind just out of his reach.

"If I have to come out there to get you," Mr. Wilde's angry words were floating through the chilled night air, "I'll wallop your backside until you can't walk!"

I finally found my voice. "What in the hell are you saying?" I yelled at Mr. Wilde. *Jesus, what an idiot!* "He's going to jump! He doesn't give a shit if you plan to beat him, he doesn't plan to be alive to see it!"

There was a silence, as Mr. Wilde glared at me, somewhat sidetracked from his original impressions. I glared right back at him, shoving past him to get to the window. Dean grabbed a branch and swung himself onto it. We watched him climb downward, for a moment, then ran downstairs to the backyard.

Dean squinted in the pale moonlight as he crossed to other limbs on the way. He looked as if he'd left his sanity back on the windowsill.

"You see? He's not suicidal." Now Mr. Wilde's voice was defensive, "he's in some sort of panic." He was monitoring Dean's progress as he addressed me.

Dean came to a point when he could go nowhere. He had leapt to the singular low branch he was now perched upon and could not reach any others. He looked down at his father standing below him.

"Hang from the limb and let go, I'll catch you," Mr. Wilde called up to him, without any notable anger in his voice. The distance of the drop was slightly longer than the length of Dean's body. He saw Dean's hesitation. "You'll be just out of my reach, but if you drop I'll catch you, I promise."

I wanted to reassure Dean that he'd be safe, but I could not.

Dean, however, did as he was told. He hung from the limb and let go immediately, not allowing himself time for hesitation. Mr. Wilde caught him, as promised, and set him down. Then he yelled into his face as he squatted in front of the boy.

"What in the bloody hell were you thinking of?" his father demanded, seemingly unaware of the glazed look in Dean's eyes. He still had his hands on Dean's ribs and he shook Dean roughly. "Answer me, what were you doing up there?"

Dean hung his head, not responding. Mr. Wilde cursed and rose swiftly from his crouched position. He swatted Dean hard and told him to go to bed.

Dean trotted off, and it was right about then that I realized I had been standing there in a state of shocked silence. I broke it. "How can you strike him like that?" I raged, stepping toward my employer. "Are you completely blind? Your son was going for that noose! And when he couldn't reach that, he was about to jump off the roof!" I was quaking with reaction to the impact of this scene.

He faced me squarely, his face giving nothing away. "I think you're overreacting," he said.

Dozens of words battled for release on my tongue, momentarily leaving me incapable of enunciation. Mr. Wilde took my arm and tugged until I followed him, letting him drag me up to Dean's room. Dean emerged from his bathroom and stopped short when he saw his father and me. Mr. Wilde pulled back the blankets on Dean's bed and motioned for Dean to get into it, obviously an unusual gesture. Dean slowly walked over and slid in. Mr. Wilde pulled the covers over Dean and then sat on the edge of the bed, looking down at him. Dean, as usual, did not make eye contact.

"Dean, how did that rope get up there on that branch?" Mr. Wilde asked him.

"I didn't put it there," Dean said.

Mr. Wilde blinked, as if contemplating briefly then shook his head. "Your governess seems to be under the impression that you were going to take your own life. Is this true?" he asked Dean directly.

Dean shook his head and said in a barely audible voice, "No, sir, I don't know what I was doing. I thought it was my turn."

Mr. Wilde regarded Dean for a moment, as if assessing the degree of truth behind the boy's words. Then he turned toward me. "You see? You were mistaken." His eyes dared me to disagree.

"I quit." I said.

CHAPTER FOURTEEN
Warped Interpretations

In my room, I was shaking.

I am not overreacting. Dean was nine years old. What could be driving him to plot his own death? I mean, obviously, he was living in a freak house, but kids that young don't instinctively seek release by killing themselves. Do they? And what did he mean by *his turn?* For what? For him to *die?*

That thought was too much for me and I began to weep openly.

I couldn't lose another precious child.

***

Mr. Wilde then knocked on my door. I opened it, but kept my distance.

"Stay." It was an order.

"No." I wiped my eyes and glared at him.

"Yes." He took a step toward me.

"No!" I took a step toward him, showing him that I wasn't threatened.

"Please."

"I can't."

"If you'd seen the look on the boy's face when he heard you say you were quitting, I think you'd agree to stay."

"What was the look?" I asked, knowing I'd lost the battle.

"Fear."

My heart pounded. I raised an eyebrow at him. "You're very shrewd," I accused, sniffing. "You knew that would get to me."

"Yes." He almost let his expression soften as he turned to leave. Then he stopped, but did not face me. "Miss Stuart," he said quietly, "I apologize for my inappropriate criticism of your cooking. I was out of line."

I laughed harshly. "Does that mean you liked my soup?"

"No."

***

The next morning Mr. Wilde was waiting for me when I returned from my early run.

"We'll keep Dean home today," he told me. "I already told him he could go back to sleep if he wished."

"Okay," I acknowledged in discomfort. I felt weird about this whole thing. Like I was missing a bunch of obvious clues to the key issue.

"I think perhaps you'd better spend more time in his company," he said, referring to Dean.

"Oh?" I returned. "Are you suggesting that there's a problem?" I dared him.

"With Dean, there's always a problem, Miss Stuart," Mr. Wilde said matter–of–factly. "Your job is to anticipate and redirect that negative energy."

"I think maybe he'd be better off getting some professional help–" I said.

"That's out of the question," Mr. Wilde declared.

"Someone's going to notify Social Services pretty soon if his behavior gets any worse," I said defensively.

"Is that a threat?" Mr. Wilde demanded, nostrils flaring.

"Not yet."

***

Dean and I were in the backyard, tossing the ball back and forth, when Mr. Wilde came out and stood observing. Dean began to throw the ball harder and harder with each successive turn. His pitches were precise and swift, and they hurt like hell when I caught them in the palm of my glove.

I called a *time out* after I had caught one that left my hand throbbing. I was certain that this sudden burst of strength had something to do with the character of our audience.

"Don't stop on my account," Mr. Wilde said, walking slowly toward us.

I shook my hand to restore the circulation. "Believe me, this was all for me," I told him, giving Dean an exasperated look. He seemed to be pleased with himself.

Mr. Wilde held his hand out for the ball. Dean handed it to him reluctantly. Mr. Wilde tossed it up and down a couple of times.

"Have you mastered catching fly balls?" He asked Dean.

Dean shook his head in dismay.

"Well," Mr. Wilde said, "trot over that way and see if you can catch this one."

Dean looked fearfully at me. I gave him a nod, wondering why he was so reluctant to let his father play with him. Didn't every boy want to play with his father? Dean walked about twenty feet away, then turned toward us with his shoulders slouched defensively.

"A little farther, Dean," Mr. Wilde chided. When Dean had doubled the distance between him and his father, Mr. Wilde threw the baseball high into the air. "Wait for it to drop, then get under it," Mr. Wilde called out. "That's it, now put your glove up."

Dean caught it. The look of astonishment on his face was classic. I wished I could have captured it on film.

"Bravo!" Mr. Wilde called out cheerily. "Now, why don't you go get yourself a snack."

"Yes sir," Dean said, still staring in awe at the ball in his glove as he headed inside.

***

"You are not the only one to see that Dean has problems, Miss Stuart," Mr. Wilde said to me when Dean was out of earshot.

I turned to look at him, wondering where he was going with this.

"He's had a tough time of it," Mr. Wilde confided. "I had difficulty keeping him out of an institution when he was younger."

"Oh," I said, giving him my full attention.

"He did get the 'professional' help that you were suggesting, you see," he told me, "and it nearly destroyed him, and me."

"Mr. Wilde, it's just that–" I started, wanting to tell him that his lifestyle was the detrimental effect on Dean's mental health.

"No, wait, Miss Stuart. Please hear me out," he requested. "I have vowed to keep the celebrity status that my books have allotted me completely at bay. My work has been used for scripts and screenplays. Did you know that?"

"No," I admitted.

"One was nominated by the Academy of Motion Pictures for an award last year," he told me. "That kind of popularity leads to absolute loss of privacy. Nothing is sacred in the media. Surely you are aware of that."

"Yes, I am," I agreed. I'd lived in Hollywood, for Christ's sake.

"I have no intention of letting my son's history be dragged through the gutters for the sake of tabloid exploitation," he declared. "Furthermore, Dean will improve with time if he is treated like a normal child."

I had to wonder where in the hell he'd found his definition of *normal.*

***

"You never came back out to play more catch," I said to Dean when I finally found him sitting in the center of the front lawn.

He didn't respond.

I walked around and stood in front of him. He was weeping with such heartfelt emotion that I almost cried with him. I knelt down in front of him.

"What is it?" I asked him gently.

"I didn't kill the cat," he said.

He's just now dealing with that? I wondered.

"Nobody thinks you did, Dean," I said softly.

"Mrs. Regan did," he said bitterly, his sadness turning sour. "She always blamed me for the things he–" he stopped, as if catching himself.

"Who?" I asked quickly.

"They always think I'm the one who does stuff!" Dean burst out angrily. Then, as quickly as it had erupted, the anger left him, to be replaced by the mournful weeping again. "I miss the kitty."

I reached out to touch his hair, testing for resistance, and found it. He jerked away.

"No!" he screeched. "No one can help me! It will never get better until it's over!"

I sat back on my heels and watched. *God dammit! What is his burden in this life? What secrets lie beneath his defenses?*

"Soon it will be my turn," he said in a thin, weak voice.

I coaxed him into going upstairs to draw then left him to go see Mr. Wilde.

***

"Please!" I implored my employer. "Please tell me what he's hiding! It's like he feels guilty for being alive!"

"Miss Stuart! Calm yourself!" he said impatiently. "If Dean is hiding anything, it's the festering of a very unsettling tragedy in his past. I've already told you he's had problems adjusting."

"That's it?" I asked numbly. "That's all you're going to tell me about him? Tell me about this tragedy! Don't you care that he's so troubled?"

"Of course I care!" he adamantly declared. "But there is no simple solution to a case of internal misery, Miss Stuart!"

I tried to think of a way to word my concerns so that he could hear what I meant. "Mr. Wilde, I agree that he's obviously battling a manifestation of his own perception of a tragedy," I said, not knowing, of course, exactly what I was referring to. "But he shouldn't be left to face it all alone."

"I agree," he said. "And that's why I'm so relieved that you've taken such an interest in him. I've seen vast improvement in his behavior since you've come to us, Miss Stuart."

Though the words were of a praise-like quality, there was no note of sincerity in his voice.

He narrowed his eyes. "I'm asking you to trust my decision to refuse to get further professional help for him. We had a regrettable setback on the only occasion that I dared to pursue an intervention from a child psychiatrist," he told me, lowering his voice to a confiding tone. "If you think the boy has behavior problems now, you should have seen him after a few treatments from that doctor."

***

Was I being manipulated here, or what?

I went into my room.

What could I do to get a perspective on the reality of this scene? This was not what I'd had in mind for myself when I'd left L.A. to get a grip on my life. I'd gone from having weird shit happen to me, to watching it happen to a little boy. And strangely, I wanted to hold Mr. Wilde responsible for Dean's disturbed character, but I couldn't get a sense of blame for him in my gut. It was as if my intuition told me that Mr. Wilde was a pawn in a larger game that I wasn't able to see.

The game of life, I guess. What goes around comes around, or so that's what I've heard.

I pulled out a pad and made some notes on his personality, thinking at the very least, I could let him influence a new character to write about.

***

By the time dinner was ready, I had written a dozen pages of a new story. It was still based on a romance, and would likely become an offshoot of the plot in my current story, but this protagonist was a jerk who'd mistreated everyone in his life. Now he'd finally met someone he could come to care about, but she didn't want him. When I made a mental picture of him as I thought out the plot, I envisioned Mr. Wilde.

Heh heh. I'd get my revenge. This guy was going to pay.

CHAPTER FIFTEEN
Deceptive Respite

Mr. Wilde was in the front hall when I entered with Dean the next afternoon. Of course, he frowned, looking at his watch. "It's late to be outside," he said sternly. "Where did you go off to?" His eyes were taking in the bag with our snacks and Dean's sketchbook.

Give me a break. "We went to watch the sunset, just off in the field over there," I told him.

"Where?" he growled.

I sighed. "Don't tell me," I started, then I imitated his voice and accent, "that's unacceptable!"

He gritted his teeth. I gritted mine too. Sometimes I really marveled at the gall I could bring up from within myself.

"Are you suggesting that I'm overreacting?" he said with a thin glimmer of self–deprecation.

I wasn't sure if I could trust the sense that I had that he was backing off. But I answered him truthfully anyway. "Yes, Mr. Wilde, that is what I'm suggesting. We didn't even leave your property."

He mulled that one for a moment, his eyes on my face. Then he glanced over at Dean, who looked like he was trying to disappear. "What were you up to, over there?" he opted for a new tactic.

"We were trying to express ourselves," I said.

"Were you successful?" he wanted to know. He really had backed off.

"Yes," I said, "I wrote a little poem." I fished my papers out of the bag I carried and read aloud,

"Don't Pretend:

These arms are reaching for you.

Reach back to me, but only if you want to.

Don't pretend to be in love when you are not.

Paint a picture of lone trees, clustered but disconnected,

like you and me. It hurts and I'm not unaffected,

so don't pretend you see what you do not.

First love is forever, sometimes loving, sometimes hating.
It's just that I never thought I'd be waiting
for you to stop pretending you feel for me, when you do not."

Mr. Wilde regarded me with amusement. "Hmm, that's what you saw when you gazed at the horizon, is it?" he asked.

"Okay, so I embellished a little," I conceded. "I'm an artist. It's my right."

"And you, young man?" he asked Dean.

"I don't like mine," Dean said with discomfort.

"But you drew a wonderful landscape," I said.

Dean looked at me with resentment, like I had told one of his biggest secrets.

"Will you show me?" Mr. Wilde asked the boy.

Dean sighed and handed over his sketch with obvious reluctance. I watched Mr. Wilde open it up, then raise his eyebrows in obvious surprise.

"He's good, isn't he?" I prompted.

"Yes," Mr. Wilde answered. He looked at Dean, "Quite good. May I have this?"

Dean looked up in surprise. "Yes, sir," he said reflexively.

Every once in a while, the man exhibited a sign of human feeling.

***

I went into the kitchen to unload the uneaten food we had brought back.

"You've probably ruined the boy's dinner," Mr. Wilde said from behind me.

I glanced over my shoulder at him. "No I haven't," I said, not bothering to explain that we hadn't even touched the crackers and cheese I'd brought. But I decided to snack on them now.

Mr. Wilde stepped over beside me. "Miss Stuart?" he asked, his tone telling me that he didn't appreciate my dismissive treatment of him.

"Yes?" I said, feeling the need to push his buttons. I spread a little cheddar cheese spread onto a Wheat Thin and passed it over to him. He took it from me in momentary confusion. Then I made one for myself and ate it, grinning at him. "Mr. Wilde, one thing you don't have to worry about is your son overeating," I said. I made another cracker for him and handed it to him. "Don't you ever eat these?" I asked him, pretending to be oblivious to the way he was assessing me. "I love having this for a snack– almost as much as chocolate chip cookies."

"And we know how much you love those," he said, back to form. He ate the crackers I'd given him, accepting a third one from me. I was enjoying the opportunity to feed him processed food. What a concept. The man was an absolute food snob. Not that I blamed him, of course, but one ought to let down his standards and enjoy some real preservatives once in a while. All I needed now was a can of TAB, and I'd be in absolute heaven.

He looked at his watch. "I'd better start dinner," he said.

"One more," I said, handing him another cracker with cheese, and then making one for myself. We enjoyed the indulgence without further comment.

And to think that at this time just three evenings previous, Dean had been working himself toward attempting suicide.

CHAPTER SIXTEEN
Tolerant

The next several days were calm and uneventful. Mr. Wilde was home, and more approachable than usual. He even told me that he would appreciate my company on Thanksgiving, which was the coming Thursday. I hadn't given much thought to the holidays, as they had never been particularly significant for me. Those I considered family were all likely to be off doing their own thing anyway and wouldn't miss my absence from a nonexistent tradition.

Mr. Wilde had a menu in mind for the dinner and believe me, I had no intention of offering anything in terms of assistance in the cooking department. He was on his own there, after the way he cut my soup up one side and down the other. I kind of had the feeling he wanted to suggest that we both cook, but he didn't do it, so maybe I was wrong.

***

During the middle of the day on Monday, while Dean was at school, I was bored. I didn't feel like going into town to hang out with Chester or see whom I could find to talk to in the general store. So I got up and started wandering around the house, restlessly looking for distraction. I wasn't really looking for anything in particular, (since I had that strong sense of boundaries about other peoples' property) but I kept hoping I'd come across something that would capture my interest.

I made the circuit through the living room, gallery, library, and ended up in the game room. On the table was a stack of books that Mr. Wilde must have left out. I glanced at the covers and realized they were texts on various forms of martial arts. But the one on top was about meditation. I snickered to myself, thinking that if the man would actually employ a pursuit of meditation and raised consciousness, he wouldn't be so uptight.

He must be researching for his current book, I thought.

***

Well, that was uneventful. I was really hurting now, so I went outside and stood staring into the vast expanse of the backyard. My eyes rested on the garage apartment where the Regans had been living. I had no idea how much repair work had occurred since they'd gone, but decided to go find out.

***

"What in the bloody hell are you doing in here, Miss Stuart?"

That startled the crap out of me. I gasped and turned to face Mr. Wilde where he stood in the doorway, glaring at me as if I had set the fire myself.

I raised my hand to lay it over my chest. My hand trembled and my heart pounded from a combination of shock and a disconcerting feeling of wrongdoing. "I was bored," I said lamely. "I didn't think you'd object to my taking a look at what's been done in here."

"Oh, is that what you were doing?" he asked in a tone that said he thought otherwise.

I looked at him levelly. "Yes, Mr. Wilde, that is what I was doing. What is it that *you* think I was doing?"

"I thought you were in your quarters, minding your own business," he said.

I stood there, feeling suddenly humiliated, like a child who is shamed for something that she had naively thought to be acceptable. I didn't know what to do or say. I had the strange feeling I was being accused of something, but that I was missing the whole thing.

Wait a minute, did he think I'd set the fire in here, then waited until now to come and assess the damage?

I bet that's it. I glared pure malice at him and walked past him and out the door. He glared right back at me, slamming the door and locking it behind us as we left. I could feel him at my heels as I walked toward the house. I was contemplating getting my car keys and taking off for an angry drive, but I knew I needed to confront him, now.

I stopped in my tracks. He nearly collided with me.

"You know," I said in a slightly abnormally high pitch, "I got the feeling back there that you were insinuating something."

"Feeling defensive, Miss Stuart?" he asked icily.

"Do you really think I could set fire to someone's apartment?" I yelled in outrage. "Do you really think that?"

He didn't answer me right away, but just looked at me with calculation. Finally he said, "Miss Stuart, I didn't accuse you of anything."

I pressed onward, "Why were you so rude to me?" I asked, realizing that my anger was getting the better of me. I'd better be careful, or I'd burst into tears.

"Was I rude?" he asked tauntingly.

I'm going to deck him. I thought in amazement. *I have to leave, right now, or I'll beat this man to an arrogant pulp.*

"See ya," I said, spinning on my heel.

Fucker.

***

I drove to the coast and parked the car, and just sat listening to music, waiting for the time to pass.

***

That afternoon at the school, Dean smiled at me as he got into the car, until he saw my morose face. He sat in silence beside me, occasionally glancing over at me.

"Are you mad at me?" he finally asked.

I was so pissed off I couldn't even muster up a reassuring smile. "No, kiddo, you're fine," I said, the tension in my voice making it sound gravely. "But I am in a bad mood though, so that's why I'm not very talkative."

He frowned, disappointed. For once he was feeling light and carefree, and here I was, being the killjoy, which made me feel even more morose.

***

Mr. Wilde was waiting on the front stairs. He said a grim hello to Dean, who scooted by and rushed up to his room. Then he stood staring down at me, while I remained at the foot of the stairs, glowering up at him.

"What exactly was that little episode that occurred in the backyard?" I snapped.

"I don't know," he snapped right back. I could tell he was regretting his accusation.

"Well, I don't know either, but I didn't like it," I declared. "And I'll be

God damned if I'm going to stay around for more of the same. I'm not a criminal, Mr. Wilde."

"Point taken," he said. He looked at me with flat, empty eyes, yet the words almost made me smile.

***

Thanksgiving. Boring. Nothing to talk about, or anyone that I really wanted to talk to.

But the food was excellent, as usual. Mr. Wilde cooked all day, and served trays of delectable tidbits as he finished them. We were constantly eating. Even Dean ate. The cable music channel was showing a collection of the best music videos of the decade. I got Dean interested in watching, and we stayed in front of the television for most of the day.

CHAPTER SEVENTEEN
Fear of Impact

Saturday, I found Dean in his playroom. He was waiting for me, wanting to show me some of his best drawings. He placed the leather bound book in my hands and pointed to the first sketch of the climbing tree. "This is my favorite place," he told me, as if having no recollection of having shown me these pages before. And as before, I marveled inwardly at the detail and dimensions of the drawing of the lone tree in a grassy field. It was similar to our special place, but a different tree altogether.

"The tree reminds me of me," Dean said disturbingly. That was when I noticed the noose hanging from the lowest branch. It had been lightly stenciled into the picture. *Okay, Amy, it's time to seriously think about going to the authorities with him.*

Oblivious to my inner conflict, Dean continued on, turning to the next drawing. "This is Albert Campbell, he's nice to me sometimes, but I don't like him much." It was as if we'd never discussed Albert or the drawings before. I instinctively knew why this boy was the one Dean felt a strong affinity for, the one for which he interpreted as homosexual attraction. Albert Campbell looked happy.

I let him go on to the next page without interrupting. "This is Rachel," he told me.

"Who is Rachel?" I asked.

"Rachel was my sister," he said.

A revelation!

"You didn't know I had a sister, did you?" he continued. "Well I did."

We stared down at the image of a beautiful dark haired girl. This was the girl in the picture in the hallway of the west wing. She was smiling warmly, making me think of an angel. I told Dean.

"She was an angel," he confirmed. "The only one I'll ever know. She died when my mother died."

I bit my tongue. *What happened to her?* I wanted to scream. But there was a real strangeness about the way Dean was behaving that held me in check. *Let him do the talking,* I told myself.

Then came a sketch of his father. "It looks like him doesn't it? But you can't tell if he's happy or sad, can you? That's because there's no difference with Father." Dean had captured his father's grim features, the handsome qualities distorted by a frown. Mr. Wilde's face looked up from the page with accusing eyes, as if Dean had been the source of his discomfort.

"It looks like he's about to say something accusatory," I commented derisively.

"I know," Dean agreed. "I tried to draw him with a smile, but even when he smiles, he looks mean," Dean said harshly, further defiling his father's image.

"These are your best ones," I said, "how about the worst ones?"

Dean seemed disturbed by my question. "No one sees the worst ones."

"Because you don't think they'll be able to tell what the drawing is of?" I asked.

"No," Dean said, as if he was incapable of drawing something indiscernible. "The worst ones aren't the ones I want to show."

"How about the second–worst ones?" I asked, not really knowing why I had gone off on this tangent.

Dean gave me a funny look then shook his head. He flipped to the mid section of the book and handed it to me. The first one made me gasp. It was him, Dean. He had drawn himself in a cage! It was one of those disturbing pictures you'd find in a psychology journal, as an illustration for an article describing some emotional disorder and the impact it had on the human psyche.

"Where did you get the idea for this drawing?" I asked casually. "I thought you only drew what you saw."

"Some things I see in my head," he told me.

***

I had the following day off and woke to head out, down the 101 toward San Francisco. I made it all the way to Marin County before the smelly exhaust of a Greyhound bus triggered a horrible flashback of memory. The fear factor burst open in my brain and something I wanted to forget got remembered.

I pulled the car off the freeway and over to the side of a quiet street. I kept hearing the sound of bone and flesh impacting with shattering windshield. I kept seeing the spray of blood and various types of human tissue. I kept hearing that pulpy splattering sound as it hit my windshield.

***

I had contemplated suicide after I had given up teaching. I had just felt so lost, I hadn't known what else to do. At first, I had thought of the easiest way to commit the act. Then, I'd thought of the least traumatic way for my family to find out about it. Then, I'd thought about how I'd feel if someone I knew and loved had taken his or her own life.

It would have destroyed me.

Then I realized that no matter how shitty I felt, that I could not inflict that kind of pain on the ones I loved.

I guess that's why the suicide that I witnessed had such a traumatizing impact on me. I guess I got to see first hand the kind of mess I would have left for someone else to clean up. And what a hell of a mess it was.

It had been an overcast day in June, in Hollywood. For once, the Hollywood Freeway, also the 101, was actually moving at the speed limit.

"What is it with these buses?" I remember grumbling in irritation from behind the pollution belching Metro Line. The bus and my car were traveling in the right hand lane. We were both going fifty–five miles per hour, but I was tired and impatient. I floored the gas and moved over to the left to go around. Much to my frustration, the bus driver seemed to speed up as I tried to gain distance on him. I couldn't get in front of him. Then, the sedan in front of me began to slow down, holding me back even more.

"Slow pokes! Some of us have somewhere to be!" I yelled from within the confines of my car.

Actually, I didn't have anywhere to be. That's just L.A. driving for you.

Tightly wound with frustrated tension, I was not watching the commotion on the overpass, which our three vehicles were rapidly approaching. Some unknown force cautioned my lead–heavy foot to lighten its pressure on the accelerator, which, fortunately for me, decreased my speed. In the flash of an instant which seemed to last much longer, a distraught woman chose that moment to take a fatal plunge into freeway traffic from the overpass.

Suffice it to say that the graphic extent of the resulting carnage is beyond my capability to describe, and certainly far more extreme than I could ever have imagined witnessing. The bus hit her, the driver slamming on his brakes and swerving to the right. The sedan in front of me also came to a screeching halt, as did I in my car, miraculously not hitting anyone or being hit myself.

There were pieces and fragments of her everywhere, especially on the windshields of all of the vehicles in the vicinity.

I shut my eyes, trying unsuccessfully to stem the shock and panic that were rapidly setting in. I felt trapped, so I opened my car door and leapt out, reflexively locking and slamming the door shut. My eyes darted around, desperately looking for an escape. By now traffic had completely stopped, and lines of cars were growing behind this scene.

I waded my way through the cars and over to the emergency lane. Voices of hysterical witnesses were screaming for someone to call the police and an ambulance. My brain dimly registered these sounds as I collapsed slowly to my knees. My hands threaded through my hair, gripping it and pulling it tightly. My stomach threatened to heave and my lungs were gasping rattling breaths. My whole body was quaking.

It was the longest moment in time I've ever known. I kept waiting for it to pass, but the horror remained with me while I knelt on the rough pavement. I couldn't stand, couldn't think straight. Hell, I probably couldn't have remembered my name if someone had asked me. I realized later that I had been in shock, which is probably why I was bitterly rude to the cop who tried to assist me. I guess I blamed him for not protecting me by preventing the tragedy. I didn't even thank him for jimmying open my locked car door.

***

I came out of my reflection crying. That had been a day in my life that would haunt me forever, both in the visual memory, and in the massive impact of violent death.

So much for my excursion to San Fran. Why not make a weekend of it next time? I could take Dean with me. Between the two of us, we could probably have a truly morbid time.

CHAPTER EIGHTEEN
Danger?

Later that evening, I was outside waiting for the black dog.

When he appeared, he was not alone. A tall, dark silhouette of a man accompanied him. They walked side by side, entering the property on the side drive, by coming through a space in the hedge. The figure stopped short when he saw me, though he managed to stay in the shadows. I bit my tongue in fear.

The dog growled.

"Hush up, Black," the dark man ordered. As soon as he spoke, I knew I'd heard that voice somewhere before. It was a deep Southern twang...

...Norman?

He changed his tone to one of apology. "Sorry, Miss. I was just a–lookin' fer ma dog. He gets away from me time and agin."

"I've seen him before," I commented in a strained voice, suddenly realizing I could be in danger. He sounded like the gas station attendant. But in the shadows he didn't look like the same man. I couldn't say what was different, exactly...

He hadn't been chasing after the dog, either. He had been following it. Besides, where could they have come from? There were no other houses within a three–mile radius, as far as I knew. A surge of panic rose up in me. I couldn't work up the nerve to ask him why he was coming *onto* the property instead of leaving it.

"Well, we'll be going on home now. Come along now, Blackie." The man gave a wave and turned to head back in the direction he'd come from. At the hedge opening, he turned back and stared at me for a moment. Then he was gone.

***

Back inside the house, I felt a quivering fear. What did that man want here? Who had he come to see? Had he been staring inside my window all of those times, alongside the black dog?

God, not again!

***

I am a firm believer that people draw things into their lives by their own energy force. Some people call it fate; some, God's will. I call it *my problem*, and therefore feel that it is up to me to deal with it. Violence and traumatic disaster had been finding a way into my life for well over a decade now, after eighteen childhood years of conservative, nonviolent living. The question was, why?

Why had I witnessed a grizzly suicide? Why had I been the only teacher outside on the playground with her students when some of L.A.'s most notorious gang members had driven by with automatic weapons? Why had I attracted a sick, demented loser who had spent months watching me undress at night before getting his nerve up to approach me?

...And most of all, why, of all places, had I chosen *this* troubled family to work for? What had I gotten myself into?

***

Mr. Wilde had been right; I needed to get away.

...He was going to be away this coming weekend, so were Dean and I. Instinctively, I knew Mr. Wilde would be pissed, but he had never actually said that I couldn't take Dean on a trip. *I approve of activities that do not disrupt the household or his schoolwork* is what he'd told me when I'd asked him for specifics. I felt quite confident that I could do this and he'd be none the wiser. Besides, I was going to leave a note on the kitchen counter.

***

"Dean, dammit, hold onto the rail!" I yelled over the head of another child who had jumped aboard the Powell–Hyde Cable Car at the same time we had.

Dean laughed, much to my surprise, and refused to hold on. The little shit tottered back and forth, his hands at his sides. He was enjoying himself, at least, but I was in a state of agitation over his antics. He was, after all, perched on the lowest step of the cable car. One perilous second of imbalance, and he'd be road–pizza.

A cruel need to be in control sent me swinging myself around the other child and wedging in next to Dean. I grabbed his ear and pulled.

"Hold on," I said harshly.

He threw his arms around my waist and hugged me with a lot of strength. I released his ear, at once contrite, and lay my hand over it.

"I love it here," he said, apparently unaffected by my disciplinary tactics. "I wish I lived here."

"I like it here, too," I said, baffled by his demeanor. He was absolutely enamored by this city. And, he'd hugged me!

Ding! Ding!

"Fisherman's Wharf!" The conductor announced. The car came to a stop. I was glad when Dean grabbed my hand. There were a lot of people out today, and I was nervous about his behavior. I watched the chilly breeze ruffling his thick brown hair as we walked.

"Warm enough?" I asked him.

"Yes," he replied immediately, already distracted by another thought. "Can we eat something? I'm hungry."

We were lucky enough to find a table in one of the small restaurants by the water. We had shrimp cocktails, clam chowder, and sourdough bread with butter. I chatted to Dean while we ate, telling him about the stores I wanted to go to while we were here to buy music and some clothes. He was in his element. I was increasingly glad I had opted to bring him along, even if I hadn't told his father of my plans. And I wasn't worried that Mr. Wilde would call this weekend, because the back apartment had been completed and the other hired help only came during the week.

"Let's go over to Ghiradelli Square," I suggested.

Dean nodded his head enthusiastically, his proper upbringing having schooled him to never speak with food in his mouth. I watched the way his body wiggled with an energy I hadn't thought him capable of. His dangling legs swung beneath his chair happily, like a normal child.

My observation was briefly interrupted by a moment of eye contact with a woman who sat at a table just behind Dean. She was staring at me intently, perhaps wondering if she knew me. I didn't recognize her, so I looked away for a moment. When I looked back, she was staring at Dean. Her blond hair and long gray coat were nondescript and therefore put out of my mind as I stood with Dean, leaving money for the bill on the table.

When we were buying chocolate, Dean picked out some samples for us, then politely asked if he could bring a bar to his teacher. Who could resist such a darling kid? There was a special carnival near Pier 41, so we went to check it out. We rode the Tilt–a–Whirl and Ferris wheel and went through the funhouse. Dean behaved as any nine year old might, yelling with startled fright at the sudden shifting of the floor and the colorful creatures that popped up in the various rooms. He kept a constant grip on my hand throughout the passage, telling me afterward that he had "really liked that place."

***

Next, we crossed the street to go to some clothing stores. I was bound and determined to get Dean to wear something besides khaki's and pressed wool slacks. He had, at least, gone for some time now without wearing the bowtie, but that wasn't good enough.

He watched me look at sweaters and jeans for a while then ventured over to the kids' section. I followed him and discretely encouraged him to try on some clothes. Four hundred of my hard earned dollars later, young Dean and I emerged, laden with packages of casual wear for him, and a new sweater for me.

***

We went back to the hotel. We took a taxi this time because we had so much to carry. Once in the room, I collapsed on the bed. I could hear Dean rustling through the packages and I smiled a secret smile of satisfaction.

"I like your new sweater a lot," Dean commented.

"Me too," I agreed. Then I sat up. "I'm going to take a shower. What are you going to do?"

Dean looked around, his eyes settling on the television. He grabbed the laminated TV directory. "They have cable TV here," he ventured, looking at his watch. "I could find a movie to watch," He looked up at me like he expected a reprimand for his outrageous suggestion.

"Well, let's see what's on." I said. I flipped through the channels and stumbled onto *Mrs. Doubtfire.* "Perfect," I declared, leaving the television set on that channel. "Keep it on this show, okay? I don't want to get charged for anything on the pay channels." I gave him a warning look. I was pretty sure I could trust him not to search through the porn selections.

Dean smiled innocently. "I will," he said, and seemed to mean it.

***

That night we ordered dinner via room service and watched movies. At ten–thirty, without being told to, Dean went in and took a shower. I turned down his bed for him, then changed into a nightgown to sleep in. When Dean reappeared, he was wearing only clean briefs. I was surprised at his sudden lack of modesty as I watched him go over to where he had neatly folded all of the new clothes. He picked up my new navy blue sweater and put it on.

"Hey!" I said. "That's mine, turkey." I laughed at him as he put his arms through the long sleeves and pulled it over his head.

"I like it," he said, as if that should mean he had a right to it.

The sweater fell to his knees and completely hid his arms. He walked over to the bed where I lay and looked at me with timid, pleading eyes.

"You should see how cute you are in that," I told him, wondering if he was finally looking for a little physical contact. Venturing to take a risk, I lifted up the blanket. "Come snuggle up with me for a while."

He did, hesitantly. I waited until he had lay down beside me then pulled his warm little body against my chest, hugging him close. The sweet clean scent of his skin and hair made a protective maternal lump rise in my throat, and I admitted that the little brat had long since stolen my heart. Now the option to quit this job would no longer be an uncomplicated one.

***

The following morning we rose at about nine–thirty then set our sites on Downtown, to buy kites to fly at Golden Gate Park. We picked up deli sandwiches to eat later and then drove my car over to the park. We spent the day there, relaxing in the sunshine, letting our kites soar high overhead. And Dean managed to break in his new jeans when we took a light hike.

"Now they don't look brand new anymore," he said proudly after he had slid bodily down a loose gravel hill.

We headed back to our picnic site to collect the kites and picnic blanket. I noticed the figure of a woman across the clearing. She nonchalantly strolled away before I really got a look at her, but she reminded me of the woman I had seen at the Wharf yesterday. I dismissed the strange thought because it seemed too farfetched, even for me.

***

I decided not to mention her to Dean as we drove back to Trinity. He was already preoccupied with the certainty that his father would be angry that we took a trip this weekend. Mr. Wilde was due back by the end of this week. I did reveal to Dean that I hadn't any plans to tell Mr. Wilde. Hell, if he truly gave a shit what we did while he was gone he'd call and ask.

CHAPTER NINETEEN
Secret Distortions

"Mr. Wilde," I said, as if he was the only person I truly wanted to see. (He'd returned the following day, long after I'd snatched the unread note from the counter, and, as planned, was unaware of my little excursion with Dean.)

"Miss Stuart?"

"I've been living here for over two months now, and I've never really had the chance to ask you about your writing," I started. He looked at me with a raised eyebrow. "Are your stories based on case study?" I asked.

"They are," he answered.

"Are you working on something new?" I asked.

"I am."

"Will you tell me a little bit about it?" I asked next. When he gave me a skeptical look, I hurriedly added. "I'm curious about how much research you put into your work."

"Hmm," he hummed, still seeming to question the sincerity of my interest. "The extent of my research depends on the basis of the story," he told me. "Like you, I write fiction. But I get ideas from real cases. When I leave town, it is often to go on site and investigate a real case. I am intrigued by the mystery of the unsolved murders. It is from the suggested scenarios that I get inspiration for my own books. My good friend, Wes Ryan, is a private investigator. He clues me in on the more interesting crimes and helps me find the background information. You'll be meeting him soon, actually. He's the one I've referred to previously. He'll arrive at the end of the week."

"I'll look forward to it," I said, impressed that he actually had some friends. "You put a lot of work into your stories. I just write from my head."

"That is the difference between you and me," he concluded.

It seemed that I was supposed to be insulted by that, but I ignored it. After all, I had been the one to make the comment, he'd only agreed with me. "Mr. Wilde, what is your current book about?"

“The murder of a young woman and her daughter,” he said. His eyes stared piercingly into mine, as if he wondered what I’d learned of his family’s tragedy.

“Is it in some way related to your own family’s case?” I asked, answering his unspoken question.

“There is no case with my family!” he said sharply.

I sat, waiting. I figured I’d instigated something with that question. Hopefully it wouldn’t cost me my job. I had a feeling he was ready to talk about it anyway, just not with me.

He had been glaring at me, breathing heavily. “How did you know about my family?” he asked icily.

“I knew only that your wife was dead. I didn’t know about Rachel until I saw a picture of her. Dean told me who she was,” I admitted. “But the only thing I know of her is that she died when your wife did.”

He closed his eyes and turned slowly away from me. He ran tense hands through his hair.

***

“I can’t erase it from my memory!” Mr. Wilde grated out, his hands gripping his head, as if to illustrate his point.

“Erase what?”

Is he having a psychotic episode?

Intrigued by this display, I stepped over to where he was now standing and laid a hand on his shoulder. This was trippy.

“It’s so loud...” his voice had dropped to just above a whisper. Unlike his son, he didn’t even react to the contact I had made. “We were shouting; each of us enraged with the other. I knew our marriage was over... had known it for a long time. And I resented her for the trap I’d found myself in. And in the middle of it was our sweet Rachel, begging us to stop fighting... I raised my hand to silence her and she thought I’d meant to strike her. So did Elaine... she left, taking Rachel with her.” He raised his head and backed away.

I let my hand drop to my side. “Is that the night they died?” I asked carefully.

"That's the night they were killed – in an automobile accident," the latter he added quickly, oddly, as if in anticipation of my next question. He raised his eyes to meet mine. They were full of deep, defensive anguish.

No wonder he was such a mess. I could only imagine the guilt he felt.

"Thank you for telling me this," I said. "It's helping me understand things so much better."

He glared at me then. "Such as?" he asked dangerously.

I sighed inwardly. What was the deal here?

I went ahead and tried to make my point, despite the obvious anger it was raising in him. "I've often wondered why you live like a recluse, Mr. Wilde." I clenched my teeth and waited.

"I have extensive privacy here," he said, narrowing his eyes. "When you've suffered a loss such as mine, Miss Stuart, you learn to be more protective of your own life."

"It seems to me that you're hiding here," I said.

"What?"

"It's a suspicion I've had, is all," I answered him. He was getting pretty pissed off. Why, dammit?

"My life and my son's–"

I interrupted him then, I couldn't help it. "What life? You're never here. Your son's life is little more than an existence, at best!"

"My son–" he tried again.

"Tried to commit suicide for Christ's sake!" I cut him off again. "That is not a child who benefits from your choices. He does not value his life. I suspect he believes you resent him for being the child who lived."

There. I'd blurted out everything. And he'd definitely heard it.

"I resent your suspicions!" he raged at me, stepping closer.

I stepped back. He glared resentfully.

"Who in the hell do you think you are?" he seethed, his voice lowered to a warning pitch. "You are not part of this family. You are an employee, an expendable employee."

"That's right," I agreed. I stood there glaring back at him challengingly. Then I realized I wasn't completely clear on what I was challenging. "That's right," I repeated, more lamely now.

"Then do we understand each other?" he demanded, his chest heaving with the attempt to calm down.

"No, I don't think that's the case," I said sarcastically. "I doubt if that will ever be the case."

He glared at me again. I left quickly.

***

Every time I saw the man during the following week, he looked at me with suspicion or displeasure. For some reason, I gained a sense of power from the knowledge that I had obviously hit home on some level with my suggestions, which he had resented.

Unfortunately, I still had no idea what I had nearly uncovered.

CHAPTER TWENTY
Tensions

"Miss Stuart," Mr. Wilde addressed me as I started to leave the kitchen Friday evening. I had been in there baking some cookies for Dean and his friends, and I kept eating them, so now I was in a hurry to remove myself from the temptation of devouring the entire batch of Tollhouse treats.

I stopped and turned to face my boss, whose presence I hadn't been unaware of. "Yes, Mr. Wilde?" I had noted a more deliberate formality than usual between us. *He must have something derogatory to say to me.* A payback was due, after all.

"I wanted to inform you that I'm having a cocktail party here tomorrow evening at six o'clock."

I frowned. *Dammit, tomorrow is Saturday, and I had hoped to take off to be on my own. And what difference should it make to me if he's having a party?* I allowed my attitude to show on my face. "Yes?" I asked, as if the significance of his comment was eluding me.

"I'm asking you to make yourself available in order to supervise Dean and see to it that he displays the appropriate social graces to my guests." Mr. Wilde stopped speaking for a moment, pensive, as if questioning himself suddenly. "You do have the suitable attire for such an occasion, don't you? Perhaps something that *compliments* your figure?"

Oh Brother. Does he think I'm some kind of social reject?

I gave him an exhausted look, saying in an ever so slightly sarcastic tone, "Hmmm, I'll have to look. I think I have a dress, but it'll need to be ironed..." then I added slowly, obtusely, "...but I don't think my tennis shoes will go very well with it... Will it be all right if I go barefoot, if I promise to wash my feet?"

That shut him up.

I was secretly pleased with my creative response, as I glared at him. Then I spun on my heel and left, leaving my sarcastic jab to hang in the air like a foul odor.

***

When I returned from my drive on Saturday evening, I was surprised to find the cocktail party was already under way. I checked my watch: six-thirty. Bracing myself to be prepared for a verbal assault, I deliberately entered through the front door, knowing Mr. Wilde would see me arrive. At the same time, some blondie GQ guy had planted himself just to the side of the doorway as I was approaching. I still wore the outfit I had left the house in that morning: clingy sweat suit, tank top, and new bright white cross trainers. It was a planned entrance, and I watched peripherally as the other man turned completely around to watch me while I purposefully walked through the passage to the kitchen. Hmmm, who was *that?*

***

After about thirty minutes, I heard the unmistakable footsteps of the boss himself outside my room. I could tell he stood before my closed door, waiting... in momentary indecision? Preparing his attack? Or, wondering if he would be subjecting himself to a potential outburst of *my* pent up wrath? Actually, I still had a bone to pick with him. *Bring it on!*

Finally he knocked on the door. I opened it and stood before him, waiting for him to speak, but he was apparently speechless. I had showered and changed into a simple, but stunning black cocktail dress. It's straight lines hung loosely, but clung to my curves enticingly when I moved. I had quickly washed my hair and applied just the right amount of mousse to control the wayward curls. I looked good.

I watched with immense satisfaction as Mr. Wilde's eyes traveled down the length of my body, noting the black nylon hose I wore on my long legs. The gaze stopped at my feet. I wore no shoes, on purpose.

"I do have shoes," I said mockingly, "I just need to find them." I turned and walked back into the room. He followed me and watched as I located a pair of black patent leather heels and slid them on. "Can I have a minute to put on some makeup?" I asked him, my tone slightly seductive, as if this was a moment of intimacy between two people as familiar as lovers.

"Certainly," Mr. Wilde answered. He made no move to leave me to my privacy.

"I'm sorry I'm late. In L.A., guests arrive for cocktail parties about two hours later than the invitation actually details. Is Dean dressed and about?" I was asking him from the bathroom doorway, casually accepting his choice to remain while I applied a light touch of earth tones to my eyelids and cheeks, followed by a dusky rose colored lipstick.

"He's fine, but worried about you," he answered quietly.

Coward.

I guess he was unable to admit his own concerns, if he'd had any.

I stopped what I was doing and stared at myself in the mirror a moment. "He's such a sweet boy," I said, deliberately evading comment to any subtle inquiry he might have intended. "Well, I'm ready," I said, turning to him, "is this all right?"

His look told me he thought I knew damned well that I looked incredible.

"You look ravishing, Miss Stuart," he informed me sincerely, "and you are doing a bang–up job of putting me in my place."

Now I grinned openly at him. "That *was* the plan," I said, and yes, I was gloating.

***

Now changed into "attractive attire," I went into the kitchen to get something to drink. We could hear the music I had just popped into the CD player coming through my opened bedroom as I poured a glass of soda from the selection of beverages displayed there. *There must be a full bar in the dining room,* I thought.

"Well, hello," a familiar voice said warmly.

From where do I know that voice? I turned toward it.

It was the Hollywood boy, Mr. GQ. He must have been waiting for me all of this time. I knew I had never met him before. I decided he must have a voice that sounded like someone else's that I knew.

I saw Mr. Wilde send him a warning look, but he was oblivious. I realized that he would be Wes Ryan, the PI who worked with Mr. Wilde.

I regarded Mr. Ryan with reserved curiosity and smiled at him, darting a look at my boss. Mr. Wilde seemed quite relaxed. It was clear that this man was a friend.

"Bryson? An introduction?" Mr. Ryan prompted.

"I'm his employee," I informed him before "Bryson" could respond. "But then, you would already know that, wouldn't you, Mr. Private Investigator?" I openly assessed him, liking what I saw. He was a babe.

"Yes, she's my employee," Mr. Wilde said, about a beat behind real time, "and I don't tend to mix my employees into my social circle."

Thanks.

Well, that had just alienated me from feeling free to socialize with his friends. Mr. Wilde frowned in frustration and left the room. What was his problem? Did he want me to be present, or not?

But Mr. Ryan stayed, giving me his attention, so I brought myself back to the moment. "I'm not sure what that was all about," I said.

"Me neither," he said. "Let's start again. I'm Wes Ryan." He extended his hand.

I took it and said, "And I'm Amy Stuart." I smiled as he raised my hand to his lips. He was very charming. I mentally fanned myself and took a sip of soda.

He stood staring wickedly at me. "So," he said, "are you going to boink your boss?"

I almost spit out my drink. "What?" I burst out laughing. "I've got to write that one down."

"You write too." It wasn't a question.

"Yes, I like to think so," I returned.

"You didn't answer my question," he reminded me, eyes dancing.

I ran my hand through my hair. "I'm not sure I'd know how to," I told him. I let my eyes give him another once–over. He was about six–two, broad shouldered and narrow–hipped, and had the best butt I'd seen in a pair of Levi's in a long time. He also had the testicular fortitude to show up to an affair at Bryson Wilde's in jeans and a white dress shirt, open at the collar. I was impressed enough with him so far to get a little giddy.

Then, I remembered what Mr. Wilde had said, and decided to put a stop to the flirting, at least for now. "Mr. Ryan–"

"Make it Wes, please," he said smoothly.

"Fine," I smiled indulgently, "Wes, have you seen Dean this evening?"

"I have," he answered slowly. "But then he disappeared."

I frowned. That was just not a phrase I wanted to hear when referring to Dean.

"You'll have to excuse me," I said, "but like Mr. Wilde said, I *am* his employee. I have someone to locate."

CHAPTER TWENTY–ONE
Silent Struggle

I went to find Dean. His room was empty, as was the rest of his wing. Where was he? I searched the entire upstairs, finally daring a peek into Mr. Wilde's room. The outside lights cast enough of a glow for me to see the elegant dark wood furnishings and fleece colored carpeting. I stepped inside and switched on a light.

"I don't want to go downstairs."

I jumped at the sound of Dean's voice. I hadn't expected to find him here, but he was sitting in a chair in the corner.

"Why?" I asked.

His face fell. "Some of those people are weird. They make me want to hide," he told me.

"Isn't there anyone down there who will be nice to you?"

"Yes, there are some," he admitted. "But what if I get cornered by the yuck–o's?"

I laughed. "Point them out to me and we'll be sure to avoid them." I held out my hand to him and coaxed, "Come on, we'll go make nice–nice and if it gets horrible, we'll come back upstairs."

***

We went downstairs together and mingled with the guests, making polite conversation. Dean seemed happy to talk about sports with one of the male guests while I chimed in comments here and there. A few of the others took immediate interest in me and managed to draw out enough information from me to get a synopsis of my writing efforts. I was momentarily distracted from Dean.

One middle–age couple, George and Therma Laughlin, persisted with the topic. "We hear you've had one book published. What type of story was it?" George asked me.

And how do you know that? I wondered inwardly.

I chuckled self–consciously, outwardly answering him with reluctance. "It was a cheesy, dime store romance," I told him, hoping that I'd just put a damper on his interest. I noticed Mr. Wilde was within earshot, working his way over to us and did not want him to hear my description of my work.

For one thing, I hadn't admitted that my book had been published, which meant he must have done some investigation to have found that out. Undoubtedly, his PI friend had taken care of that for him. I wonder what else Wes knew about me? That felt weird, like I was now totally exposed.

George was still waiting for my response and here came Mr. Wilde with his eyes on me. I could feel the heat on my face as I tried to hedge my way out of this conversation. I was fairly certain that the caliber of my writing was far inferior to my employer's. A man like Bryson Wilde, with all of his intellect and knowledge, would find much to criticize in my silly, meaningless efforts.

"Really," I tried to tell the Laughlins, "It was nothing to brag about, I wasn't even offered a contract. I guess my publisher didn't think I had another book in me."

Mr. Wilde had reached us by now and had obviously heard everything I'd hoped he wouldn't. "But what do you think, Miss Stuart?" he asked in a deceptively inquisitive voice. "Do you think you have another book in you?" He was raising one eyebrow as he regarded me. He looked like Mr. Spock.

I studied his handsome features, so deceptively gorgeous, yet so unlike the man within. Then I glanced at the Laughlins. The older couple seemed genuinely interested and nonjudgmental, but I was not certain of Mr. Wilde's motives for asking and could not gauge his sincerity. "Well, yes," I admitted with hesitation, "I've been working on my second one for a few months now."

"Oh? And will this be another cheesy dime store romance?" Mr. Wilde inquired, deliberately using my own belittling phrase in a way that left one with the impression that he was making fun of me!

Nervy.

"Actually, no," I responded with a warning meant only for him, "this one's about an absolute bastard of a man who is extremely sarcastic and arrogant and wonders why he has no friends." I gave him a challenging look, then allowed my lips to form a smirk of satisfaction when he narrowed his eyes. He had caught the innuendo in my words.

George and Therma laughed delightedly at my audacity. "Score one for Amy, Bryson," Therma teased. Then she directed her next comment to me. "Don't let him intimidate you with his insinuations, my dear. Not everybody is always interested reading a piece that is so complicated that one needs to reread it to get the full meaning. I like a good romantic novel every so often. If you've got the imagination to write them, more power to you. There's definitely a good audience out there waiting to lap them up."

"Absolutely," George seconded his wife's statements.

"They would know," Mr. Wilde told me. His tone was friendlier now, as if I had successfully put him in his place, "George and Therma are both editors for my publisher."

"Really?" I was impressed. "You came over from London?"

"No," Mr. Wilde answered for his friends, "they work for the American sister company in Chicago."

Right about then someone put some music on in the game room and people were beginning to dance. Mr. Wilde frowned through the doorway, clearly not interested in the loud music and voices. I couldn't help the attraction I felt toward the scene, though. I loved to dance, especially to the kind of music that was playing on the stereo. I glanced around the room for Dean. He was listening to an older woman, acting enchanted.

There was a crowd of people moving toward the commotion, some wanting to join in, but most too reserved to do more than watch and comment. Three couples were dancing in the open space between the television and the coffee table. Wes Ryan appeared beside me and took my hand. "May I have this dance?" he asked formally.

"Absolutely," I gave a wave to Mr. Wilde and the Laughlins and then headed into the crowded room. I saw Dean look over at me as I passed by some people standing around the perimeter of the room. I held up one finger to him to signal I'd dance to one song only. He nodded reluctant approval and seemed to be okay for the moment, so I left myself open to Wes Ryan's charm.

We began to dance. Wes coordinated his movements so that he was matching mine, dancing dangerously close, but never quite touching his body to mine. I stuck to a safe variety of twists and gyrations, but managed to keep up with his endless energy. We laughed at each other, sharing private amusement at the other's efforts.

And then...

I felt the steady heat of someone's eyes boring into me from the crowd and hoped that they were not Mr. Wilde's. But when I looked around the room, he wasn't even present. I still felt as if I was being watched. It was a like strong, eerie sensation of a presence of evil.

I'd felt that before, in another time and place, and had, to my own detriment, ignored it.

Then the feeling was gone before I could identify its source.

***

I pulled Dean out onto the dance floor next. He did okay out there. I was surprised. He also was enjoying the attention he was getting. His face was alight with pleasure.

Then the happy expression on Dean's face fell. We stopped dancing.

"It's time you were in bed, son," Mr. Wilde said from behind me. "It's late for you to still be up."

Dean didn't argue. "Yes, sir." He left quietly.

I started to follow him out of the room. A hand on my arm stopped me. "Dance with me one more time, mystery lady," I heard Wes request. Again his voice had a familiarity to it from some other time. It gave me a brief queer feeling. I hate those unexplainable feelings of déjà vu.

"Mystery lady?" I repeated mockingly, covering my momentary disquiet. But I followed him to the clearing for one more dance. Wes was a good dancer, actually quite sexy on the dance floor. He was awfully handsome, in a store bought sort of way. When the song was over, I thanked him and allowed him to kiss my hand again, but then I hurried to see that Dean was safely off to sleep.

I stopped in my room to kick off the heels I'd chosen. I never wore dressy shoes and these ones always gave me blisters. I guess I'd danced my last twist for the evening since both heels had tender spots on them. I snuck up the back stairs in my stocking feet.

I found my boss waiting for me in the hallway a few paces down from Dean's door. He had a somewhat amused look on his face.

"What's the matter, Miss Stuart?" he asked jokingly. "Just a country girl at heart after all?"

Humor? From this guy? Unheard of!

"Blisters," I confessed then winced for effect. He smiled at me. I looked at him warily for a moment. "You know, whenever you've called me aside lately, I've been insulted by what you've had to say. Are you about to nail me with some more negative appraisal?"

To his credit, he looked surprisingly contrite. I might have almost believed he was sincere. He shook his head, watching me without speaking. I waited with a raised brow for another moment, then decided he had nothing to say and turned to go toward Dean's room. I entered to find Dean in his pajamas and lying in his bed already.

"Tired?" I asked him as I sat on the bed and suppressed the urge to smooth his hair from his brow.

Dean nodded. "Um hmm. It was fun," he said shyly smiling at me.

What a cutie.

I was truly moved by his timid admission. He might just be the most precious being I had ever encountered. I bent down and kissed his cheek, that familiar lump rising in my throat. He accepted my kiss without reaction.

Mr. Wilde appeared next to me. I guess he had been watching the two of us together. "I regret spoiling your fun, son," he said sincerely to Dean. "I just worry that you might become ill if you don't get your proper rest."

"Yes, sir," Dean acknowledged respectfully.

I moved aside, not expecting Mr. Wilde to bend down and kiss Dean's forehead. His gesture surprised his son, as well, neither of us having read his intent. I made a face of surprise and winked at Dean, saying goodnight. Mr. Wilde followed me out of the room, switching off the light on the way.

CHAPTER TWENTY–TWO
Contraindications

In the hallway I turned to him.

"If you have no objections, I'll call it a night," I told him.

"So early? My guests will be disappointed." He omitted any preference of his own for my company.

"Well, as you yourself said, your employees don't mix with your social set," I reminded him, deliberately letting some of my anger put a slight edge in my words. I was learning to confront him as a method of preservation of my sanity.

"Actually, I said I don't *tend* to mix my employees with my social–" he attempted to interject.

"What's the difference?" I hissed caustically. "You still insinuated that I have no place in your circle of friends, did you not?"

He sighed, "I didn't mean for you to interpret it that way."

"Huh!" I gave a low guffaw. "Hey, you're the one with the refined vocabulary, why don't you say what you mean then?" The truth was, he'd hurt my feelings.

"I was attempting to warn Wes against pursuing you," Mr. Wilde explained patiently, honestly. He might have even been feeling somewhat intimidated by my apparent wrath.

"I can take care of myself, Mr. Wilde," I informed him, quite indignant. Who the hell was he to interfere with my private life? On the other hand, I had no intention of revealing any attraction to Wes, especially when I'd not yet analyzed it myself. "I remember my commitment to my job and will continue to keep my private life private." I said forcefully. "On the other hand, I'm not about to let you dictate when and where I can get attention from the opposite sex." The latter was probably not the best thing to say. Nevertheless, I *was* free to pursue male interests in any way I chose to. He did not get to oppose me.

"Very well, as you wish," he said, not wanting me to have the upper hand. "But this is a good opportunity for you to meet some new people who stand for something larger than themselves, and have aspired to do more in their lives than just–"

My eyes opened wide with indignation as I once again interrupted him. "Stand for what? Wearing 'suitable attire?' You are a snob, Mr. Wilde." My tone had a razor sharp edge to its careful control. He'd hit a raw nerve in me. I knew it, and I was giving myself away.

My employer appeared to be struggling to contain his contempt for my insignificant, anemic, unseasoned perspective. I was sure he saw me as having no concept of my own lack of culture and subliminal importance in a world like his. He narrowed his eyes at me. "If that is so clearly the way you see things, why are you here?" His words were cold and biting.

Blinking, I was silenced. Then, "I'm here because I'm looking for something," I said quietly. *All this time I'd been telling myself I wanted answers, but I'm actually looking for a place to heal,* I realized.

I left him standing there, watching my retreat. I wondered if he had any idea that he had stabbed a knife into an all too sensitive spot. He really had no notion of what made me function.

***

When Mr. Wilde finally decided to rejoin his guests downstairs, I was taking a load of laundry from the dryer. I heard Wes approach him in the kitchen.

"You don't have any designs on that nanny of yours, do you?" he asked my employer.

Wes couldn't have chosen a more appropriate time to inquire about me, I thought to myself. *If he's truly interested, I can take advantage of the opportunity to get out of the house... and maybe get a little background information on the Wildes.* So much for healing, Amy.

I could hear the exasperation in Mr. Wilde's voice. "Don't go there, all right? Just stay away from her. She's got responsibilities here." I couldn't recall ever hearing my boss address someone with the degree of familiarity and confidence he was using with Wes. Like they were legitimate buddies.

Apparently not one to pass up competition, especially for a woman, Wes persisted. "Wait a minute Bryson, you're not telling me that she's not allowed to date while she's in your employment? Is that legal?" he goaded good–naturedly.

I peeked through the doorway to witness Mr. Wilde's response. He opened his mouth to rebut then changed his mind. Instead he half smiled and shook his head. "You always do whatever you please anyway. Why am I even trying?" He didn't sound bitter.

"Where's your charming friend?" Therma Laughlin called to Mr. Wilde from a few feet away.

***

Many of the guests were staying for the weekend, apparently. Dean filled me in on the missing data the following morning. Wes was using his usual accommodations, which was one of the two apartments over the garage, and the Laughlins were in the guesthouse with another couple to whom I had not been introduced.

***

I was out running with Dean. No one else was up yet, but there had been a crew of people preparing breakfast in the kitchen when we'd gone out. I'd had another brief feeling of déjà vu when I came face to face with one of the hired caterers. She had blond hair, pulled severely back from her face, and when she'd met my eyes, she had darted her own away in discomfort. I had stared at her for a moment, but couldn't tell if she was the same woman from the cleaning crew I'd seen in the strange clothes. Well, it was a small town. People probably had more than one job around here.

Dean and I reached the end of Wilde Lane and turned back, slowing to a walk. I was pleased that Dean had improved his stamina enough to be able to keep up with me. At least I could see some positive changes in *him.*

"Hey Dean, what do you know about Wes Ryan?" I asked as the thought of him entered my mind.

Dean looked up at me with an expression of disdain. "He's weird. I don't like him."

"Really?" That surprised me. "What's so weird about him?" I asked, my curiosity aroused.

"He looks at me funny, and he always pretends he's the boss of me,"

Dean said.

"He tells you what to do?" I asked.

"Yes," he grumbled.

"Has your dad left you with him a lot?"

"No," he seemed somewhat defeated now. Maybe there was a bad chemistry between Dean and Wes. Maybe Wes didn't have the patience to try to gain Dean's trust. I certainly knew it was not an easy task.

"Well, sweetheart, we'll try to make sure he doesn't need to boss you around too much while he's here, okay?" I wanted to reassure him. Dean's expression didn't change. "What's wrong?" I pressed.

"He bugs me when he changes his voice. He can do impressions. He can make his voice sound like other people," Dean explained. "Father says he's a master of disguises."

"Oh really?" I wasn't sure what to think of that. "Does that mean he can fool people into thinking he's someone else?" I asked. I've never been one to be amused by practical jokers.

"He made me think he was Father once, and I got in trouble," Dean confirmed bitterly.

"Well that's not cool," I in a sympathetic tone. "Do you think it was on purpose?"

"I *know* it was."

I've always believed in honoring children's instincts, even when the subject was a cute guy. I'd keep Dean's opinion in mind.

***

I showered and dressed in jeans and white denim blouse. When I went into the kitchen, there was an impromptu comedy skit going on. I stopped to watch Wes Ryan impersonate both Presidents Bush, and also Clinton, Reagan, Carter, Ford, and of course Nixon. He was marvelous, and very funny. I've always admired people who could make others laugh like that. Then he went into a Bryson Wilde rendition that nearly had me in tears. And then I remembered Dean's convictions about him and again resolved to keep my guard up, in spite of his appeal. Still, Wes may be the one with the real answers.

CHAPTER TWENTY–THREE
Insight

Therma Laughlin took my arm. "Join me for a cup of tea?" she asked.

"Ooh, love to," I said with a smile. I got a good feeling from her.

"You fit in well here," she commented to me as we sat across the table from each other in the empty sunroom.

"I do?" I laughed. "I feel like a square peg here!"

"Don't you believe that for a minute, darling," she said. "I've never seen Bryson take lip from anyone, before you came along."

"This is good?" I asked. "We're at each other's throats so much of the time."

"He's a tough one to challenge, though, isn't he?" she asked knowingly.

"Yes," I agreed with feeling. "But I fear that one day, one of us will go too far, and then I'll be out of a job; which is a strange thing to hear myself say, because I'm always contemplating quitting."

"Oh, you mustn't!" she said with a wicked grin. "He needs to be riled up a bit. Keep pushing. Break down his rigid rules and routines."

"I have, to quite an extent," I said smugly, smiling conspiratorially along with her.

"He's a good one for you to know if you want to write, my dear," she added. "Association, on any basis, with Bryson Wilde will be recognized by the best publishers."

"I don't want to owe that man a thing," I said forcefully. "Can you imagine how he'd hold something like that over me? I'd never hear the end of it, nor could I ever satisfactorily return the favor."

"Oh please, you've done wonders with Dean," she said.

"How can you tell?" I asked her. "I think he's a very disturbed child."

"Well of course he is," she laughed. "Look who he has as a father." But by the affection in her voice, I knew she'd do anything for Mr. Wilde.

"But still–"

"Amy, Bryson is very impressed with you, believe me," Therma declared. "He showed me Dean's drawing. It's wonderful."

"I didn't teach him to draw though," I said.

"No, his mother did that," she agreed. "But you brought his talent to his father's attention, at least to the degree that Bryson has the drawing in his office, where he can see it every day. That is quite significant."

"Yes," I said. "It is significant."

Now I felt a renewed commitment to my job. I wondered if maybe she would tell me something else. "Therma, was Mr. Wilde happy with his wife?" I asked then regretted the question. It was putting her on the spot.

"I don't think he was," she admitted reluctantly. "But it was a very complicated situation, and very damaging to Bryson. He shut down to quite an alarming degree after he lost Elaine and Rachel. And truthfully, he's never disclosed his feelings of that loss to me, so I'm not able to represent him to you. Just know that he *is* human, somewhere deep down inside that handsome, yet brutal exterior of his."

I grinned at her. In all honesty, I was already certain of that. The question was, would the human within him ever resurface, or would I be caught in a power struggle for the duration of my employment here? And what about his son? Would Dean ever get a break and be free to be the child that he was?

CHAPTER TWENTY–FOUR
Facade: The Calm Before the Storm

"Where is Dean, Miss Stuart?" Mr. Wilde asked impatiently.

I looked around the kitchen. "He's not here," I said impishly. When my eyes met his testy glare, I skipped out to find my charge.

After twenty minutes of searching the house, I finally became concerned. Where the hell could he be? And why would he choose now to disappear, when he knew he was expected to be present to say good–bye to his father's guests?

I circled around the yard, coming to the front drive just as the Laughlins were saying their farewells. Therma gave me an affectionate squeeze.

"Give me a call anytime for advice on your work," she said quietly. "Consider me a *connection.*"

"Thank you!" I whispered back. Then I shook hands with George.

"Tell young Dean good–bye for us," he said.

I stood away from Mr. Wilde as they drove off, waving.

"Miss Stuart, I would like you to find Dean, please, and then send him to see me," he instructed.

***

I found him in his playroom, working on homework. He was wearing his dork clothes again. He even had the bowtie on. What was wrong here?

"Dean?" I asked in exasperation, "Why didn't you come down to say good–bye to the guests?"

"I had homework," he said coldly.

Okay.

"Well, your dad's ticked at you," I informed him. "He wants you go to him."

Dean got out of his chair and slammed his pencil down, stalking angrily out of the room. I followed him, thinking I might be able to play buffer between him and Mr. Wilde. We found Mr. Wilde in his study. He raised his glance from his work without raising his head. His look was uncomplimentary.

"Young man," he said icily to Dean, "when I give you instructions to be present at a specific time, I expect you to follow them."

"Fine," Dean said, unconcerned.

Uh oh.

But Mr. Wilde did not reprimand Dean. Instead, he turned on me. "Miss Stuart, have I not made it clear to you that I expect you to directly supervise him?" he demanded.

I batted my eyes. "Why, yes you have, come to think of it," I said in a dumb bimbo voice. Too late, I realized I'd probably gone a little far with that one.

Mr. Wilde dropped his pen and stared at me with an open mouth.

"Sorry," I muttered then I turned to Dean. "From now on, mister, the only privacy you'll be getting is in the bathroom." I grabbed the shoulder of his sweater vest and started to turn him around.

"That wasn't quite the extreme I had in mind, Miss Stuart," Mr. Wilde said drily.

I looked over at him. He was amused, apparently, at my behavior. "What would you consider to be appropriate then?" I asked him. It was difficult to look him in the eye this morning.

"An understanding with Dean that he is to check in with you if he intends to go off on his own," Mr. Wilde answered. Then to Dean he asked, "Can you be trusted to do this, Dean?"

"Yes sir."

"Did you forget that you needed to be downstairs this morning to say good–bye to the guests?" his father inquired.

"No sir."

"Why were you missing, Dean? Did you have a problem of some sort?" Mr. Wilde asked.

"Yes sir, I had a problem," Dean answered. There was an edge of sarcasm in his words. I wondered what he was thinking.

"May we hear about the problem please?" Mr. Wilde wanted to know.

Dean didn't respond.

Mr. Wilde looked at me with eyebrows raised in inquiry. I still avoided eye contact. "Well, if you've nothing to say, Dean, you may go."

Dean practically bolted from the room.

Mr. Wilde addressed me as I turned to leave. "Do you know if something's wrong with him?"

"He wouldn't talk to me either," I told him, averting my face, as if I were impatient to leave also.

"Miss Stuart, do you have anything that you'd like to say to me?" he asked, persistently.

"Not at the moment, Mr. Wilde," I told him. "May I go now?"

"Certainly."

***

I almost collided with Wes as I skipped down the side porch stairs. He caught me with one hand on my upper arm.

"Hey, sweetheart, where are you headed?" he asked lazily.

"I'm just looking for something," I said evasively.

"Oh?" he asked, letting go of my arm and stepping back a step. "Need any help?"

He was carrying a fishing pole and tackle box. Judging by the deck shoes and heavy cable knit sweater he had tied around his waist, I figured he was going fishing.

"No thanks," I said, squinting at him in the bright sunlight. "Where are you off to?" I wanted to know.

"I'm going out to fish on Mac Greyson's boat," he told me.

"So you know people in town?" I asked him.

"Oh sure," he said. "I spend a lot of time in town when I'm in Trinity. I get bored here at the house."

"I know what you mean," I agreed.

"Well, my lady, we could do something about that," he said.

"What do you have in mind?" I asked.

"How 'bout shooting some pool later tonight?" he suggested.

"Now that sounds like fun," I mused. "It's a date."

"Great, I'll come by for you later, after dinner," he said.

***

It was unusually warm again, considering it was two weeks after Thanksgiving. I was out on the pool deck, debating whether or not to swim. I was acutely aware of my employer shuffling his manuscript pages around in his game room, and suspected he was working his way into a frustrated frenzy. Did I really want to be in the vicinity?

***

When Mr. Wilde emerged wearing a pair of blue surfer style swim trunks and an unbuttoned cotton shirt exposing his chest and flat belly, I was on my final lap. I had seen him come out, but continued to swim while he observed from a chaise longue until he decided to take a dip as well.

He tossed his shirt over the chaise longue and stepped into the water onto the first step of the pool, and then walked down the rest of the steps and struck out for the other end. He returned underwater, flipping his hair when his head broke the surface. He opened his eyes to my stare. I could feel the heat of exertion on my flushed face, and was breathing hard.

"How many did you swim?" he asked me.

"Forty." I wanted to ignore him, but for some reason I found myself giving him my attention. "Dean's drawing upstairs." I told him before he could ask.

He ran a hand through his hair, smoothing it back in a practiced motion. "Uh, Miss Stuart... Amy," he started, not meeting my eyes, and surprising me with the unexpected informality of using my first name. "I don't know how I repeatedly manage to get myself onto your black list, but it's not my intention."

"Oh yeah?" I asked, genuinely surprised again, the frown on my face must have told him that I was reluctant to believe him. "You really don't know me, Mr. Wilde," I said, not taking the same liberty he had. "Why do you measure me by my accomplishments? Why don't I qualify for respect because of who I am at heart? What if I came from a wealthy, well–established family? What would that change? I'd still be thirty–one years old, single, childless, and with no current career goals other than a pipedream of being published again. Why am I lacking in aspiration by taking a position as a governess for a year or so, and spending some time writing my next book?"

He shook his head and shrugged his shoulders. "Do you really come from a wealthy family?" he asked. When I sighed in exasperation and rolled my eyes, he chuckled softly. "Only a joke," he told me.

Another joke!

He moved to the stairs and sat on the top one. He looked me in the eye and asked, "You told me last night that you were here because you were looking for something. What might that be?"

I glared at him. "Do you really expect me to confide in you?" I asked incredulously. "I don't feel that I can trust you! You'd turn around and use my weaknesses to taunt me when you're feeling disadvantaged."

Shocked, Mr. Wilde opened his mouth to rebut, but apparently found that he could not because I was right: He did use my confessions to taunt me. He had attacked my cooking, writing, clothing, even my methods of taking care of Dean. "I see your point," he finally said with a sigh. "But if it's any concession to you, I feel deep regret for having offended you."

I raised a skeptical eyebrow. "You do?" *He does?*

"Yes, I do." He edged a little closer to me and rested his elbows on his knees, cupping his chin in his hands. "I've read your first book, you know," he informed me, carefully.

My face flushed a very self–conscious red. "You have?" I asked unhappily. *Oh my God. That would not have been my first choice for an introduction to my abilities.*

"Um hmm," Mr. Wilde responded, enjoying my discomfort, I suspected. "It was very...enlightening." He smiled, amused with himself.

My guard was up. "How exactly were you enlightened?" I asked reluctantly. *Perhaps he might offer criticism of my simple writing style and vocabulary,* I thought bitterly.

He cleared his throat and looked at me through squinted eyes. "I assume that the heroine is based upon you, she certainly has your quick tongue."

I smiled ever so slightly at his assessment.

He continued, "She's very naive and inexperienced, however."

"I started that book over ten years ago," I explained. "She's based on a persona that I created as a teenager, so of course she's naive. But that was most of her appeal."

"Oh, I didn't think so," Mr. Wilde contradicted me. "I think she appealed to the hero because she was so strong willed and determined. She's autobiographical, is she not?"

I stared at him. I would not answer that question. If his PI buddy had done his homework, then they both knew I had a history that was rich with fodder for story.

"She also had a very passionate nature," he prodded when he couldn't get a response from his last comment.

This one I could take on. I rolled my eyes. "Oh, brother," I said sarcastically. "I know you can do better than that."

"What do you mean?" he feigned innocence.

"Oh please! Don't patronize me! I'm much more complicated than the character in the book, okay? And I'm not a sucker for a compliment."

"What are you insinuating? That I'm making a pass at you?" He demanded.

Actually, yes, that's what I'd been insinuating. Now I wasn't so sure.

"No, of course not." I said, backing down.

"I'm trying to give you a fair assessment of your writing," he threw back at me, "what's so bloody patronizing about that?"

***

He made crab cakes and brought them out to the patio.

I had put on my denim shirt and jeans and brought a book out to the poolside. I was seated in a chaise longue and had managed to become absorbed in the paperback. He brought a little table and set it between us. The plate of crab cakes was set on the tiny table, along with two gin and tonics. *Is he psychic or what? How did he know I love gin and tonic?*

"This is quite a treat," I commented pleasantly, realizing he was making an effort here. To do what, I was uncertain.

"You've undoubtedly realized that I've had you 'checked out', so to speak," he said, not acknowledging what I'd just said.

"Yes," I was glad he'd brought it up. "I've wanted to ask you about that."

"The information you gave me when I hired you was confirmed, by Wes. It was he who found out that you'd been published to a greater extent than you'd admitted," he said. "Why didn't you tell me about the book?"

"Because it's fair game for criticism from a writer of a higher caliber," I told him. "I'm self–conscious enough, without your *constructive* input." Then I changed the subject. "So Wes knows as much about me as you do, eh?"

"Undoubtedly he knows more," Mr. Wilde said.

That might not be good.

***

He was trying to get something out of me.

"You said before that your were here because you were looking for something. I want to know what it is," he spoke in a gentle tone.

I sighed wearily then bit into a crab cake. It was delicious. "Haven't we already been through this?" I said after I'd swallowed. But when I looked at him and saw how open he was, I realized I was willing to tell him something.

"I was the victim of a violent crime before I left Los Angeles. I–"

"What sort of crime? Were you injured?" he interrupted, his frown deepening.

"I was nicked with a bullet in the back of my neck," I told him quietly. "The other three bullets struck my favorite student, killing him." I realized I felt detached from the pain of it, which allowed me to continue. "I am not prone to violence," I said. "I've tried to avoid the criminal element all of my life, but over the past year, it's been finding me more and more frequently. Once it had actually left me injured, I knew I had to go away."

"You speak of this criminal element as if it were a force, with it's own free will and power," he observed.

"I guess I do think of it that way," I agreed, although acknowledging it out loud made me want to rethink my mindset.

"And now you're looking for what? Resolution?" he asked.

I shrugged. "I'm looking for a new trust in my instincts about people." I said, pausing to formulate my true thoughts. "I'm looking for peace, and

I'm looking for freedom from fear."

He nodded with understanding. "As am I."

After a long, contemplative silence, I asked him about his good friend Wes. "Who is he to you? How long have you known each other?"

Mr. Wilde took a long swallow of his drink then reclined back in his chair. "We started our investigative careers on the same case. Did you know I have a background in journalism?"

"I'd heard something to that effect," I acknowledged.

He looked at me sharply. "From who?" he asked.

Paranoid!

"From that old man at the general store," I reminded him. "The day I asked about the job, I also asked about you." It felt funny to admit that, as if I'd taken a liberty I'd not been entitled to.

"Wes Ryan and I met just after I was married," he told me. "He's been a trusted friend ever since."

"I see," I acknowledged. "So will you be in town this week while he visits?"

"No," he said. "I've got to run over to Sacramento tomorrow for another signing, and then Wes and I will fly to Chicago to interview two families who've lost loved ones to unsolved murder. We should be back by Wednesday."

"I notice you're telling me more detail about your trips," I commented.

"Perhaps," he agreed. "But I've not revealed the name I am published under, have I?"

I supposed if I was willing to snoop, I could find out that little tidbit on my own. But the thought of violating his space was just plain abhorrent.

***

It struck me later how very similar my life had become to Mr. Wilde's. We were both hiding and afraid.

***

Wes came for me at about eight forty–five and we drove into town in his black Jeep. He had the stereo on moderately loud, glad that I approved of his music selection. At Lucky's there were 5 tables. We were one of the only two couples playing pool. This town was so dead, for Christ's sake.

For some reason, I had lost interest in the whole idea of a night out, and was not at all interested in the game at hand. I found myself thinking about my boss, and the way he had tried to make amends with me today. I felt like I needed to sit alone in a quiet space and analyze this whole bizarre situation. The solution, or explanation for the unhealthy, dysfunctional, clinically certifiable behavior of the two male Wildes had to be amidst the information I had collected thus far. I felt like I was just being obtuse, and not seeing the obvious.

Wes picked up on my distraction. "What's the matter, mystery lady?" he asked.

I smiled, in spite of myself. "Why do you call me that?" I asked.

"Because I can't read you yet," he answered with a gentle voice.

"Of all of the people here," I declared, "I am the *least* complicated."

"Afraid not, sweets," he informed me. "On the contrary, you're quite the puzzle."

"Wes, it's kind of been giving me the creeps, the way you know as much about me as you do. Or at least I'm assuming you do."

He strode over to me and planted a warm smooch on my cheek. "I'm sorry, Amy. I should have seen that I was making you uncomfortable," he said with sincerity. I waited to feel aroused by his touch, but it did nothing for me. He reached up his hand and gave my arm an affectionate squeeze. Nope. Nothing. Man, I needed to unwind.

***

Playing pool on a first date can be dangerous. All that bending over the table and rubbing chalk onto the tip of the stick... associations and connotations constantly come to mind.

I caught Wes eyeing me appreciatively on more than one occasion. I kept hearing Mr. Wilde's words about keeping my personal life out of his house, and then acknowledged that if I let him, Wes would probably take me to his bed tonight. I didn't want to sleep with Wes yet, and I really didn't want to give him any encouragement inadvertently.

After our fifth game, I suggested we leave.

"So soon?" he asked, disappointed. "I was just going to suggest we start making the game more interesting, by betting kisses, or backrubs for the stakes."

"I was pretty sure that's where you were headed," I said with an indulgent smile. "Sorry, friend, but I'm not going to go there with you. Tonight you get to be a Private Dick." *Clever, Amy!*

He dropped his pool cue and grabbed his heart. "How could you be so heartless?" he asked dramatically.

"Because it's ten–thirty, and I get up at six in the morning," I responded. "I could use a good night's sleep," I added with an apologetic tone.

"Okay, my girl, we'll get you home."

CHAPTER TWENTY–FIVE
Indiscretions

I saw Mr. Wilde off early Monday morning. He said he would likely return in the afternoon, to meet Wes, then leave for Chicago.

Whatever. At least we were being friendly to each other.

***

Instead of dropping Dean off at school, I decided to walk him inside the school building to say hello to his teacher. She was quite glad to see me, and told me that if I preferred, we could have the parent–teacher conference right now.

"Conference?" I asked. "I hadn't even known they were scheduled."

"Oh yes, Miss Stuart," she said with a frown. "I sent home notices two weeks ago, and the pupil free day tomorrow is on the school calendar that goes home the first week of the school year."

Pupil free day? Calendar?

I looked at Dean questioningly. "Why didn't you tell me about the conference?"

He shrugged uncomfortably.

"Dean, you could have told me," I told him chidingly. Then to Miss Carter I asked, "Is it all right with you to confer with me, rather than Dean's father? You see, his father is out of town for a while."

"Why not?" she said amicably. "Besides, I seem to get a much more receptive audience with you."

So we conferred. Dean was doing better over all. He still turned in the odd homework assignment that Miss Carter could only describe as unacceptable. However, she did emphasize that he was socializing more with his peers, and participating more in the group projects. This was a vast improvement over the past, when Dean had apparently insisted on working independently, and had brilliantly out shone his classmates, thus completely alienating himself.

"Now he seems to want to be a part of the team sometimes, which makes him popular because he's so bright," Miss Carter added.

I looked over at Dean, who had been silently following the whole discussion. He wore a frown until he saw my impressed smile then he let his face relax.

"I think we'll have to take advantage of this pupil free day," I told him, "and celebrate that you're doing so much better."

"Okay," Dean said, almost smiling back.

Miss Carter thanked me for the meeting and then stepped out to collect the children from their line outside. I told Dean that we'd take another trip to San Francisco tomorrow on his day off. His dad was going to be gone again, and this would just be a daytrip. We'd be back in the early evening. Dean agreed to the plan with some reservation.

Children began to file into the room as I left. I looked back at Dean, pleased to see him greeting some of the kids with a smile.

***

I sang along to some oldies on the radio as I drove away, thinking about what I could do with Dean tomorrow. *I'll wait until the boss and Wes are safely gone, then I'll pack some snacks and extra clothes and load the car for another trip to San Francisco, by golly.* Well, that covered tomorrow. But for now, I was already bored and I had hours to kill before picking up Dean. There was nothing to do at home. I'd been feeling blocked with my writing, so that wasn't on my "to do list" for the day. I decided to go into town and look for Chester. Maybe he'd invite me out on his boat.

But when I found him, Chester was fishing off of the pier. I looked out at his boat, moored in the bouncing sea. Well, there *were* a lot of angry looking clouds rolling in from the horizon. Maybe it was a good day to stay on land after all.

"Too dangerous to take her out?" I asked him sympathetically.

He was bummed. "Yeah, I've got to play it safe," he said sadly.

Now this was a man who really loved the sea.

"Is anyone else out there?" I asked him, suddenly getting the willies at the thought of being trapped on a boat in a storm.

"No one that has any sense," Chester said.

CHAPTER TWENTY–SIX
Evil Permeations

I went home and tried to write. I ended up with a few decent segments, so that gave me hope that day wouldn't be a total wash. At about twelve–thirty, the front doorbell chimed. I wasn't even sure what the sound was from, because I'd never heard it before. I made my way to the front of the house and saw a woman whom I recognized to be Mrs. Campbell peering angrily into the house through the leaded glass window.

"Mrs. Campbell?" I asked, opening the door.

"I want to see Mr. Wilde!" she said in a frenzy of anger, shoving inside the house. She stopped and looked around, as if shocked by the sophistication of the manor.

"What's wrong?" I asked from behind her.

"My son was attacked in the woods today!" she exclaimed, then burst into tears.

I felt my own eyes water in sympathy. "Oh my God! Attacked?"

"A man in black clothing and a black ski mask grabbed Albert and tried to force sex on him!" she cried.

"Jesus," I said. My stomach turned into such a tight knot, I almost lost my balance. "But Albert got away?"

She nodded, covering her face with her hands and sniffling. "He said the man was tall and had an accent," she muttered.

"And you're suspecting my boss?" I asked in amazement.

"Amy– can I call you Amy? He's very strange and unfriendly! He's weird!" she pointed out.

"I agree," I said with irony, "but that doesn't make him a child molester."

"The whole town suspects him," she informed me.

"Are you serious?" I asked. This was absurd. I felt compelled to defend Mr. Wilde. Why, I'm not certain. I guess if he was going to have to pay a price for his arrogance, I figured it ought to be a legitimate one. That man was not a pervert! An introvert, maybe. But not a pervert.

"Mrs. Campbell, it wasn't Mr. Wilde who assaulted your boy this morning," I told her again, remembering his daytrip. "He's in Sacramento for the day."

"Can you prove it?" she demanded. She was so distraught she was shaking. When I gave her a helpless look in response, she concluded, "Then I'll have to go to the sheriff with my suspicions. And I'm not the only person in this town who thinks it is Bryson Wilde. Some of us are asking for an investigation."

***

An hour after Mrs. Campbell left, the sheriff arrived. I was close to tears now with anxiety about my employer getting caught in the middle of all of this. I truly don't know why I was so completely certain that he was innocent, but I was. And I was determined to protect him. Charges of child molesting were the same as a conviction. He'd always be a criminal and a danger to the children of Trinity in the town's eyes.

Sheriff Caldwell was sympathetic to my distress and he assured me that no charges had been filed, but that Mr. Wilde would be required to provide proof of his whereabouts over the past several weeks. Apparently, there had been quite a few reports of a pervert in the woods lately.

"But he won't want to prove that he was out of town," I anxiously told the cop. "He's been traveling for book signings and if he reveals those locations, anyone could find out his pseudonym. And he's dead set on protecting his identity as a writer."

"Now Miss Stuart, even you can agree that this is rather extreme behavior for an author, no matter how popular," Sheriff Caldwell reasoned.

"Yes, I can," I said reluctantly. "I have a hard time understanding his need for so much privacy. But as time has gone by, I've learned more about him and his family, and I suspect that he has very *good* reason for his behavior– extreme as it may seem."

"Well, ma'am, there are lots of ways to interpret that. I'll still need to bring him in for questioning," he said.

***

I met Mr. Wilde at the front door. He gave me a weary look, and was not pleased that I had something very important to tell him.

"That's absurd!" he said sharply, when I told him of the town's suspicions. "What a pathetic group of individuals."

There was a knock on the door. It was Sheriff Caldwell.

"He went to Sacramento for a book signing!" I declared as the officer led Mr. Wilde out of the house.

"I can easily verify my whereabouts on the times in question, Miss Stuart," Mr. Wilde said icily, as if embarrassed by my behavior. "You need not concern yourself." He followed the sheriff out the door. I watched him get into the back seat of the sheriff's all–terrain wagon. They drove off without any further reassurances from Mr. Wilde.

***

Where in the hell had he gone?

He hadn't shown up for dinner. Dean and I hadn't touched our food, each tense for a different reason. When had I asked Dean what was wrong, he had grumbled that he just wanted to go to bed and then had done just that. Now I had no distractions and I was too tense to think straight, so I sat on the bottom stair in the entrance hall. I don't know why I still had the urge to talk to Mr. Wilde. I had nothing more to say in my own defense, anyway. He had positively railed on me when he'd returned from the Sheriff's Station. I had gone way too far by revealing those few facts, apparently.

Thump. Thump. Thump.

It was a very faint but distinct sound. I looked toward his office doorway. That second door just beyond it was the only one downstairs that I'd never opened. I'd just assumed it was a closet the first time I'd seen it. Now it became apparent that it wasn't.

The door opened onto a descending stairway and as soon as I opened it, the thumping became much louder. I went slowly down the stairs and found Mr. Wilde in his basement gymnasium, slamming agitated fists into a punching bag. He was covered in perspiration, wearing a sleeveless sweatshirt and boxing shorts. In spite of my inner turmoil, I duly noted that the man could sweat like a normal individual.

He saw me and stopped.

"So you've found my gymnasium as well?" he demanded.

Obviously. "So I did," I said carefully. "I was wondering how you stayed in shape."

"I wonder why you are so bloody curious about my personal life!" He was fit to be tied.

My hands started to shake. I didn't know what to say.

"Now I'll never be certain that you're not blurting out information about me wherever you go!" he rasped resentfully.

"I won't be," I said earnestly. "I would never have–"

"Spare me the reprisal, Miss Stuart."

Then my indignation finally kicked in. "How can you be so self righteous?" I demanded. "You've had me *investigated* to get your answers about me!"

"I'm you're employer," he said, as if that were all he needed to say.

"Yes, but I'm not working for some secret government agency," I said acidly.

"There is no comparison, Miss Stuart," he said in a level tone now. He faced me squarely and let his glare bore into my defensive eyes.

Shit.

Well, I'd tried. What more could I do? I stomped back to my "quarters".

Fuck!

Was I being unreasonably defensive here, or had I not saved my employer a lot of grief by exposing a tiny excerpt of his life to the world? As a writer, he exposed his inner self in his work, what the hell was such a big deal about my referring to a book signing? But even as I tried to defend my actions in my mind, the bottom line was that I had breached the contract that I had signed. He would be completely in the right to fire me now if he chose to.

It didn't help that he was such a bastard. Even worse, I couldn't explain my loyalty and the degree of determination to protect him that had arisen earlier today.

I paced back and forth in my room.

"I've got to get out of here," I said aloud.

***

I went to Lucci's and ordered a slice of pizza and a draft beer. I sat grumpily at the polished oak counter, making sweat circles with my beer mug in the shape of the Olympic rings on the surface.

"I've been calling the house looking for you," Wes said in my ear.

I jumped.

"Let's get a table," he said with a frown of concern that looked somewhat forced. "You need to blow off some steam, I can see."

***

"Wes, what is the story with Bryson Wilde?" I asked in exasperation.

We sat facing each other across the checkered tablecloth. He smiled in amusement. "You're not the first woman to wonder, I'll tell you that much."

"I'm not wondering as a woman," I insisted, refusing to let him try to say I was hung up on my employer. "I'm wondering as a human being. He's hiding *something.*"

"What do you think it is?" He asked with interest.

"Does this mean you won't tell me anything?" I demanded.

"I'll hear your ideas, and if you're correct, I'll tell you so," Wes said companionably.

"Wonderful," I said with cynicism. Then I sighed, not really wanting to say anything against Mr. Wilde that could come back to further slap me in the face. "I just wonder why he's so concerned about his privacy," I finally said. I looked at Wes. "Sometimes I've thought he might be involved in the witness protection program, or something like that. He's so proper. Sometimes I think he's full of shit."

"I'm surprised to hear you say that," Wes commented.

"Why?" I asked defensively. "Outward appearances can be deceiving. Did you know the town is supposedly abuzz with the rumor that he's hiding in the woods waiting for unsuspecting kids to pass by so that he can molest them?"

"The whole town?" Wes chided, as if I was being melodramatic.

Maybe I was.

When I didn't respond, Wes said, "Well, the boys I hang out with, who happen to be volunteer deputies, told me that was the latest scuttlebutt, but it isn't going anywhere."

Thanks to me, dammit, I thought.

"Did they also tell you he'd cleared himself by proving he was in Sacramento today? That's what the current upheaval at the house is all about, because I told Sheriff Caldwell that he didn't want anyone to figure to out his pen name."

Wes winced sympathetically. "Ooh, big no–no," he said. "Now, that comment would promote gossip, which triggers curiosity. You know how people are about celebrities. Right now, he's rich and reclusive, but add a popular author's name to the equation and suddenly everyone wants to know everything about him because he's also famous."

"I know," I returned unhappily. I thought about Mr. Wilde's admission to me that Dean had had some psychological problems. That would make a nice cover for one or more of the tabloids.

I'd blown it, and I knew it.

After a moment, I told Wes, "I don't believe the rumors even if the description fits."

Wes looked at me in surprise. "You don't sound like you know what you believe."

"The kids say he has an accent, but they don't know what kind. That covers a lot of territory, even in this small town." I said in response, feeling perhaps it was time to get on board the loyalty train again. "Personally, I'd be inclined to suspect a few other local townsmen before I'd turn on Mr. Wilde."

"Good for you," he praised. "Bryson's really found himself a gem in you."

***

I left Wes at the bar after my third beer. I probably shouldn't have driven home, but I felt sober, so I did. I hoped to hell he wouldn't relay any of our conversation to Mr. Wilde.

I entered the house through the front door, finding it still unlocked. I guessed that meant the big boss was awake and about. I drew the bolt on the door and tried to sneak by his study quietly, thinking it might be in my best interest to avoid him just now.

"Miss Stuart?"

So much for that idea.

I went to the doorway and leaned my shoulder against the frame. "Yes?"

"Did you lock up?" he asked.

"Um hmm," I told him. "Am I fired?"

"No."

"That's nice," I said with a small smile of relief.

"I thought perhaps we could have a chat. Are you interested in a cappuccino?" he offered.

"Uh, okay," I said, knowing by now that when he invited me to join him for food or drink that he was in a better mood. But I still felt like I was on shaky ground, mostly with myself.

We went into the kitchen.

***

"I think it's about time you told me about the things you are running away from, Miss Stuart," he said to my surprise as he measured freshly ground coffee.

"Oh!" was my response, accompanied by a troubled frown. "Haven't I told you enough?"

"Hardly," he said chidingly.

"Are you wondering if I'm running from the law?" I asked, evading his initial request for information.

"I've already told you that I know you're not."

"Did Wes tell you that I'd been shot?" I asked him.

"No, you did," he said derisively. "Come, Miss Stuart, tell us all about yourself." He leaned back against the counter and folded his arms over his chest.

The tables had indeed turned again, and it was my move.

I sighed in defeat. Where to begin?

***

"This is not an easy subject," I informed him. "I've really never fully disclosed this information to anyone."

"I'm listening," he said, intrigued.

"Am I going to find that I'm the protagonist of your next book?" I asked, stalling again.

"If your story is interesting enough, perhaps," he conceded. "Talk." It was an order.

I told him about the suicide on the Hollywood Freeway. I did not disclose the extent of the effect it had had on me, only that the carnage had disturbed me. "It was a sick twist of fate," I said, "that I should have ended up at that very spot in that very moment in time, so soon after the day that Eduardo had been gunned down."

"Indeed," he concurred. He was observing me closely.

I continued. "Not long before all of that, a male neighbor in my apartment complex had been demonstrating an overt interest, trying to get to know me," I said, slipping into a self–absorbed reverie. "I was not impressed... he was very strange. Pretty soon, he began to make insinuations that he had been watching me. I didn't understand what he was telling me until I realized that he was following me– and *peeping* me."

"I beg your pardon?" Mr. Wilde asked.

"The creep had been watching me undress through my windows." I stopped talking. An involuntary shiver raced through me. The familiar feeling of invasion was spreading over my entire body.

***

I flashed back on a memory of his washed out, baggy–eyed face. It was a victim's face that spoke of a life that had never gone his way. I remembered how I had at first been open to occasional chitchat with him, thinking it wouldn't hurt to be on friendly terms with my neighbor in that grungy Hollywood apartment complex. But I had soon found out how needy he was, and had been repelled. I'd had enough to deal with, without enabling a loner to cling to me for life support.

Unfortunately, he'd taken that one concession as an invitation to approach me, again and again, and again. He just couldn't seem to get rejected enough.

That had been the beginning of a three month nightmare that had begun with unwanted phone calls and knocks on my front door and had ended with my catching him peering in through my bedroom window while I was naked. I had been trying to decide whether or not to wear a g–string under my nylons. He had watched me try them on, then check out my ass in the mirror, then take them off, then put them back on and check my rear view again.

A lovely feeling, performing for an unknown audience.

***

Coming back to the present, I looked over at my boss.

"Do you think that once a person has experienced such violation, that she becomes more sensitive to a potential reoccurrence?" I asked him, thinking of the dark stranger. Now was the time to tell him about it, but I suddenly felt a resistance that I can't quite explain, as if I'd be admitting to finding myself in yet another role as the victim. I'd been trying so hard to get control of my own safety.

"Not necessarily," he said in grim answer to my question. He had his hand on his chin, contemplatively listening to my story.

"I was trying to find some peace," I said. "I thought that a small town like this would be the perfect place, but it's really no better."

"It's probably worse," he said with a touch of irony.

I looked at him. *Now, what is he referring to?* "You know, I often feel as if we're each talking about two different things during the same conversation," I said.

"I'm quite certain that we are," he said with an odd smile.

Strange.

"Now, how about those coffee's?" he asked, returning his attention to the preparations.

***

"When did you get your first break?" I asked him as he poured steamed milk to top off each cup of cappuccino.

"When I uncovered a child pornography ring," he answered. "It was the first case on which I'd collaborated efforts on with Wes. I didn't know him well then," he reflected. "I thought for a time that *he* was actually involved with it. But he was far more capable than I'd ever surmised. He has a talent for disguise."

"What happened?" I asked Mr. Wilde.

"We broke open the case and our story made all of the major publications," he told me. "I made reference to my accomplishment when I submitted my first manuscript to my publisher, and I made the best seller list overnight."

"You've really earned your fame," I commented, thinking of how little effort I put into my own work.

"You have talent, Miss Stuart," he said generously, as if reading my thoughts. "But you've yet to put it to good use. I'm certain that you're capable of much deeper work than you've produced thus far."

He was right. I nodded in agreement. I was somewhat surprised that he had put enough thought into the subject of my abilities to have made that conclusion.

"What's your pseudonym?" I asked him on impulse.

"Morton Dunleavy."

I grinned. "Oh my God, *you're* Morton Dunleavy," I declared. "You're a very famous man."

"I know, I've tried to impress that fact upon you repeatedly," he said ironically.

I wanted to pursue the subject. "Someone is eventually going to recognize you by the author photo on the book jacket–" I stopped, thinking. "You don't put a photo in your books, do you?"

"Not since my first release, no." He told me.

"And no one in town has figured it out yet?"

"Not so far," he acknowledged with a touch of irony.

I looked at him for a long moment, thinking that I really preferred moments like these, where we were more compatible. I truly didn't like for him to be upset over something I'd done. I felt my remorse for my earlier indiscretion rise again.

He kept his eyes on mine, as if he could see my thoughts forming, but just shook his head in mild exasperation.

"It was an inadvertent blunder." I said apologetically.

His eye flashed with anger. "You've made that clear, Miss Stuart," he replied with a hint of his customary arrogance. "We can let it go. I've no sense that any harm was done."

"I *am* sorry," I told him.

"You've made that clear as well," he returned.

"But am I forgiven?" I pressed, holding my breath.

He inclined his head, gave me a half smile, and left me wondering, as usual. By now, I ought to be used to this.

I sighed, wanting him to understand that I'd been trying to protect him. "I wanted to prove that you were far away from here when these incidents were occurring."

He gave me a look of reproach. "Certainly you can understand the violation of my privacy," he said.

"Absolutely!" I emphatically agreed. "I felt sick doing it, but I felt I had no choice. They were falsely accusing you."

"How can you be so sure?" he asked.

I looked at him with reluctant honesty. "Truthfully? ...I can't imagine you participating in any sort of sexual activity, no matter what form of expression," I said.

"I'm flattered," he responded drily.

Was that an insult for him? I couldn't see why. The man hadn't an ounce of compassion to give. Well, maybe he did. Something was definitely changing in him that was bringing him out of his hiding place a little bit. And he had come to be more tolerant of my company as well. But I still couldn't get a sense of his sexual side.

He'd informed me that he'd delayed his departure to Chicago because of today's events, but that he and Wes would leave early in the morning and return late Wednesday night. He'd also said that this was his final trip for research for a good while. I'd told him I wasn't sure if I was pleased to know he'd be around more or not.

CHAPTER TWENTY–SEVEN
Sensory Impact

But the following morning, for a brief moment, the departure for Chicago seemed to again be in jeopardy. I was heading out for my run, when I heard Wes talking to Mr. Wilde. I stuck my head into the kitchen to say good morning, and was told that there was a tragedy in town.

"What is it?" I asked, my stomach clenching.

"Mac Greyson's boat turned up late last night, but Mac's nowhere to be found," Wes told me in a strained voice. He looked pale and worried.

I looked from him over to Mr. Wilde. My employer had a pasty complexion, he looked positively ill. I felt quite certain that he had no relationship with Mr. Greyson. So why was he this bothered? Don't get me wrong, I felt the weight of worry myself, and just knowing that Mac's wife and children were probably scared to death was enough to make me feel deflated and upset. But Mr. Wilde looked like he had seen a ghost.

"What's happening in town?" I asked.

"They've got a search and rescue team coming in from the county," Wes said. He shook his head in defeat. "There's not much hope that he's alive, if he fell into the water somehow."

"And the sea was kind of rough yesterday," I added.

"I heard it was extremely rough," Mr. Wilde corrected me tensely.

"Are you men still going to leave this morning?" I asked, successfully hiding my hope from my voice. I had plans of my own, after all.

Mr. Wilde looked at his watch. "We'll be gone by the time you return from your run," he said.

Good.

***

Dean and I went into the city. We saw two movies. We bought candy. We had Chinese food at a restaurant on Broadway. We walked up to Coit Tower and looked at the view of the city, Alcatraz, and the Bay and Golden Gate bridges. Then we drove over both bridges, two times each.

***

I called Chester when we got back to Trinity.

"Have you heard anything about Mr. Greyson?" I asked him.

"Yeah, Amy," he said in a tight voice. "He's gone to be with the big kahuna."

"They found his body?" I asked, a rush of mournful tears forming a lump in my throat.

"It washed up late this afternoon," Chester said. "I still can't believe he took his boat out..."

We paused, letting our silence express a million thoughts of solace for his family and friends.

Chester cleared his throat. "There's a community service tomorrow, at the Town Hall," he said. "Then the family will announce the funeral plans. Do you want to go?"

"Yes," I said. "Shall I meet you at the pier in the morning, and we can go together?"

"Please do, Amy."

***

I attended the meeting of the community and partly expected to be shunned because I worked for a man some people considered to be weird at best, and at worst "the pervert." It was my first experience with such a gathering, but I was warmly received. It was wonderful. People really reached out to each other to give, as well as to receive comfort. We took up a collection for Mac's family. His wife was there for a short time. She told us that she was very grateful for our support, and that following a brief funeral, we were all invited to the burial and then to her home afterward.

Chester was unusually silent, although I'm sure he was preoccupied with the tragedy. On our way out, I asked him how he was feeling.

"Very angry, Amy," he said forcefully. "Mac Greyson was no fool. He knew the sea better than any man in town. He had no business taking his boat out. I just can't believe he died for nothing."

That made me uncomfortable. "Do you think there was foul play?" I asked with dread.

"Well," he said, relenting slightly, "I can't go accusing someone of something I know nothing about. But I feel really unsettled."

"I think time will ease that," I said without much conviction.

At my car he gave me a companionable hug. "Take it easy, Amy," he said in my ear.

"You too, Chester," I said, suddenly emotional. "You take good care of yourself. Don't take any risks for a while, okay?"

He gave me the *hang loose* sign with his hand and walked off.

***

Thursday morning after I returned from driving Dean to school, I met up with Wes in the back yard and stopped short in my tracks when I saw the sweatshirt he wore. It had a logo for some oyster bar and the words *Shuck me, suck me, eat me raw* written across the chest.

Good God.

Normally, I would have laughed and complimented him on his audacity. But today, considering the mood in town, it gave me a weird feeling of kinky perversion. I couldn't ignore the rising anxiety I was feeling lately, and I wanted more information from Wes about his history with Mr. Wilde. I had to be getting close to a breakthrough. Wes' shirt and love of flirting set the stage for the topic of conversation I wanted to take up with him, so I forged ahead.

"Mr. Ryan," I greeted him amiably.

He curled his lip in mock disgust. "You've been hanging around your boss too much," he joked.

"You're probably right," I agreed. "What're you doing? Anything interesting?"

"I'm heading into town to go for a boat ride with Chester. Want to come with?" he asked, holding his arm so that I could link mine with it.

"Hell yes," I said.

The sea had been calm since early yesterday. I knew we'd be safe out there.

***

I took my own car and parked it beside Wes' Jeep in the Marina lot. We sat in Wes' car, until Chester showed up. I took the chance to shake off my weird mood while we sang along to the classic rock songs playing on his stereo.

Too bad I still really felt no physical chemistry with Wes. He was sure a lot of fun to be with. We had a blast on the boat. The sea was like a sheet of glass and the sun was shining through the crisp air. We drank Pepsi and ate Doritos with Chester, who kept us amused with horrific surfing tales.

***

Chester got us back to the harbor at about two o'clock. We parted company then, with Wes walking me to where I'd parked my car in the small parking lot.

"I think someone killed Mac," Wes said out of the blue.

"What?" I was stunned. Coming from him, this was credible.

"I think someone sent him on a mad dash out to sea for something he was willing to risk his life for," Wes said.

"Such as?" I asked, but I really did not like what he was saying.

"Maybe someone told him one of his kids was out in the dingy, or that his bait had just been ripped off by a passing vessel," he continued.

"How likely do you think either scenario is?" I asked him.

He shrugged his shoulders. "I don't know. But between the incidents in the woods these past weeks, and now Mac turning up dead, I just think there's some bad blood in this town," he declared forcefully.

I felt my anxiety rise again.

"What time do you have to get Dean?" he asked.

"In a little bit," I said. I still wanted to turn the topic of conversation to that first case which Wes and Mr. Wilde worked on together. I decided to try to nonchalantly bring it up now. "Hey, Wes?"

"Yeah?" he responded, leaning an arm against the roof of my car so that his face was level with mine.

I looked into his eyes and hoped madly that I'd get a real clue from him to justify once and for all the way my boss behaved. "Tell me about you and Mr. Wilde. You know, when you two worked together on your earlier cases."

"He told you about that?" Wes seemed genuinely surprised. "He must really like you."

"I'm not sure I'd classify it quite that liberally, but nonetheless, he did kind of tell me that you two have worked together in the past," I said.

Wes turned and rested his back against the car, stretching his legs out at an angle in front of him. "Bryson's slipping in his old age," he muttered wonderingly to himself.

"You mean he wouldn't have ordinarily admitted that much?" I asked in amazement. What did that man think he was protecting about himself?

"We worked together on a couple of homicides that had been unsolved," Wes said, answering my question. "But our biggest glory was the porno ring. That got Bryson his publishing contract."

"Really?" I asked, acting as if this were new information. "You guys found a porno ring?"

"It was an impressive set–up, let me tell you," Wes said with remembered admiration. "They were using kids from all over the country, ...these fresh, innocent kids..."

Why was there appreciation in his words? Surely not!

"Bryson was relentless. He even suspected me before he was able to get the whole organization broken up and the ringleaders arrested and tried," Wes said harshly. "That was the end of that."

"Wes, the way you said that sounded like you resent–" I started to question what he was admitting, but he cut me off.

"You know, there have been times when Bryson has acted so holier–than–thou, I've been tempted to wipe that arrogant smirk off his face," Wes said. He was talking, but not necessarily to me. He seemed to have gone off on a distracted tangent. "He's so brilliant, that's the problem."

Wes stopped speaking and stretched his hands over his head. He didn't look back at me, but just walked off.

What was that about?

CHAPTER TWENTY–EIGHT
Impact

"You look rather wind–whipped, Miss Stuart," Mr. Wilde commented as I walked into the house with Dean a while later.

"I went sailing with Chester and Wes," I informed him.

He frowned in disapproval. "It's not safe out there," he commented.

I didn't want to debate with him. I needed to be alone with my thoughts.

"Have you learned nothing from the Greyson drowning?" he went on. "That was a sensible man who drowned because of a poorly thought out decision."

"I've listened to a lot of speculation," I said absently. *But what I've* heard *is a lot of creepy obsession with murder and child porn from Wes,* I added silently. *God! I have so much on my mind!*

"How did you learn he'd been found?" he wanted to know. "I received word they found him Tuesday afternoon. Where were you when everyone was notified?"

"I was uh–" *Think, Amy!* This was not that hard. *A quick white lie... come on!* Nothing.

"Where were you?" he repeated in a sharper tone. "I called the house to check that all was well, but no one answered," my boss declared, ire rising.

Uh oh.

I shifted back and forth on my feet, trying to think of something that I could have done to take me away from the phone that wouldn't have been against the rules. I had a brain freeze. I couldn't think of anything I could tell him that wouldn't have included taking Dean with me, or having left him behind. I wanted to kick myself in the butt. Why had I slipped up like this?

Because my conscience was bugging me.

"Where were you, Miss Stuart!" he rasped.

"Uh, that was the day when Dean and I were in San Francisco." I said then clenched my teeth, bracing myself.

"What do you mean, *when you were in San Francisco?*" Mr. Wilde yelled in astonished rage.

"I've taken him into the city two times," I said calmly. I felt like a naughty girl confessing to her father. "We saw movies and went to the wharf and Golden Gate Park." I had known he'd be angry, but I hadn't been able to conceive of a valid reason for him to be, other than the fact that I hadn't informed him of my intentions.

Obviously he had his reasons.

"Bloody hell!" He bellowed again. He raised his face and hands upward beseechingly, as if asking the powers that be to explain my stupidity. "You've made us all vulnerable! I knew you'd be destructive to our lives! Get out of my house– NOW!"

I stepped backwards in shock. What in the hell was he talking about? What a paranoid loser!

"Wait a minute, asshole!" I yelled right back at him. (If I was out of here, I was at least going to go with a feeling of satisfaction that I'd stood up for myself.) "I'm not a mind reader! Since when, is it a crime to take an excursion to the city? You left us a thousand dollars, for Christ's sake. What did you think we'd *do* with it?"

He balled his fists, lowering his head so that his piercing glare could skewer me like a laser beam. "Apparently you didn't hear me–"

"I heard you!" But I wasn't leaving without an explanation. "You accused me of making us all vulnerable. What were you talking about?"

He didn't answer me, but just stood there heaving agitated breaths in and out of his chest.

"I'm not leaving," I said in a defiant tone not unlike a child's.

"Miss Stuart, did I not make it clear that I want Dean to remain at home with you during my absences?" He rasped with marked control.

"Truthfully, Mr. Wilde, I thought that your main concern was that he be under my direct supervision," I said, slightly more humble now. "I really wanted to give him an opportunity to get out and have some fun. You have him under such confining conditions, and he's such a brilliant child. I wanted him to get some stimulation. And, quite honestly, he loved every minute of it."

He sighed in exasperation throwing his hands up. "I can't talk to you!" He turned his back on me and walked out of the room.

"Mr. Wilde, I'm sorry I've angered you," I called earnestly after him. But to my own ears, I lacked credibility. "I will not go against your wishes again, as long as you clarify what those wishes are." I added the last part as a weak afterthought.

He didn't even acknowledge having heard me. He left the house through the front door, the tires of his silver Jag squealing on the cobblestones as he tore off.

***

I went to my bedroom and slammed the door.

God! What the hell was it about this place, this family, that had kept me from making a hasty retreat a long time ago? It seemed that the more time that went by, the worse things got, in spite of the progress that I was making with Dean. The things that I wanted to discuss with Mr. Wilde, I never did because of these stupid, senseless arguments that always arose out of the blue.

That was the third volatile argument I'd had with him this week. I'd never argued like this with anyone. And I certainly had never anticipated such extreme emotions in myself. In any other situation of conflict in my life, I had always left well enough alone and moved safely away from scenes like these. I couldn't understand why I was involved in this mess. Why didn't I pack my things and go?

I didn't know, truly.

I felt pretty certain that I still had my job. I knew the boss would cool off, spend some energy making a few derogatory comments to me then be almost nice again. In the meantime, I didn't want to quit. I was just bound and determined that I would not leave this place wondering what in the hell this man was hiding. His son was hiding stuff, too. His own stuff.

I wasn't going anywhere.

***

I lay in bed staring at the ceiling while two voices argued in my head.

One said I was reading too much into everything and looking for evil where it didn't exist. The other voice said, *What if it does?* Something about that case, where Mr. Wilde had suspected Wes as one of the culprits, just left an unsettled feeling of doom in my stomach. But as paranoid as Mr. Wilde was, he must have concluded with complete certainty that Wes was reliable. With all of the care he took to stay safe and secluded, he'd be sure he could trust Wes Ryan.

There was more to this. I decided to do a little undercover investigation of my own. Maybe I could lure Wes in, if I approached the topic of pedophilia from another perspective...

***

I heard rustling outside my window.

Fuck! What does this guy want? This was scaring me.

Shaking and panting with a fear that threatened to buckle my knees, I went outside. A menacing growl sounded as soon as I'd left the last stair. It was the black dog, this time not acting so passive.

"Hey, don't give me any of your shit. You don't even live here, asshole." I was attempting bravado. Big mistake.

With a snarl and a bark of anger, he charged at me and leapt up at my face. This was a big dog. My hands shot up to protect myself and I took a painful bite on the right palm. I fell back onto my behind and back. Angry adrenaline drove my foot up into the dog's belly, and he yelped and backed off momentarily. I jumped to my feet.

"Fucker!" I yelled. The dog didn't react, but I felt slightly vented.

"Black! There you are!"

The figure appeared, not completely coming out of the darkness at the back end of the house. Again, I had the eerie feeling of déjà vu... like I knew this guy. The dog trotted over to him and sat at his feet.

"Did he hurt ya?" The dark man asked, the accent very prominent.

I didn't let the low grade menace in his tone affect my rage, quickly telling myself that an aggressive offense was my best defense here. "What in the fuck are you doing here?" I raged. "You are trespassing on private property! And don't give me that bullshit about chasing your dog!"

"Gosh I'm sorry, Miss Amy," he said with an insincerity that made my stomach turn almost as tightly as the realization that he knew my name. "We were just out for a walk–"

"A walk from where?" I interrupted him harshly, using my teacher–confronting–a–lying–child voice. "You don't live around here!"

"Now how do you know that?" he asked, taking a few slow steps toward me, but never coming into the light.

"I know that you don't." I said, controlling myself better now. I didn't like the way he was moving closer. "I also know that I could have your dog quarantined and destroyed for an unwarranted attack on my property."

"Now, Miss Amy, this isn't your property, is it? You only work here. And let's not have any talk of destroying Blackie here."

"Then get yourself, and your fucking dog, out of here now!" I blared out, this time taking a step toward *him.* The dog growled again. "And you shut the fuck up!" I said to Blackie.

They didn't move.

"Go!" I commanded.

The guy shook his head, his voice turning cold. "You know, I thought I liked you, but now I see you're just a bitch that needs to get fucked up the ass." There was a very serious threat in his words.

"I don't need you to tell me how to get fucked," I told him, adrenaline fueling false bravado. Then I got even more brilliant: "And don't make the mistake of thinking you can stick your dick anywhere you want, either. You never know who might be waiting with an ax, or a butcher knife, to teach you proper dick etiquette."

Proper dick etiquette? Where do I come up with this stuff?

I ran into the house, making it just in time to the bathroom before I wet my pants.

***

And *God dammit!* Why was it that this freaky creep always showed up when Mr. Wilde wasn't around?

I looked down at my hand as I let cold water run over the bite from the dog. *Jesus, I hope that thing has had his shots.* Now I'd have no choice but to tell Mr. Wilde about the dog. Surely he'd see the marks from the bite.

BOOK THREE

ILLUSIONS OF SILENCE

"...I thought silent meant safe..."
–Bryson Wilde

CHAPTER TWENTY-NINE
Perspectives

I talked to Wes again Friday afternoon. He had come upon me while I was brooding. This whole dark stranger thing felt like it was about to come to a head. But since my ego was still smarting from the tongue–lashing I'd been given, I had yet to approach Mr. Wilde. I guess I'd chosen to be out in the chilly air on the pool deck in an effort to cool my own smoldering temper. I was still wondering what had been going on with Wes when he'd gone off about Mr. Wilde the other day as well. That had been weird, too. So once again, I yielded to the temptation to see what Wes might reveal to me.

As if he had finally taken pity on me, Wes finally confided his perceptions. He confirmed that Mr. Wilde was indeed unhappy, and had been so since long before his wife Elaine had died. The dreams of his youth were now far out of reach, and the treasures he had created as an adult, he held at bay. His writing was decreasingly satisfactory, although his editor still worshipped him. He had even confessed to Wes that he felt his work lacked the depth of a healthy human mind.

"I'm not surprised he told me that," Wes had said then. "He certainly has made a mess of his life. He'd alienated his brother, turned on poor Moira, as if she were a misfit, less than human...." he had drifted off in that vague way again. "...He really needs to get laid..." He'd shaken himself then, looking at me meaningfully. "All of the women in Bryson's life have been very sexy," he said in a low tone. "But unlike me, he's never known what to do with his urges."

Ugh. I didn't need to hear that, especially if I was supposed to infer that he'd released his urges with Elaine or Moira. What drives people to betray their best friends over sex?

Wes had then told me that he'd be leaving after a few more days.

***

Wes' perception of my boss sounded well grounded and it gave me food for thought. Unlike anyone else that I had ever called an asshole, I was still in a business relationship with Mr. Wilde. At least I hadn't been *convincingly* terminated yet. A definite pattern had developed between the two of us. It seemed we could blow off steam at each other, and then speak civilly at our next encounter.

What a novel concept.

I decided to try one final time to make friends with my boss. I planned to wait until he appeared to be congenial, perhaps the next time we ate together. At that time, I would very carefully win his trust.

Right, Amy.

***

I watched Mr. Wilde take down his favorite pool cue from the bracket on the wall and rack the balls for the break. He took aim and shot the cue ball in a practiced motion. The perfect triangular formation scattered sharply around the table, two balls slipping into corner pockets. He walked around the table, expertly firing the white cue ball at those still remaining upon it.

Seeming to be smugly unconcerned as usual that I was observing, he racked the balls up again and prepared to break. He was bent over the table about to begin when I walked further into the room. At first I let my surprise show as I stopped and looked at him. I grinned, then smothered it, all at once unwilling to admit that I was affected by the difference in his appearance. He was dressed in a pair of relaxed fit jeans, white T–shirt, and a navy cotton sweater that looked an awful lot like the one I had bought in San Francisco. The heavy black lugger boots on his feet made soft clunks on the floor as he moved around the table again, firing expert shots that sent balls zipping into the pockets.

Mr. Wilde straightened up and regarded me, waiting to see what I wanted.

"Sorry to bother you," I said, trying desperately to hold back my smile. But, my God, he looked really good.

"Are you laughing at me, Miss Stuart?" he asked lightly, apparently unperturbed by my expression.

I let my eyes widen and shook my head, "Oh, no," I said smoothly, "it's nice to see you looking so informal."

"Hmmm." he hummed, raising an eyebrow.

I continued to stare until he prompted me, asking, "Was there something that you needed?"

"Yes," I answered, although I was having trouble recalling just what it was. "Oh yeah, it's Friday night." I waited to see if he had any clue as to what that had come to mean for Dean and me: that Bill and Todd were spending the night again. He gave me a blank look, of course. "I was about to go into town to pick up a pizza for the boys. I'm getting another for myself, care to split it with me?"

"Would you mean pizza from a box?" Mr. Wilde asked in mock arrogance, seeming almost playful enough to smile at me. Despite my resolve to make an attempt to be friends, by now I was becoming disconcerted by his friendly demeanor. He was making this too easy for me!

"I love anchovies," he told me.

I wrinkled my nose. That was definitely where I drew the line. "I'll have the guy put them on your half of the pizza," I told him. That said, I decided that now would be a good time to leave, giving him one last appraising look as I turned.

"Wait!" he called after me. I turned back and watched him walk toward me. He reached into his pocket and pulled out a couple of twenty–dollar bills. "You'll need this," he said. I grinned and took the money from him.

***

I thought about that sweater as I drove into town. I hadn't seen mine since the weekend I'd bought it. How in the heck could Mr. Wilde have gotten hold of it?

***

I called the boys down over the intercom as I set out plates and napkins on the table in the booth. I sensed my employer's presence in the doorway, and was all at once thankful that I'd not been talking to myself just then. If I had been, he would have heard me say how fine he looked in his jeans, and then wonder if he was acting so amicable because of my vibes, or because he had made a resolution of his own.

Dean and his two buddies clamored down the back staircase. Dean did a double take when he saw his father's casual stance and informal attire. I looked back to see the cause of Dean's distraction and jumped slightly, for effect, when my eyes met Mr. Wilde's. "Dean, has your father ever been properly introduced to your friends?" I asked, knowing full well that he hadn't. He had avoided the boys every weekend since this ritual began.

Dean shook his head, his eyes still on his father's face. He was probably searching for signs of disapproval, but found none. His friends were looking at him expectantly. Finally he said carefully, "Father, this is Todd and this is Bill. Bill and Todd, this is my father."

Unaware of the tension between father and son, Bill and Todd both approached Mr. Wilde with their hands extended. He inclined his head, taking Bill's hand first. "I'm pleased to make your acquaintance, Bill," he said in a friendly voice. He shook hands with Todd next, making similar pleasantries. Then he looked at Dean again, who stood unmoving, and staring. He managed a rare smile, and then he made a slight jerk of his head toward the table, gesturing for Dean to rejoin his friends.

Dean turned back toward the table, his face an unreadable mask.

***

"Where do you want to eat?" I asked him, smiling again. It felt like the tables had turned, and that Mr. Wilde was the one making the effort to connect with me.

He blinked and looked at me. "Hmm? Oh, uh, would you care to join me in the game room?" he asked. "We could take in a movie, I've a pretty sizeable collection." He seemed to be holding his breath while he awaited my response.

"That sounds great," I returned, easily.

Then I took the risk.

I inclined my head and looked at him with narrowed eyes. "How about listening to music instead of a movie? That way we could talk."

He nodded agreeably. "I approve of the idea," he said, with a touch of his familiar arrogance. "If you'll carry in the pizza, I'll get the plates." He crossed over to the kitchen cabinet and took out two plates.

He led the way back into the game room. He set down the plates, then went over to the wet bar's small refrigerator and took out two bottles of beer. Grabbing the remote for the stereo as he sat, he clicked on the music. Jazz. He faced me and started right in with the topic of Dean while opening the bottles.

"Now, I'm sure, at the very least, you have some heartfelt observations and comments to offer on the subject of my son, hmm?"

I grinned at him, giving myself a little shake to make sure I wasn't fantasizing this whole scene. "Of course I do," I admitted. But I took the time to hand him a slice of pizza on a plate. We ate our first few bites of pizza in silence, which of course I broke first.

"You know, Mr. Wilde–"

"Call me Bryson, to hell with formalities," Mr. Wilde's words were self–mocking.

What's gotten into him?

"Okay," I paused to smile uncertainly at him. "Anyway, Bryson, your young son has become quite an interesting study for me." I was deliberately light. "He's incredibly gifted, both academically and in art. He's not a bad athlete either."

"And I haven't taken much time to notice," *Bryson* added with surprising candor.

I nodded my agreement, not trying to soften the reality with a soothing comment. *So we're being honest now.* I surmised that, like his son, that if I let him talk without prying too hard, Bryson would probably reveal quite a lot of information to me.

"Did you know he has nightmares regularly?" I asked next.

"No."

I couldn't tell if he was concerned by this information. I went on, "He woke me up one night, shortly after I started working here. He was moaning and crying in his sleep and–"

"You were with him?" Bryson interrupted.

Confused by his question, I shook my head. "No, I heard him all the way in my room," I felt my eyebrows rise way up as I relived my own interpretation of what I had encountered. "I literally thought that he was being raped, that's how hideous his cries were." I paused to gauge Bryson's reaction, but his eyes were hooded now, hiding. He was taking in what I said very carefully.

I hoped my face didn't betray my inner musings as I continued. "When I got up to his room, Dean was still lost in some terrifying dreamland. He came out of it a few minutes later, but was very defensive and hostile, demanding to know what he'd said in his sleep. The next day he apologized for the way he'd spoken to me, and said it was a recurring dream. He also insisted that I not tell you about it. He's obviously afraid to admit what the nightmare is about."

"I've never heard him cry out at night before," Bryson confessed with a frown, "but it's never occurred to me to listen for him or to check on him, either. He's so self contained all of the time."

"But realistically," I chided, "he's a child. He's got to have needs. The biggest ones are to feel safe and secure. The nightmare must result from him feeling vulnerable."

"He has nothing to fear from me," Bryson responded defensively, inappropriately.

I rolled my eyes. Then looked at him levelly. "He's lost an awful lot already, and knows you have, too. If he asks for too much, he may push you to the point of rejecting him, then he'd lose you as well." I told myself to refrain from my next comment, but lost the battle to my own impulses, "Frankly, he lost you the same day your wife and daughter died, because you shut down."

His stubborn side kicked in then. "I give him everything he could possibly need– the finest clothes, a good education, he could have any toy in the world if he wanted it–"

"How about a hug?" I interrupted him, my voice dripping with irony.

Bryson looked away. He apparently had no answer for that one, dammit. *When had he turned into such a cold bastard?* He had obviously felt deeply tied to his daughter, hadn't he been capable of the same with Dean?

"Is the thought really all that repulsive?" I tried again.

Nothing.

Is the conversation over?

Bryson finally blinked twice and returned his attention to me. He sighed tiredly and shook his head. "No, it's not repulsive at all. I love Dean. It's just that..." he sighed again, "there are circumstances... things that keep me at bay... I don't know...." He stopped, seeming to consider how much to reveal to me.

"I had a rather shitty marriage," he finally admitted.

I wasn't particularly surprised to hear that. I sat watching him, waiting for further explanation.

"You see, we were married right out of university," he continued. "Elaine was pregnant with Rachel and we felt obligated to marry. I loved Elaine in a lot of ways, but never without reservation. I think she felt the same about me, but we were never intimate friends, never shared our dreams or fears, or deepest emotions with each other..." He paused to see if I was following him. I was intrigued.

He continued. "I was very close to my father, and he died three years after we were married. I couldn't even cry in front of her, we were that detached."

The man can cry?

"I had a brother who was eight years my junior," he continued. "Our mother had died when Corbin was a toddler, so in the year after our father passed, he seemed to become lost. He had married foolishly, to a girl who was a heroine addict. I convinced him to leave her, and file for divorce. Then I had Corbin come to live with us. He was just out of school. Elaine fell for him quite obviously the day he arrived. It destroyed my relationship with him, and what was left of my relationship with her, as well. They had a fling, you see. I never forgave either for that. It came between us to the end. I forced Corbin to leave after I'd found out the truth. Moira, his ex–wife had been causing disturbances, anyway. It was a relief to have him go away and take his problems with him. Apparently he went to London to return to university for an advanced degree."

"When was the last time you saw him?" I asked.

"At his funeral," Bryson told me.

I was shocked to silence. I just stared at him, painfully unable to think of something to say.

"Corbin was murdered in Downtown London ten years ago," he revealed.

"What happened?" I asked in a whisper.

"He was beaten to death in an alley."

Jesus Christ!

"Was his killer ever captured?" I wanted to know.

"No," he said grimly. "I knew who was behind it as soon as I'd heard he was dead," Bryson told me. "I instigated the investigation, and put the London police force on his ex–wife's trail. It was a sick, twisted act of revenge, very well planned and executed. There was no evidence to be found. The perpetrator had known what he was doing.

"In the end, Moira confessed to having hired someone to kill him, but she wouldn't reveal the identity of the murderer. She went to prison for her crime, but the killer remains a free man."

"What a horrible story!" I exclaimed. I suddenly remembered how Wes had spoken fondly of her. I kept my thoughts to myself for the moment.

He nodded in agreement. "Unfortunately, it doesn't end there," he went on. "Moira lost her sanity shortly after she was imprisoned. She was transferred to an institution for the criminally insane."

"Aren't they all?" I asked ironically.

"You came upon me a several weeks ago," Bryson said, completing his train of thought, "just after I'd heard some bad news. Do you remember?"

I nodded, and he continued. "I felt little reason to admit it then, but I'd just found out that she'd escaped. I went over to London to try to get the case reopened."

Jesus.

***

I had been thinking about something. "You said that before Corbin left for England, his wife had been giving you guys problems," I remembered. "What kind of disturbances had his ex–wife been causing?" I asked, very intrigued with his story, despite the shock it caused me to feel.

"Mostly threatening phone calls and demands for money," Bryson said dismissively. "I never took her seriously, she was such a misfit. She never liked me, and let me know in very certain terms that she held me responsible for the break–up of her marriage. I told her she was very astute."

I can just hear the sneer in his voice as he said the words, too.

"What made you suspect her involvement in the murder?" I asked.

"She had vowed to take revenge. I guess I'd been expecting something slightly more... juvenile," he confessed. "It was then that I realized how much I'd underestimated her wrath. That is one disturbed creature."

"You've experienced a lot of loss," I said. My voice was tight with restrained sympathy.

Bryson nodded in agreement. "Dean has never known the compassionate side of my nature; it's been locked away for quite some time." He stopped speaking and regarded me.

"Something is changing, though, or this wouldn't be coming up." I fed him his next line, anticipating what he was leading up to.

Bryson raised an eyebrow at my perception. His lips curved up slightly as he spoke without humor, "You've forced the issue, my dear. We were fine before you arrived."

"What?" I asked as if I hadn't heard him correctly. Why is it that people always want to blame someone else for their bullshit? "How can you say that you were fine? Look at the way Dean interacts with you."

"He's very guarded against me, I sense that quite strongly."

What a brave admission!

"He doesn't know you," I countered, "and you don't know him. It will take time and careful patience to work through that." I felt the need to talk him into approaching his son. "He's a very loving boy, very affectionate. But he's got a very cynical outlook on the world." I thought of another incident. "The morning you left for your first trip, Dean got in trouble at school again. His teacher waited to speak with you, but had to talk to me instead. When I told her that you had left the country, the look on Dean's face really disturbed me."

"Why, was it one of relief?" Bryson's tone held no humor in it.

I ignored that. "No, it was...hard to read. Dismay, fear, rejection, disbelief." Seeing that I had Bryson's attention, I gave an edited version of what had happened afterward. "That night when I called him for dinner, I found him asleep. He had been crying in secret and apparently overwhelmed himself with his own intensity. I had told him that I would want to talk very seriously with him about his problems. I guess that's what had set him off. He was extremely agitated when I woke him, nearing hysteria, insisting that he wouldn't tell me anything, no matter what I did to him."

"Did you threaten him with punishment?" Bryson asked in amazement.

"No, actually. After his outburst, I told him he didn't have to say a word. That seemed to earn his trust, because he's been progressively warming up to me ever since. When he finally did tell me about his mother, he said that the subject was not discussed." Bryson nodded tensely when I paused, confirming. "He doesn't seem to know where he stands with you."

Bryson knew I was right.

I pushed on. "Bryson, you expect him to live like a hermit. How can your son ever thrive in such a setting?"

"What would you have me do, Amy?" he countered patiently. "Like you observed, I have lost a lot. More than I'd ever thought possible."

"You haven't lost your son," I said then added, "yet."

"But what I *have* lost has left me helpless to help him."

"I don't understand," I said truthfully. "Are you saying that you've lost your ability to love?"

"No," he answered grimly. "I've lost the ability to protect."

"From what?" I asked, suddenly reluctant to hear any more.

"From evil."

A cold chill whipped up my spine. So, he felt it too. A presence of evil.

***

"Have you ever gone for therapy?" My words broke the long, reflective silence.

Bryson shook his head firmly, "It's not for me," he said with finality. He waited for me to argue my point, but I gave up easily, sensing his stubbornness. Bryson looked at his watch. "It's nearly ten o'clock. How late do the boy's stay up?"

"Until they get sleepy," I said, shrugging my shoulders, slightly miffed at his predictable rejection of my suggestion.

***

I next saw Bryson as he came downstairs the following morning to make breakfast, only to find the three boys already engrossed in the task. I was supervising while I read the paper and drank coffee.

Surprised, Bryson asked what they were making.

"French toast," Bill answered him. "Would you like some?"

"Yes, I believe I will," Bryson told him.

I looked at Dean, wearing big jeans, oversized bright yellow sweater, and a red baseball cap turned backwards, kneeling on the counter, watching his father warily. He had been mixing eggs and milk together for batter when his father had interrupted them. Bryson raised an inquiring eyebrow at Dean. "Do you have enough eggs there? Could I get you some more?"

Dean shook his head slightly, then as always, remembered his manners. "No thank you, sir. This will be fine." He seemed nervous and uncomfortable under his father's scrutiny.

Bryson shrugged casually, "Very well, if you have everything under control, I'll go into my office for a bit. You'll call me when it's ready?"

"Sure thing, Mr. Wilde," Todd called out.

***

We ate around the large dining room table. The French toast was delicious, and both Bryson and I thoroughly complemented the boys' abilities. After breakfast, Bill and Todd changed into their soccer uniforms. Bryson became his old terse self when I told him about the game. I left with the boys at noon. I had invited Bryson to join us, but he was barely able to conceal his disapproval of Dean's attending, and so declined the invitation. It irritated me that he had gotten so pissed about the game. Where were those other pieces of the puzzle that was Bryson Wilde, which still kept me in the dark?

CHAPTER THIRTY
Stranger

Monday morning I took Dean to school, noting that Bryson's car was not in the garage. Had he left town again? He'd said nothing to me...

That's it! The time has come for the bullshit to end. I'm going to insist upon knowing where to contact Mr. Wilde when he's away from now on, I declared in my head. I would base my demand on the threat I had received from the dark stranger. It was time to admit to that one, anyway.

***

"What dark stranger?" Bryson snapped, stepping closer to where I stood. "When has there been a stranger on the grounds?"

"On numerous occasions!" I snapped back. I felt like one big, stupid jackass for not having informed him sooner. But I hadn't known whether or not the guy really *was* an intruder, or an employee, or what. "That's why I want to be able to get hold of you," I added resentfully.

He peered angrily into my eyes.

"What are you doing?" I demanded.

"I'm trying to ascertain the location of the brain cell leak," he said.

"I resent your attitude," I told him, insulted. "I wasn't sure that he was an intruder. You've been so unwilling to give me any information. For all I knew he was a guest, or a tenant."

He wasn't even listening.

***

"Hello?" I answered my phone with a bored voice.

"You sound like a girl who needs a night out," Wes said on the other end of the line.

"Hi Wes," I said, forcing a smile into my voice. Wes would be leaving soon. I was running out of time. "What do you have in mind? Please don't say pizza."

"How about some pizza?" he suggested.

Great. "Why not?"

***

I met Wes outside after calling to my employer that I'd be skipping dinner tonight. Bryson hadn't been pleased, but he hadn't tried to tell me that I couldn't go.

We drove in Wes' Jeep. He had a good cassette tape playing a collection of hip–hop and rap songs. We sang along to the songs, trying to keep up with the lively rhythm of the music, and laughing at each other when one of us would forget the lyrics.

"You seem to be pretty upset about something," Wes observed.

"I've just been arguing with the boss a lot lately, is all," I said drily.

"Bryson can be a prick at times," Wes said.

"Yes," I agreed wholeheartedly. "I find it hard to believe that you two have been such close friends for so many years. You're so liberal." I was trying to get him to tell me more about his competitive drive to knock Bryson down a peg.

"Well, you know what they say about opposites," Wes said dismissively. "So tell me about your book– is there any sex in it?"

I sputtered. "Actually, there is," I admitted slowly, "but it's mostly perverted and criminal." Though I'd deliberately phrased it that way, I was instantly uncomfortable with the whole subject.

He, on the other hand, was intrigued. "What kind of perverted sex?"

"The kind that occurs between an unwilling child and an adult," I said, trying not to squirm.

"What do you know of the subject?" he asked invasively.

"Only what I've read," I told him.

"Are you going to give graphic details?" he asked.

This wasn't going quite the way I'd intended.

"Um," I started then feigned hesitation. "I'm kind of paranoid that I'll make myself a target for the FBI or something if I research it too extensively, so I'll probably limit the descriptions to secondary references, rather than depicting the acts as they occur."

"Chicken," he teased.

"Gross!" I complained, feigning a much milder reaction to his responses than I actually felt.

The subject matter was awful enough, but now Wes was giving me the creeps.

***

Wes was to leave the following morning to go back home to Southern California where he based his business. He assured me I'd see him again soon. I jumped at the chance to keep the good–bye moment light and brief.

CHAPTER THIRTY–ONE
Survival Instinct

My conversation with Wes gave me nightmares. In the dream, I was the one in danger. Everyone else carried on as if I was overreacting to the fact that I was being pursued by the dark stranger. After such a fitful night, I desperately needed to burn off some stress. It was only about ten o'clock Tuesday morning when I put on my bathing suit and wrapped a big towel around myself, then went outside to the pool. Bryson was already there.

"It's getting to you, isn't it? This incessant tension?"

He didn't have to explain what he meant. "Yes!" I declared, dropping the towel and diving into the lukewarm water. I swam about twenty laps, then stopped in the shallow end, still feeling pent up and tightly coiled. The chill air did little to cool my agitation.

"This is all your fault, you know," Bryson said to me. "You forced everything out into the open."

I realized he was teasing, but didn't see any humor in his accusation. "A typical comment from a typical male," I said cynically.

"A predictable, defensive retort from an emotional female," he returned. He waited, a challenge in his eye.

Oh no, he would not have the last word. I made a mental grasp, but I was drawing a blank from the swift response section of my brain. So, I grabbed a plastic ball that floated beside me and threw it, deliberately bouncing it off the water's surface. It sent a sharp splash into his arrogant face.

I watched, as if in slow motion, the gleam of triumph he directed at me turn into a brow arched in surprise, to a wincing grimace as the splash struck him square in the face. His hand shot up and caught the ball, palming it like an NBA pro, and holding it in threatening poise. My face undoubtedly registered my shock at this sudden and completely unexpected display of agility.

"Never engage a water polo champion in a pool battle," he growled. I could see a glint of alert, cunning glee in his eyes.

"I don't believe it!" I said, finally reacting to his remarkable recovery. It was very obvious that he was about to retaliate, and I just hoped he wouldn't try to nail me in the face with the ball.

In the flash of an instant, his arm whipped downward, shooting the ball in a rocket–fast arc so that it barely grazed my shoulder, before bouncing out of the pool and landing just out of reach on the lawn surrounding the deck. I stood staring at him with a look of amused shock, silently acknowledging to myself that in the fleet of an instant, Bryson Wilde had been the sexiest male specimen I'd ever encountered. *I'll have to analyze that one later, I thought.*

He started to move toward me very slowly, an unreadable spark in his intent stare. I held eye contact for a brief moment, and then shuddered at the force of my physical response. *Oh my God, Amy! Your asshole boss is turning you on!* My heart was pounding! I spun around and made a dash for the ball, my only plan to get it and throw it back at him. I darted through the waist–high water to the side of the pool and hoisted myself up and leaned over, resting my hips against the edge so that I could stretch out my arms for the ball.

Amy! Are you crazy? Never stick your ass out at a man who is leering at you! Especially when you are totally aroused by him!

Too late.

I felt his hands on my waist. His fingers spread downward and his palms pressed into my hips. I froze, not wanting to move away from him. He took that as an invitation and pressed warm lips to my shoulder. I shuddered again and my elbows gave out so that I began to slide back into the water.

"No, Amy," he whispered in my ear, his face in my hair. "Stay right here, don't move away." An arm encircled my waist, bringing our bodies together so that I could feel his full arousal, erect in his loose trunks, pressing between the backs of my thighs.

"Oh God," I gasped, knowing I was ready whenever he was.

He slid his hand down the front of my bikini bottoms, letting his fingers caress me and find for himself that the wetness between my legs was not from pool water. "I want you!" he whispered raggedly into my ear. And he was panting as hard as I was.

I'm not much of a talker during sex, and I knew he was requesting my consent. I arched my back so that I was pressing firmly up against him then rotated my hips. His sharp intake of breath told me he'd gotten my meaning. His hands pushed down my bikini bottoms and I stepped out of them, letting them float away in the water.

He cupped my buttocks and lifted me slightly, then lowered me down onto his erection. And then he thrust upward and into me. I think it was at that moment that I truly understood the meaning of primal need. I didn't need to be kissed or caressed. I just braced my hands on the side of the pool and held on for the ride.

But I didn't get *fucked* with the indifference that I thought I would.

He had a very sensual rhythm to his movements that by itself brought me close to orgasm. He created a smooth force that was neither harsh nor gentle, but it worked me until I was moaning out loud – something I'd thus far been too inhibited and unexcited to do with previous lovers.

He slowed his thrusts, putting an arm around me and drawing me up so that I was almost standing upright.

"Amy," he whispered roughly to me. His other hand slipped down to caress my clitoris lightly. "Amy, I want you to climax for me."

He drew in a sharp, sexy breath as he again thrust inside me. I gasped again; one more of those and I'd be ready to sing. His hands moved to my hips as he rasped into my ear, "Bend over again, so I can make you come."

His body was rigid with barely held control, his fingers grasping my flesh firmly as I bent forward and arched my back so that I could take him in deeply.

Thrust. Thrust. Thrust.

"Amy!"

It happened. I actually experienced a spontaneous, simultaneous orgasm with him! I couldn't believe the power of it. I actually cried out his name. Hell, I might have called out my own and twenty others, as well, I was so out of my mind.

***

We reveled silently in the glory of the aftermath, the intensity of it keeping me stunned. Then he pulled out of me and drew me back against his chest. We sat on the nearby stairs, still not facing each other. I sat on the step below his, between his legs, liking the warmth of his now flaccid penis against my back.

"I hadn't planned on that happening," I said finally. My mind suddenly conjured up a significant list of likely consequences to this indiscretion.

"I hadn't either," he said, resting his chin on my shoulder. It was an endearing gesture, and out of character. I got another burst of arousal out of it.

"Might you get pregnant?" he asked after another moment.

"No," I said. I had just finished calculating my cycle. I was safe. "Might you be carrying a sexually transmittable disease?" I regretted the way that came out as soon as my own ears heard it.

But he didn't take offense. Instead he chuckled. An endearing trait that I'd was become privy to more often. I lurched forward and twisted around to look at him. He grabbed me, smirking derisively. "Come back here, Amy," he growled playfully as he pulled me back and repositioned me so that he could again put his chin on my shoulder. "I couldn't be completely certain, but I highly doubt that I'm carrying any diseases," he informed me.

"I can't believe how turned on I got by that," I said. Too late, I realized the extent to which I had just opened up the all too touchy topic of my past sexual experiences. He chuckled on my shoulder again. It sounded really good to my ears, too good. And the vibrations from his neck on my skin felt both erotic and familiar.

"Nor can I," he said.

His arms felt solid and secure in their loop around my torso. The fingers of one hand caressed my belly. "You're very different when you've got your pants down," I said, needing to comment on the effect he was having on me.

"And you're very sexy when you're out of control," he said.

You're out of control...

I turned around and faced him, keeping my body submerged in the warm water.

"Now I'll get a chill," he protested. I moved closer, tentatively inviting another embrace. He didn't reach for me...as if holding me face to face was too intimate.

Why was I surprised? *A good screw in the pool does not love make,* I thought cynically.

"I must be crazy!" I said lightly, hoping my tone sounded as unaffected as I desperately wanted it to. "Screwing the boss – doggy style at that!"

I felt that I had to degrade it out loud, so that I wouldn't glorify it in my mind. We hadn't even kissed. Hell, we hadn't even made eye contact during the entire encounter.

I shot past him, climbing the stairs with my bikini top still on and my bare buns jiggling behind me. I felt like an easy lay all of the sudden, ashamed that my feelings were hurt. Where had they come from, anyway? Until about an hour ago, I'd never even thought about him in a sexual way, only in a physically attractive sort of way.

You ask what's the difference? None, obviously.

I heard the gentle churning of the pool water as he got out of the pool, but kept my back to him as I wrapped my towel around my body. *Now what do I do?*

"You're not handling this very well, Miss Stuart," he said chidingly, his arrogance returning as if on cue.

Fuck you! I raged silently. But out loud, I replied sarcastically, "Does that mean I'll be docked my Christmas bonus?" Then I scurried into the house and shut myself into my "quarters".

CHAPTER THIRTY–TWO
Storm Front

The phone rang at two–thirty that afternoon. Bryson called to me that he'd get it in the kitchen. I had been hiding in my room for an hour now, and he was, for a change, the one with the writer's block.

I heard him answer and listened absently to the changing tone in his responses. Then the phone slammed down.

"Miss Stuart!" he bellowed. He was still calling me that when he was tense. I could hear the storming approach of his footsteps. "Dean is missing from school! Come with me to find him!"

Great. Proximity was not the thing I wanted with him just now. And, oddly, it did occur to me that Dean might not want to be found.

***

Standing beside Mr. Powell, the school principal, Miss Carter nervously wrung her hands. "Dean was sent to the office after lunch, for fighting, and never arrived. We think he left the campus."

Bryson listened to her in shock. "He must still be here," he said calmly. He looked doubtfully around the front of the campus, then toward the road. It was pouring rain. Nobody said anything about the recent incidents with the children in the woods surrounding the grounds.

"No, we've searched the entire premises," Mr. Powell informed us grimly. "He's not to be found."

***

"What do you suppose got into him?" I asked Bryson as we rushed back to his car.

"With that boy, one never knows." He said.

We jumped into the car and sped away from the school toward the highway. Bryson squinted down the road, searching. "Let's just hope we'll be able to get to him before – there he is!"

Dean was creeping along the side of the road, avoiding puddles, and appearing absolutely lost. He was quite startled when we pulled up beside him. Both Bryson and I jumped out of the car and ran over to him.

"Dean! Are you all right?" We said in unison. My voice was filled with concern while Bryson's was incredulous with shock.

Dean nodded, but didn't look at either of us. He was soaking wet and filthy, and shivering dramatically.

We put him in the backseat and headed back to Wilde Lane. Bryson dialed the school on his cellular phone and told them we'd found Dean and were taking him home. He made an appointment to meet with Principal Powell the following morning.

"What are you going to do to him?" I asked Bryson quietly when he'd disconnected.

"I've no idea," he said. At least he sounded calm, relieved actually.

When we entered the house, Bryson opened the door and followed Dean and me inside, closing it with a deliberate slam. Dean stopped in his tracks and turned slowly around to face us. He looked terrified and confused. I was all set to take charge, but Bryson acted first.

"Up to your room, quickly," Bryson ordered brusquely.

Dean averted his face and walked past us. I knew he was dreading punishment. I waited for the right moment to intervene. We followed Dean into his room. He stopped in the middle of the floor and waited, but Bryson walked right by him and into the bathroom. I heard him turn on the bath water.

"Come in here and get out of those wet clothes," Bryson called out to Dean. Dean hustled into the bathroom to do as he was told. I kept a protective vigil in the doorway, letting the shower curtain shield Dean's nudity from my view.

"Is the water too hot?" Bryson asked after he had let the tub fill a few inches. Apparently Dean indicated it was not. "Then get in, what are you waiting for?" Bryson chided gently. "You must be nearly frozen."

It was a deep bathtub. Bryson let Dean sit in silence until the water had reached his shoulders then finally began to speak. "It's been a while since I've supervised your bath, hmm?" he started.

"They're going to kick me out of school," Dean's sullen, unmoved monotone got right to the point.

Bryson raised an eyebrow, but kept his voice level as he asked, "What happened? It must have been something severe for you to have left school on your own."

Silence.

"You haven't answered me," Bryson reminded him softly after a moment. "Is it that bad?"

"You might as well get your belt ready, I was the one who started it." Dean's voice was cold and emotionless.

"Ah, I see." Bryson said. "Dean, I need to know what happened today, so that tomorrow, when we go to see Principal Powell, I'll know what to say on your behalf."

"I got into a fight with Albert Campbell," Dean finally admitted. His voice was strained with his own suppressed rage.

"Was it something that he said?" I asked, unable to stay uninvolved any longer, wondering whether the fight had to do with Albert's considering Dean to be gay, or the Campbell's suspicions of Bryson being a pedophile. The whole town seemed to be falling apart. Even the children were feeling it.

"Yes."

"What was the fight about?" Bryson's eyes shot a questioning frown toward me. Didn't he think that Dean would know of the rumors that had gone around? That they were probably still plaguing the school?

"He took my book of drawings. He looked at the private ones," Dean started, his familiar monotone back in check as he spoke. "He said I knew who the pervert was. The one in the woods."

Bryson frowned again. "What book of drawings are we referring to, here?" he asked, apparently not willing to discuss the "pervert".

Silence.

"May I have an answer, please?" there was a checked impatience about Bryson now.

Dean answered. "He had no business looking at them. He said he was going to show the teacher. He said the man in the mask had tried to hurt him in the woods."

"The man in the mask? What are the drawings portraying, Dean?" Bryson wanted to know.

Silence.

Bryson sighed, finally allowing an edge into his tone. "You can tell me," he said, "or, I can have a look for myself."

Dean's response was sullen and uncaring. "He said he was going to show the teacher. No one was supposed to see those."

I was certain that the shit would hit the fan now.

But Bryson only chuckled. He looked at his son intently. "Do you feel better?" he asked.

"Yes, sir." Dean's shuttered facade was up for protection. He would take no chances.

"Here," Bryson said as he reached for a towel, "come out and dry yourself off."

Dean dried himself silently, as usual hiding all signs of the turmoil he must be feeling. We left Dean to dress in jeans and sweatshirt. I knew he was hiding something that was very large in his mind. What burden was this child carrying? I wondered once again.

***

"Dean, come stand by me," Bryson instructed softly from where he had been seated on the bed. When Dean was standing before him, he asked again to see the drawings.

"I don't want anyone to see them," Dean responded firmly, his head hanging.

"Miss Stuart has seen them," Bryson pointed out.

"Not these ones."

"Dean," Bryson said reasonably, "has it escaped your attention that I've been uncharacteristically patient with you? I'm prepared to be careful not to overreact to what I see. Show me the drawings."

"No."

That's when Bryson's hand shot up, but he stopped himself from smacking Dean with obvious restraint.

"Go ahead and hit me, Father. Child abuse is just one more thing I can hide for you." Dean faced his father squarely.

I watched. My lips formed a large, surprised "O".

What was up?

"Child abuse?" Bryson raged, all restraint on his temper lost completely. He leaned threateningly closer to Dean. "You don't even begin to know the meaning of the word!"

"I don't?" Dean cried. "How would you know? You don't know anything about what I know! You just want to hide from the world forever! But the truth will come out soon!"

Bryson looked up at me defensively, as if I had an explanation for Dean's accusation. I shrugged and shook my head. He returned his attention to the boy. "What truth, Dean? And what do you mean, *hide from the world?"*

"You know why you're hiding," Dean said.

This was getting intense. It's like they say, the kids can always see through the parents' bullshit. I finally broke in. "Who has been feeding you your lines, Dean?"

"That's what I was going to ask *you,*" Bryson said accusingly to me. "There is a very familiar ring to this encounter."

I gave Bryson a dismissive wave. Then I addressed Dean again, "Okay, turkey, spill it out. What's going on with you? You're shutting us out, why won't you give your father an explanation?"

"You shouldn't align yourself with him," Dean said to me. "You're a fool."

I laughed in spite of the tension. That was an impressive line from a nine year old. He was probably right, too. I turned to Bryson, who had risen to his feet. "He's definitely got your gift for verbal sparring."

"Which is second only to your own," he returned acidly. Then to Dean, "What's happened? What do you think I've done that angers you so?"

Dean looked up at his father, his bravado finally failing. He hung his head, then dropped to the floor, bringing his knees up and rocking back and forth. He looked up once, then down again, shaking his head.

"God Damn! Answer me, lad!" Bryson had lost it again.

I put a hand on his arm, silently urging him to calm down. "Dean, we can't make it better until you tell us what's wrong." I said.

Dean continued to rock as he spoke, "You can't make it better at all." His words were filled with that all too familiar tone of confused despair.

"What in the devil are you referring to?" Bryson almost shouted.

"Bryson..." I whispered my plea for him to get back in control.

"I'd better leave now, or I'll *resort* to child abuse," he said, glaring down at Dean's bowed head as he stepped away.

"Do what you want. It will all be over soon," Dean mumbled.

That scared me. Was he thinking in suicidal terms again?

Bryson charged back to Dean, bending down and grasping the boy by his upper arms, and raising him up to his own eye level. "You had better decide to be more cooperative and honest. I won't tolerate another scene like this from you. You've been warned." His words held absolute threat. He set Dean down and was gone.

Dean was as white as a cadaver. I think he had been nearly frightened to death by his father's wrath.

"Sweetheart, please talk to me!" I begged, leaning down to his level.

"Just leave me alone!" he rasped, turning his back on me.

I stood looking at his small, tense body, trembling with such intense emotions, carrying such enormous secrets.

"Just go!" he repeated.

I did, but only because I felt that Bryson needed to get a grip on his own emotions and come to Dean's aid.

***

I heard the doorbell ring as I went down the front stairs. I came upon Bryson talking to a boy about Dean's age. It was Albert Campbell.

"Tell Dean I'm sorry I got him in trouble," he was saying nervously. "Here's his book. Tell Dean I wasn't really going to do what I said. I told Mr. Powell it was my fault, too." He turned and ran down the stairs to where his mother was waiting in the car.

Bryson closed the door and turned to find me watching him. I started to tell him he ought to return it to Dean without looking, but perhaps that was not correct. Perhaps enough was finally enough. He opened the book and flipped through the stenciled drawings created by his son's very talented hand. I could see recognition in his eyes, as he passed over the ones of Rachel and Bill and Todd.

"I've never seen any of these. He's better than his mother was," Bryson said, a note of pride barely audible.

He stood beside me and turned the pages slowly. He stopped at the last section. There were four drawings that said "Father's Way" in Dean's perfect printing on the top of each page. The first depicted a car, smashed into a tree. The tree trunk was fractured at the point where the car was crushed against it. A faceless man stood off to the side, hands in his pockets, waiting.

I looked at Bryson. "What does 'Father's Way" mean?" He shook his head to say he didn't know, but I didn't believe him. "Is that man you?" I asked.

"I don't know," he answered in a haggard voice. "I hope not."

"Do you know what this is depicting?" I asked, because I did not.

"I believe it's the accident that killed Elaine and Rachel."

"Was Dean there?" I asked, confused now.

"No," Bryson said adamantly.

We looked at the next picture. This time, "Father's Way" was written on the bottom of the page. There were the tree, and the car, and a woman's head and arm dangling out of the opening left by the detached and crumpled car door. The man stood with his back to us, facing the scene. He had the same stance of hands in pockets, watching.

Drawing number three showed a girl's body, crumpled on the street, some distance from the car. The man stood beside her, staring down. In the fourth one, the man stood behind a boy, who wept beside the body of the girl, which now lay next to the car. The woman's hand hung close by from the interior.

I looked at Bryson. His mouth was trembling. He couldn't look at me.

"Take this book and destroy it," he said with a deadly command.

I took the book from him. There were more drawings following the "Father's Way" section, but I dared not look at them just now.

"What a callous monster that child has become," he said.

"Bryson, there is a very disturbed little boy inside your son, but not a monster," I said.

"No son of mine could be so vicious," he declared.

What the hell does that mean? "Why are you so adamantly certain that the drawings were done to be spiteful?" I demanded to know. Jesus, he could be so far off on stuff.

"Why else would a child denigrate the memory of his mother and sister? He wants to taunt me."

"*Taunt* you? That sounds like a guilty conscience talking, to me," I said. He was making no sense. "Besides, he never intended for you to see those pictures. Look at the extremes he took to prevent it!"

"There is so much that you don't know, Amy, about what drives me, and the direction of my thoughts," he said, somewhat deflated.

"Well, that's a relief to hear because–" I started sarcastically, but was cut off.

"But obviously, there is much that Dean *does* know, as is apparent in his artwork. He knows that it was I who found their bodies," Bryson said almost to himself. "But, how? I'm quite certain I've never discussed it with him."

So the faceless man *was* Bryson.

"Well, I'll believe *that,*" I said. "Listen, children are just as complex as adults. When they display what we perceive to be inappropriate behavior, there's a reason."

"You know," he said thoughtfully, "I was like you once. I, too, used to think that things happen for a reason, but I've since learned that things happen, period, and any other connotation beyond that is merely speculation and superstition; a weak ego trying to blame the world for its unhappiness."

"So," I summed up, my buttons now pushed beyond my tolerance peak, "in other words, life happens to us. We have no control over our destiny."

"No, it's not that simple, Miss Stuart," he said in exasperation. "Please don't put words into my mouth."

"I'm only trying to get a perspective on your way of thinking," I returned.

"It's simply this: We have choices in life. We make them, then we stand up and face the consequences that follow."

"Are the consequences always bad?" I had to know.

"No, Miss Stuart," he sighed. "Consequences are results."

"Are you quoting the dictionary?" I asked, perversely needing to continue to agitate him.

"Your sarcasm is uncalled for," he said, unbending. "I'll remind you that I'm your employer."

CHAPTER THIRTY–THREE
Dark Forces

I came awake with a start. There was a tremendous noise around me. It sounded as though a steam shovel was driving on the roof.

And then there was the shaking.

My mind took this in for about three tenths of a second before I flew out of bed and rushed to stand in the doorway for the duration of the rather significant earthquake. I could hear glass breaking and objects falling throughout the house. The shaking stopped after about twenty seconds. I grabbed some sweatpants to pull on under the large denim shirt I had worn to bed and raced up the back staircase. The light was still on, as I had left it several hours ago. I took this electrical display to be a good sign that the quake had not been that destructive, that and the fact that the house was still standing!

I reached Dean's room and flipped on the light. Bryson's body barreled into mine from behind, jarring me roughly aside. He leapt over to the open window and thrust his head outside. I narrowly registered the oddity of the window being open when the temperature was about thirty degrees outside.

I turned to Dean in confusion and saw him sitting erect on his bed, clutching his pillow to his chest. His china blue eyes were as wide as saucers and his body was quaking in fear. I walked over to him, reaching out a hand to place on his head. He grabbed it and was suddenly climbing up my body like a monkey. He clung desperately to me, arms around my shoulders, face buried in my neck, legs in a clamped vise around my hips. He was heavier than I expected, his body not as thin as it was wiry. I carried him to the doorway, knowing that the first aftershock was due any moment. It struck as Bryson finally pulled his head and shoulders back into the room.

He jogged over to the doorway and braced himself with his hands on either side of the frame. He was facing me, the grim look in his eyes as he held my gaze not clearly expressing his concern to me. I let my eyes travel down to the gap that his hastily wrapped robe left open to expose his torso.

The walls and floor were swaying more gently this time as I finally broke the verbal silence.

"You wanna close that up?" I asked, as if it was his fly that was open.

Bryson looked down at himself then glared at me. I grinned at him and chuckled to try to break the ever–present tension. His expression softened reluctantly when he registered that I had been teasing. The shaking ceased, but we continued to stand still. Bryson assessed the walls and ceiling.

"I think we'll feel safer downstairs," he said to me. Then he put his lips to the top of Dean's head, which was still pressed into my shoulder. "Dean, why don't you come to me, and I'll take you downstairs, hmm? You're too heavy for Amy."

"No!" Dean's muffled response sounded like a wounded animal.

Bryson and I frowned at each other. I assumed Dean was probably still angry with his father over the explosive scene the previous evening. Maybe Bryson thought the same as he stared at the back of his son's head with determination.

"Dean, in a crisis situation, people who care about one another must put their troubles aside for the moment and come together. I want you to come to me so that I can keep you safe."

Good speech, I thought.

Dean slowly relaxed his hold on me and allowed Bryson to transfer him to his father's arms. Another, milder tremor hit then, which sent Dean scrambling to grasp Bryson as tightly as he had clung to me. Bryson's arms gave Dean a reassuring squeeze. I was touched by the unlikely scene then was taken completely off guard when he reached out a warm hand and cupped my neck. There was a tremble in his touch that alarmed me. I met his gaze and found an intense message of urgency, and suddenly the cold air in the room, and the open window became suspicious elements of question.

"Will you please close and lock the windows in here, then meet me in the game room?" Bryson asked me in a low voice.

I nodded and he left with Dean. The room now had a creepy feeling of violation about it. I closed the sash window and turned the lock until it caught on the top frame. My chilled fingers smarted from the pressure of the cold metal.

Why had that window been open? It finally occurred to me to wonder. I took Dean's pillow and comforter and headed down the hall toward the front staircase. Bryson was there, below in the entrance hall, still holding Dean while he looked for quake damage and checked all of the locks. I followed him and we made a circuit through the living room, gallery, and finally the game room, bolting and securing every possible entrance to the house. It was now very apparent to me that Bryson had sensed that there had been an intruder in the house before the earthquake.

The dark stranger?

***

We settled ourselves in the game room. I put Dean's pillow against the arm of the couch so that he could recline against it. Bryson set Dean down and covered him with the comforter. He stood staring down at Dean, studying him. I propped my thigh on the arm of the couch by Dean's head, and sat one–bun–on, letting my hand rest on Dean's shoulder.

"Dean," Bryson said in a tight voice. He caught himself and cleared his throat as he started again. "Dean, I saw the figure of a man running across the roof outside my window during the quake."

I stared at Bryson in alarm, the pit of my stomach turning and twisting with that all too familiar sense of dread. He glanced my way, but continued speaking to Dean. "Did you see that man?" Dean did not answer. "Was he in your room? Did he hurt you?"

"No," Dean said evenly, sitting straight up to respond to his father. "No, sir, he hurt me a long time ago," Dean said then shook his head in confusion. "No, he didn't hurt me... that didn't happen, remember? ...There was an accident." He seemed to be talking to himself.

"What's he saying?" I whispered to Bryson.

Bryson's face was draining of all color. He came over to the sofa and knelt down on the floor. "Dean?" he said softly. "Tell me about the accident. Who is the man in those drawings? It's not me, is it?"

I waited with baited breath for Dean's response, but it never came. He collapsed back against his pillow and drifted off to sleep. I watched Bryson as he gaped at Dean. Something big was about to be revealed. I could feel it. Then I thought about the dark stranger and his dog and wondered again if he had been in Dean's room this morning.

"Do you know who that man was?" I asked Bryson. That faceless man had threatened to hurt me. I was beginning to shake from the residual fear that was swelling within me.

Fear of violation.

"Amy, I know you're frightened," Bryson said, looking up at me now. He was guarded, not wanting to reveal certain information.

"I am," I agreed. "Look, Bryson, I'm not going to flee, if that's what you're wondering. But I'm afraid that this man you saw is the same one who threatened me before."

"He threatened you?" Bryson asked, almost snapped actually. "You didn't told me you saw someone on the grounds."

"Well, he did," I admitted willingly now. "He threatened to rape me, but in more unflattering terms."

Bryson clenched his jaws. "I can't believe you didn't tell me that!" He was pissed.

I looked at him with uncertainty. "I'm sorry," I said honestly. "I was mortified by the things he'd said. I didn't want to repeat them." Why did it make a difference that I'd been threatened? The fact remains that there has been a stranger on the premises on a regular basis for weeks.

He shook his head as he stood up. He put a hand around my arm and drew me a few paces away from the couch. He folded his arms over his chest and stared into my eyes as he spoke. "Miss Stuart, Amy," he said, "contrary to what you have no doubt come to believe, I am not a paranoid, housebound freak. I have been quite certain for some time now that I was being stalked."

"Stalked?" I reacted with a jolt of shock.

"Yes, stalked." he reclaimed the floor. "And I don't mean by an obsessive, love–struck fan. I'm referring to a person who wishes to do me or my son grave injury or worse."

I was panting with effort to conceptualize the enormity of what he was confiding. *No wonder! No fucking wonder!* Tears welled up in my eyes. I was overwhelmed.

"No, no," he said softly, chucking my chin. "I need your help; your proven strength."

Dean moaned in his sleep. His head jerked from side to side as if dodging an assault. His lips were pressed tightly together, trapping his frightened cries inside his head. I crept over to Dean's side, forcing myself not to pull him protectively into my arms. Instead, I spoke in a low voice, calling his name.

"Dean, you're dreaming, sweetheart. Open your eyes, baby."

I watched his face continue to contort, his mouth finally opening to let out a silent wail of despair. I tried again, repeating the words. Finally, he opened his eyes.

"No!" he whispered in anguish.

Bryson picked Dean up with trembling arms.

***

"What could make him fear telling me about it?" Bryson asked. He masked his agony now, although I had been privy to a peek at his compassionate tears while he tried to comfort Dean.

Dean had remained silent.

***

We sat close together on the couch. Dean lay sleeping soundly with his head against my thigh on one side. Bryson sat with his shoulder and leg pressed to my other side. The television was on at a low volume, the reports of damage from the quake seemed to be minimal. The room was chilly, but we were reluctant to move to turn up the thermostat.

Bryson finally tossed the afghan from the couch around us, arranging it so that it didn't cover Dean's face. A comforting heat spread under the blanket. It helped me to relax a little, but I was still close to very frightened tears. I knew that if I gave in to them, I'd lose whatever edge I'd managed to maintain throughout this whole ordeal.

"The stranger has a big dog he calls Black," I said softly.

"How do you know?" Bryson asked in an equally quiet voice.

"The dog always stares at me through my window. That's why it took me so long to become alarmed. It seemed like he belonged here, and Dean had told me he was the guard's dog." I looked at him. "But now, I'm beginning to wonder if maybe the dog was keeping guard on *me* while the stranger prowled around. He's only appeared at night, usually when you've been away and after Dean's in bed."

"I dread the thought of what this man's been doing to Dean," Bryson said sadly.

"Oh God, me too," I said, squeezing my eyes shut. "We've got to get him to tell us more about it."

We sat in silence for a while. Then it was Bryson who spoke. "I'm not going to involve the police, you understand," he said.

"You don't feel you can trust them," I guessed.

"No. For all I know, they've helped this thug track me down."

"Is there any connection to this man and the deaths of your brother? Or your wife and daughter?" I asked carefully as the thought occurred to me.

Bryson turned pained eyes to me. "Most definitely," he said, swallowing against a catch in his voice. He looked away, clenching his jaw. "Amy, there was no car accident. Rachel was kidnapped and brutally murdered. I found her body out in the woods behind our home. She had been raped and beaten savagely. When Elaine found out, she drank a fifth of vodka and slit her wrists. I told Dean they had died in a car accident to spare him the impact of the tragedy."

Tears rolled simultaneously down each of our cheeks. I listened in stunned silence as the parts of the picture were almost completely together. I reached for his hand under the blanket and we laced our fingers together. It occurred to me that we were more closely bound now than while we'd had sex in the pool.

***

"Bryson?" I whispered after a time.

"Yes?"

"Did you ever suspect me?" I asked him. I had been crying quietly for a few minutes now, the fear of the danger we were all in was too overpowering.

"All the time, I'm afraid," he admitted.

I sighed, insulted. But then, I realized how troubled he must have been over my refusal to cooperate with his restrictions. "How come you never fired me?"

He laughed softly then, ironically. "I tried to, if you will recall," he reminded me.

"But I wouldn't go."

"No, you wouldn't," he agreed. "And truthfully, your indignance in the face of my wrath seemed genuine."

"It was," I said, suddenly seeing the irony as well.

"Amy, will you come away with Dean and I?" Bryson asked, his voice full of unspoken tension.

"Right now?" I questioned, trying to make a decision with a clear mind.

"Yes."

"How long will we be gone?" I asked.

"As long as necessary."

CHAPTER THIRTY–FOUR
Stalked!

The destination was Mammoth Mountain.

It had not been difficult to avoid Bryson as I busied myself packing clothes for Dean and me. In addition to my primal fear of death and violence, I was seriously angry with myself for having let a sexual encounter occur between us. I had lied to myself and denied the changes that had taken place in my relationship with the boss. I had come to care about him. But Bryson had nothing to give me in return. At least now I could see why he held himself at bay from emotional bonds. He'd lost so, so much.

***

Knock. Knock. Knock.

"Amy?" he called through my door. "Are you ready to leave?"

"Yes," I said. I opened the door and faced him.

I started to move past him, but he put a hand on my arm. "Uh, before we get in the car, I have something to say to you," he said, taking my duffle bag from me and setting it aside.

I quickly raised my hand to silence him. "Bryson, please, let's go back to being the reluctant, unlikely friends that we seem to have become, and get through this ordeal, okay?"

"And what about yesterday?" he asked skeptically.

"Yesterday is a memory," I said dismissively.

He grinned, cocking his head, "Oh, and a lovely memory it will always be."

Inside I wanted to cry, but outside, I matched his grin with one of my own as I responded lightly, "Yes *indeedy.* Now let's go."

I led the way out of the house.

"Does this mean we're partners?" he asked from behind me.

"To whatever extent we're able to be," I confirmed.

***

Well, we were partners now, which meant that we were to take trouble on, side by side. In my opinion, the first priority was Dean and getting him to spill his guts. I quietly suggested this to Bryson as we drove. Dean sat in a catatonic state in the back seat.

"He's really clammed up, now," I said.

Bryson nodded in agreement, thinking. "You've gotten much more out of him since you've known him than he'd ever have told me," he said. "Of course, I've only asked for information when he was in trouble."

His comment gave me food for thought.

Thus far, my most common error in judgment had been based on incorrect assumptions on my part. Perhaps I was doing that again now. I was assuming that Dean was afraid to upset his father with his secrets. Maybe there was more to it than that. Dean was a very intuitive child. Maybe he sensed that Bryson was resisting him, that there was a very good reason for the distance between them.

"Maybe there's something else with Dean that bothers you," I said out loud to Bryson.

Bingo!

All at once, Bryson slammed on the brakes and pulled the Range Rover off to the side of the road. His face was set in a grim mask as he opened the door and got out, slamming it shut with an angry force. I watched him walk off, ahead of the car, hands on hips. I think he had convinced himself that revealing his last secrets to me would make him irrevocably vulnerable to the whole world, rather than just to me. What would be so bad about being vulnerable to me? He was so stunningly attractive, even now, in this setting. His form was in perfect visual contrast to the silvery sky and the wet, tree–lined road.

I got out of the car and reluctantly followed Bryson to where he had stopped with feet planted apart, hands still on hips, eyes glaring cold frustration toward me. I bravely returned his look with one of curious inquiry. "I hit a tender spot, didn't I?" I asked him.

"What in the bloody hell do you want from me?" he seethed through gritted teeth.

I sensed that my question had provoked a reaction to a deep issue – one that was too deep to delve into during a casual conversation. I also tempered the self–defensive urge to tell him that I didn't want a damned thing from him.

That wasn't the truth.

"I want to *know* you," I said.

That was the truth.

"You do know me," he visibly tried to relax as he spoke. But his eyes, though they met mine, were guarded.

"I want to know your truths, not your cover stories–"

"God dammit!" he cut me off, all worked up again. "Why can't you just leave things alone?"

"Bryson, I need to know that you trust me enough to talk to me!" I was unable to keep my voice down now, as we sparred, out there on the empty road.

"Don't you see what's bloody happening here?" he yelled. "I can't take care of your needs at a time when everything I thought was stable in my life is emerging as the core of its worst crisis!"

I knew he meant that to be directed toward my feelings about the sex we'd had. "For Christ's sake, Bryson, this isn't about my needs, this is about our three *lives,* my friend. Your stability has been based on bullshit. The choice is yours now, to either cut the crap or leave me for dead, because I'm not a mind reader." I glared right back at him now. "I *know* you're still keeping secrets –"

"There's nothing more for you to know!" he declared.

"Then there's no point in continuing this farce," I responded, more to myself than to him. *I'm really only making things worse for all of us if I stay in this,* I realized. *If I'm sensing that there's still missing information, then there is.*

I had to protect myself first and foremost. I would look for an out.

***

We were driving again.

"When I came to you in the pool, I was looking for a human connection in the middle of all of this terrific chaos," Bryson said quietly, so that Dean couldn't hear.

"I wanted a connection too," I told him in a loud whisper. "I guess my interpretation of connection encompasses more of me than what's between my legs."

"Amy, I'm sorry I can't offer you more."

Story of my life.

***

I pushed aside my confused emotions and tried to think rationally. There was still a missing link to this chain of events that was unfolding. Bryson was intent on making me find out the hard way. Perhaps there was a way that he couldn't control...

I thought of Dean's drawings. I had brought along the book, still having decided not to look through the last several pages. Truthfully, I knew there'd be a dramatic realization in them, the key to Dean's emotional lock box. I also knew that I didn't want to deal with the enormity of what the drawings would reveal. The *fear factor* had taken control of me again, convincing me that I was not strong enough to help him through his problems.

But now, all I could think of was how alone that poor child truly had been all of this time. I knew that kind of alone.

I had barely survived it...

...How could a little boy?

***

"Dean, are you hungry?" I asked over my shoulder into the back seat where Dean sat, slumped and shut down.

No answer.

Bryson sighed in defeat.

***

We pulled into a rest area about twenty minutes later. I had to pee. Bryson got out of the car to stretch his legs. Dean stayed in the car.

I sat on the toilet, feeling numb. I knew I wouldn't be worth a damn to the Wilde's much longer. My own defenses were kicking in and I was zoning out. I needed to feel safe again. Now.

I emerged from the restroom and tried not to look over at Bryson, who seemed to be waiting to talk to me. A piercing shriek broke through the brisk mountain air. I shot a look of surprise at Bryson, to find that he in turn was gaping at me.

"Bastard child! You were never meant to be!"

The shrill voice came from the car.

We bolted over to the passenger side, where Dean lay pinned beneath a blond haired woman who wielded an enormous butcher knife in the vicinity of his chest.

Someone protect that boy!

***

Bryson tore open the door to the backseat, trying and failing to pull the crazed creature off of his son. She squirmed away, squealing to let her "take the boy". I watched, as if from a distance, deafened by the pounding of my terrified heart, as Bryson grabbed a handful of her dusty gray coat, and then of her very familiar fuzzy blond hair, and dragged her kicking and screaming out onto the ground. The stench of her unwashed body and clothing was nauseating.

One of her flailing feet had clipped Dean in the mouth. He sat unmoving, staring at nothing, a trickle of blood dribbling down his chin.

***

Bryson was fighting the woman for the knife.

She screamed like a banshee, "Let me take him! He's Corbin's boy! His bitch mother stole my husband! He–can–go–to–hell–with–her!"

CHAPTER THIRTY–FIVE
Moira

"If anyone's going to hell, Moira, it's you! Drop the bloody knife!" Bryson grated out. He had one heck of a time wrestling that blade from her.

***

Moira!

I stood watching, mesmerized – paralyzed actually. The *fear factor* had found me again. I looked at Dean's bleeding lip, then at Bryson's bloodstained shirt and realized she had injured him as well. What if she overtook him by mortally wounding him?

I really didn't know what the hell to do, except dive into the melee, so to speak.

Instinct took over then, moving my feet toward their thrashing bodies. I looked down at my steel–toed Dr. Martin's, then took aim and shot a swift kick to the side of Moira's head. It stunned her long enough for Bryson to slam her knuckles onto the rough pavement, inducing her to release the damned knife.

"Get in the car now!" Bryson hollered as he scrambled to his feet and dove into the front seat. I piled in beside Dean and locked the doors. Moira was on her feet too, her eyes wide with psychotic rage, tearing at the door handles, screaming threats and obscenities at me. Bryson struggled with the keys in the ignition, drawing the terror of this drama to an extreme frenzy. Finally, the engine turned over and he slammed into reverse. The car's motion yanked the unprepared Moira off her feet again, nearly running over her body.

I watched Bryson shift into first gear, then jam on the gas, releasing the clutch too quickly. The engine stalled.

Dean screamed.

***

Moira charged at the back passenger window. She slammed her face *hard* against the panel. Blood spewed from her nose and lips, but she held herself against the glass, her eyes glaring first at Dean, and then me. I could hear her scream that she would find us and kill us.

Bryson restarted the engine.

Moira was circling around the back of the car, approaching the driver's side.

"She can't get in," I said, oh–so–calmly. "Take your time." But inside my head, I screamed, *get us the fuck out of here!!*

He did. We flew, leaving a cloud of dust around Moira.

***

"Holy Christ!" Bryson exclaimed in a rattled voice. "Where in the bloody hell did she come from?"

"Behind the back seat," Dean answered. Then he burst into tears.

***

We drove all day on Interstate 5. So much for the early season ski trip. There was only manmade snow anyway. Bryson didn't stop driving until we were in Portland, Oregon. We checked into a hotel under a fake name and paid cash.

***

I took a look at their injuries. Bryson had a hairline slash across his chest, just missing his left nipple. Yeow!

Dean had a puffy lip.

We iced Dean's lip and sponged Bryson's cut. Neither warranted medical attention.

***

I cradled Dean against my chest, trying to make him feel safe. He eventually fell asleep. I sat with him in my arms, listening in a dull fog to the conversation that Bryson was having with Wes Ryan on the phone. I was sweating with tension and cold fear. There was something *off* here. Shouldn't Bryson be questioning Wes' reliability by now? How the hell else could Moira have known where we'd be?

Then I realized I'd seen her in the city and again at the house.

He hung up and directed his attention to me.

"Wes is going to get a couple of the lads in the San Francisco precinct to help get a manhunt out for her," he told me, referring to Moira. "He says we're safest here."

"I don't think we are, Bryson," I said.

"Why not?" he frowned at me.

"I don't know," I said shakily. "But my gut is screaming at me to get out of here. I don't trust Wes."

He walked over and sat on the edge of the couch, facing me. "I'm certain that your nerves are frayed to the fibers, you know," he acknowledged. "But Wes, despite his faults, is the only person that I *have* trusted in five years. He's kept us safe for this long and..." he stopped speaking as he saw my expression.

"I don't think we can trust *anyone* right now," I said softly. I suddenly remembered the day that Dean had told me he didn't like Wes. Dean seemed to be the only one who had known the absolute truth all along.

Bryson moved closer, his face paling. He must have known what I was thinking, but he asked me anyway, "What is it?"

"Wes is somehow involved in all this, Bryson, he has to be." I said in a strained voice. I wanted to cry and hide, and the effort to keep a grip was exhausting. "He told me about having known Moira in the past, when all of the problems in your marriage occurred," I admitted. "He knew her well, and cared about her."

Bryson shook his head to deny my words, but then stopped. "This is becoming more than I can handle."

"I think it always has been," I told him.

***

We slept for three hours, then checked out of the hotel and began driving back. Bryson told me he would rather trust my instincts and be wrong, than to find out they were right. Somewhere in the vicinity of five o'clock a.m., we pulled over and stopped for coffee in an all night diner. Dean woke up and asked what we were going to do.

"We're taking a break," I told him.

"May I get something to eat?" he asked timidly. Poor thing, he hadn't eaten since yesterday morning.

"Of course you may," Bryson answered. "You may have whatever you would like." He lifted Dean out of the car and kept a grip on the boy's hand.

Dean smiled.

CHAPTER THIRTY-SIX
Corbin's Boy

We all had pancakes. They were terrible, but we ate them with relish.

Then Dean asked Bryson about what Moira had said yesterday. "Is it the truth?" His little face looked slightly saddened.

Bryson stopped sipping his third cup of coffee. He set the cup down and looked very seriously across the table at Dean. "Yes, son, it's true."

***

"Why didn't you tell me before?" Dean asked.

"I didn't want you to worry that I didn't... care for you..." Bryson's voice tapered off and he sat silently, looking defeated.

"Uncle Corbin is my father," Dean said, seemingly unaffected by Bryson's revelation. "Where is he?"

Bryson cleared his throat. He shook his head, saying gently, "This is not the time to discuss it, son."

"When is it a good time?" Dean asked. He looked down at his empty plate, as if uncertain that he was safe from upsetting his father, uncle, now.

When Bryson looked at me, I shrugged my shoulders. "He needs to know," I said meaningfully. I'd been silently reflecting on the fact that I'd been right in my suspicions that there were more secrets. I hadn't commented on Moira's declaration yesterday, mostly because I had been on overload. I still was.

Bryson sighed. "Corbin is dead, Dean. He died several years ago, before your mother and Rachel."

"Oh," Dean responded. He kept his gaze fixed on his plate.

"I'm not certain that he knew he had fathered you, Dean. I didn't speak to him about it, but your mother might have. She and I had some problems, but they were not about you. I wanted a son and she gave me one. In my mind you have always been my real son."

Dean nodded his head, seeming to accept Bryson's declaration. "What's going to happen to us?" he asked.

"We'll need to make a plan," Bryson admitted, not revealing anything but confidence in his statement.

"Let's just go back home," Dean said. "The bad lady thinks we're gone."

"But maybe she'll wait for us to return," Bryson pointed out.

"Then let's be ready for her," Dean said.

Bryson laughed. "If only it were that simple!"

I piped in my thoughts now. "I think there's also a man involved."

"You mean Mr. Ryan," Dean said.

I flashed a look at Bryson.

"I think maybe I should show you my drawings now, Father," Dean said solemnly.

***

I pulled the book out of my knapsack. We put it in the middle of the table and opened it to the back. The truth was there in two separate drawings.

"I draw what I've seen, Father," Dean said quietly.

"You saw them?" Bryson asked. He looked at me with tortured eyes. "Rachel..."

"I was with her," Dean said. "That man took me, too."

"What?" Bryson was in anguish now.

"He made me watch him hurt Rachel," Dean explained slowly. "Then he just hit her and hit her..." his words trailed off.

"You never told me," Bryson said. He reached across the table and took both of Dean's hands, holding them tightly. "I came home and you were in your bed, asleep."

"He let me go. He said it wasn't my turn yet."

There it was! That key phrase: *not my turn yet.*

Dean continued. "I couldn't remember any of it until last summer, when Mr. Ryan started staying in the guest house. Something about him reminded me of it."

"Was he the man who hurt you and your sister?" I asked.

"I think so," Dean confirmed.

***

"I saw Mother, too," he added. "She did suicide, right?"

"Yes," Bryson whispered. He was sweating with the effort to maintain control.

"I didn't remember what I saw," Dean went on. "And you told me they died in the crash, so I thought that's what happened. Then the nightmare started coming whenever you went away on a trip. In the nightmare, I saw them again, the real way they died. But there was a car there, too...and then two times when the dream came, it lasted until the man came too, and he hurt me too in the dream." He looked at each of us for a solemn moment. "You saw me have those dreams."

"Did you see the man's face?" I asked. I sensed his helplessness and wanted to keep him on a factual level.

Dean shook his head. He cast a forlorn look at Bryson. "Sometimes Mr. Ryan talks like you and I think it's you."

What was he saying?

"Did you think it was I who had hurt you and Rachel?" Bryson asked then wiped wet eyes on his shirtsleeve.

"Not until Amy came. That's when I really started to remember things, and I got mad at you. Mr. Ryan kept saying that you had wanted me to die, instead of Rachel. I tried not to believe him, but..." Dean started to cry then, saying earnestly, "I'm sorry for what I said the other day."

That just about did Bryson in. His breathing became ragged with the effort to restrain his emotions. He held out his arms to Dean. Dean slipped off the seat and went cautiously around the table, not sure what to expect. Bryson pulled Dean onto his lap, embracing him tightly.

"You didn't do anything wrong, Dean," Bryson said. "It wasn't your fault, I'm the one who lied. I thought I was protecting you."

***

"We'll have to set a trap for them," Bryson said at last. He waved away the waitress when she offered him more coffee, asking for the check.

***

"I should have trusted my suspicions of Wes back when we worked on pornography case," Bryson murmured to me as we drove. "My God. He's a serial killer." The weight of his comment hung like a cement cloud over our heads. Aware that Dean might hear, we had waited until he had drifted off in the back seat to continue our discussion.

"I know what you mean about instincts, Bryson," I told him. "I'm only just beginning to realize that I've always had them, but have ignored the voice in my head that told me to take care of myself. It seemed the selfish route so much of the time that I left myself open, trying to be nice and good."

"Exactly," Bryson agreed.

For once we were on the same wavelength.

"Wes was very likely involved in that child porno ring," I said. "He told me about it, too, and admitted that he had known you were suspicious of him. He never forgave you for that, and seemed to me to feel vindictive toward you."

Bryson took his eyes off the road to look at me. He was scared.

"I think it was Wes who killed Corbin," I said, shaking as the words came out. My whole body trembled now. I hugged myself, but could not calm the tremors.

"Then he killed my girl, and terrorized my son," Bryson concurred. His hands gripped the steering wheel. "That's a pretty extreme need for revenge. I can only conclude that he's a pedophile and murderer, and used his disdain for me as a reason to act on his desires. We're probably not his only prey. But I think we'd have a difficult time persuading the law to investigate him. We have no proof of any of this."

"He's the dark stranger," I declared.

"I wonder why he didn't kill Dean that night?" Bryson said.

"I get the feeling he'd planned on tormenting you for as long as he could," I suggested. "Remember Dean said the man had told him it wasn't his turn yet?"

"Yes," Bryson responded in a rasp.

I thought back to the night that Dean had tried to commit suicide. "Dean told me the voice had told him it was his turn, that night when he went out on the roof."

"What voice?" Bryson asked in alarm.

"He couldn't remember."

Bryson sighed. "I knew you were right about his behavior," he admitted. "But I wasn't letting myself see the obvious clues, only thinking about how a steady routine would keep our lives together."

"It sounds like I came into the picture just as Wes was beginning to turn on the heat. He must have been bothering Dean at school as well as at home. Poor Dean was always in a state of defensive confusion. His memory has learned to shut down to protect his sanity."

"I wavered between reading his behavior as defiant and manipulative, and downright disturbing," Bryson acknowledged. "I realized that I wasn't going to be able to pretend that he was functioning as normally as I needed to think he was, as long as you were in my employment." He growled in self–contempt, "Look at what I've become! I've been so weakened by this terror."

***

"I'm trying to imagine what that night must have been like for Dean, and how his subconscious has compensated by blanking out everything he had saw and experienced," I commented.

"It must have been unfathomable," Bryson said brokenly. Then he finally gave the true recap of that night: "I was away, but due home that night. The children were kidnapped and taken off without their mother's knowledge. Dean was deliberately spared from death, while his sister was mauled and destroyed. Dean was returned home where he crawled into the sanctuary of his bed. I came home and found that Rachel was missing and Elaine was hysterical. Dean continued to sleep. We left him alone in the house to search for our daughter.

"I found her. Elaine came upon me as I wept over her body. She took one look at her baby and lost her sanity. She tore back to the house. I couldn't bring myself to follow her, knowing I could offer her no comfort. When I finally returned to the house, I found her in the bathroom, hanging from the exposed rafter. There were slits in her wrists and an empty bottle of Vodka. She had taken no chances.

"Dean slept through the police inquiry and when he woke, I told him that his mummy and sister had died in a car crash. He seemed to believe me. With all of the secrets surrounding his existence already, I thought I could spare him the worry that he had somehow been responsible for their deaths, as children often think."

"It seems that Wes was setting up the ultimate torture for you," I surmised. "He forced you to live with your wife and brother's treachery single handedly."

"Yes," Bryson agreed. "Only he underestimated my love for Dean. Still, he completely manipulated my fears and left me virtually powerless for five long years."

"And how do you feel now?" I asked.

"Decisively empowered."

CHAPTER THIRTY–SEVEN
Powerless

We were back in Trinity by ten–thirty.

I could smell the perspiration on my skin; that clean, wet, pre–body–odor that changes as the moisture creates a breeding ground for bacteria. My entire body was slick with it, causing my jeans and sweater to cling uncomfortably as I slowly padded through the larger of the two bedrooms in the guesthouse.

There were no indications that anyone had been here in the past forty–eight hours. The air had an unventilated quality to it that smelled more of dust and damp walls than of the various human residues. I went to the bathroom and felt the surfaces of the tiles in the shower, the tub, and basin. They were bone dry, as were the shampoo and hand soap containers.

***

"No one's been here," I told Bryson when we regrouped in the living room.

"No," he agreed, looking out the bay window behind the couch, to the side yard where Dean sat on the grass. He watched the boy pluck blade after blade of grass, hold it up very close to his eye then cast it disdainfully aside. Bryson blinked and shook his head as if to clear it. "Let's check the apartments and the garage," he said.

When we emerged from the house, Dean rose from the lawn and followed us at a distance.

"Maybe we should ask the Campbells to keep Dean until this is over," I suggested to Bryson.

"No!" Dean screamed from behind us.

We turned toward him.

"He knows where to look!" Dean shouted. Tears tumbled down his rosy cheeks, splattering over his trembling lips. "There's no place for us to hide! We can't keep running!"

Bryson nodded in agreement as he walked over to Dean and put a hand on the boy's shoulder. Dean was bawling now, completely out of control.

"Any more brilliant ideas, Amy?" Bryson asked in a mocking tone. His wink told me he would have agreed with me before Dean had set us both straight, however.

"No, that's the only one I had," I said. Then to Dean, "You're right, sweetheart. We work best as a team. We'll stay together."

Dean stopped crying almost instantly. But his body continued to be wracked by shudders for at least a quarter of an hour after that.

***

We searched the two apartments and the garage. There was nothing to go on. No clues.

We didn't know what to do next, so we made a late breakfast.

***

"Someone in this town keeps him abreast of the goings–on over here," Bryson surmised over the scrambled eggs and toast we were forcing ourselves to eat. "We should go into town and make our presence obvious to everyone."

"Sounds good," I said shakily. My nerves were frayed. I was surprised my stomach was holding my second breakfast. "We'll hit every place of business, including the service station. I've had a bad feeling about Norman since the day I drove into town."

And I knew just who to ask for some background information on him. My good friend Chester.

***

"He's *pilikia.* You know, trouble," Chester said, not about Norman, but of Wes Ryan. "Make a *hei'au* to help you see the truth about him."

It was like speaking to the town wise man.

"How do I know this truth?" I asked shakily.

"In the Hawaiian language, we call it *kuleana,*" he told me. "It's something you sense in your gut."

"But Wes is your friend," I reminded him.

"There was a change," Chester said carefully. "I feel his dark energy. It's right in front of us."

"Have you seen Wes in the past twenty–four hours, Chester?" Bryson asked him.

"Not," Chester responded, Hawaiian style.

Dean laughed.

***

We went to the general store and said hello to the proprietor and several customers. They all gave Bryson surprised looks when he approached them, but all responded cordially. He could be rather charming when he tried to be. No one had see Wes for a couple of days now.

***

Nightfall was upon us and we really had no plan. Bryson and I secretly agreed that Dean was the main target, but that Bryson would probably be approached first, and then made to watch Dean suffer at the hands of Moira and Wes. We also agreed that for the time being, we probably had the stalking duo on a tailspin, no doubt having followed us to Oregon, only to arrive and find that we'd gone. I figured this bought us another twenty–four hours. And likely, they would also have expected us to go to the police for assistance, and so would be waiting for an opportunity to strike when our guard was down.

CHAPTER THIRTY–EIGHT
Raging Silence

I could feel my blood pressure rising under the force of my unrestrained anxiety throughout that endless day. I was dog tired, and needed rest so badly that, when Bryson suggested we all sleep in the same room, I refused. I told him I needed one solid night of sleep then I'd cooperate with anything he suggested.

***

I finally drifted off, that eerie feeling of disquiet never really relenting, only total exhaustion giving me a break.

***

Was I dreaming? I could feel the bed sag slightly as someone slid in behind me. Cool hands gripped my hips possessively.

Bryson? Had he not been able to contain his true desire for me? Was he finally admitting he needed me?

Yes!

Now I could let myself enjoy him again, and feel the powerful elation at his inability to show restraint.

...But Jesus, the man could be kind of rough... His fingers were biting into my buttocks, pulling me by the cheeks toward him. He shouldn't have made himself wait so long to come to me...

With my eyes closed, I wanted to let my senses respond to the feel of him. The roughness of his jeans scratched pleasantly at the skin on the backs of my thighs. I waited for his fingers to caress my breasts, belly, clitoris...

...But, he didn't. He unzipped his fly and pushed roughly inside me. The first thing I felt was a tearing pain.

Wait a minute! This is not Bryson! I realized this with the certainty that only a woman can have.

But now his hand was over my mouth, his arms in a clamped vise around mine, and he thrust roughly inside me. It hurt like hell and I moaned in pain. I squirmed and struggled, but he had me pinned so that I couldn't get any leverage with my legs. The man was built like a cannon. After a minute or so of *that* torture, he tried to push me over onto my stomach.

Oh God, *not* to sodomize me!

Somehow in my frenzied resistance, my flailing leg made contact with his hardened testicles. He gasped and let go of me. I scrambled out of the bed, knowing without having to see him who he was. Panic seeped into my shocked senses, but I frantically searched for a weapon, hoping survival instinct would prevail.

"What's the matter, Amy? I know you like it from behind, I saw you take it that way from Bryson," he said menacingly. His words were calculated to break me down, to give him the power to hurt me.

It worked.

The bedside lamp was a two foot tall brass pipe, with a socket at the top. It would have to do. I grabbed it and yanked it away from the wall. The plug shot out of the electrical outlet, and the cord whipped around furiously, wrapping itself around my legs as I flung the shade off the top, shattering the light bulb. I wriggled my legs furiously, trying to free them from the cord. I almost forgot about my assailant as I prepared myself for battle. I held the lamp like a baseball bat, waiting to swing with all of my might.

The dark stranger had risen from the bed, holding his nuts, and muttering something about how he'd see to it that I had no asshole left when he was through with me. He came at me, stumbling as his open pants slipped down his legs and tangled around his calves and ankles. His enormous penis danced with his body's motions, still hardened with arousal at the twisted, hideous pleasure he was getting out of this scene.

I looked into his eyes and almost fainted from the immeasurable terror that his psychotic expression brought up in me. He was enjoying the chase, feeding on the fear he sensed in me as he licked his lips with pleasure. I knew that was just what I shouldn't have revealed to him, but I was too freaked to act nonchalant anyway.

"I'm Norman, Amy, just like I was the one in the woods, just like I've been the one outside your window," he said tauntingly. "And I killed Mac Greyson, because I felt like it. I told him about how I liked to watch you at night, and he said he was going to tell you about it. So I told him I'd raped his daughter and left her in her little dingy out at sea... and off he went!"

Disgusted and mortified at what he'd just revealed, I swung the lamp–base like an ax and somehow managed to make a chopping contact with the tip of his member. He bellowed angrily, almost falling over in pain. I bolted, bringing my knee up into his face as hard as I could on the way.

I heard rather than felt his teeth cut into my flesh and crack against my kneecap. My foot slammed back down on the ground, too hard. The force of the impact almost jammed my knee joint. He came at me again, hurling himself bodily into my midsection and knocking us both to the floor. Still gripping the lamp base, I jammed the broken bulb into his leg. He yelped, but managed to use his weight to pin me down. I screamed, a loud animal cry of terror. My fingers found his eyes and I dug my nails in. Now the cries were his. He batted my hands away, and I rolled onto my side and onto my knees. I managed to fling myself past him, running through to the kitchen.

The lights came on. I stumbled to a stop.

***

Bryson was there, a robe thrown hastily over jeans, hair disheveled from sleep. His eyes sharply assessed my appearance, seeing at once that I had been attacked.

"*I'm not through with you, bitch!*" Wes Ryan rasped from behind me. I spun around. There was no vestige of sanity about the man, at all. His eyes looked past me to Bryson. "And you're next, and then the little bastard upstairs." Blood trickled from the corner of his mouth and from one nostril. He had pulled his pants up, but had not fastened them as if still expecting to use his penis as a weapon. "You've been so easy to manipulate, old friend," he said to Bryson, his attention no longer on finishing me, but on feeding on the tension in the room. "You're so oblivious to the boy – undoubtedly because he's your bastard nephew. It's been so fulfilling to watch the terror in his eyes while I talked about how he'd die, when it was his turn."

Bryson stepped between Wes and me. He had removed his robe, and used one hand to motion me backwards. The complete picture of this hell called *living with the Wildes* began to take a very defined form in my terror filled senses, and suddenly a lot of questions were answered in those few informative sentences Wes had just delivered. Preservation of life surged beyond my instinct to flee, and I backed up a few steps, again considering the weapons at my disposal.

There were plenty of knives.

"*Move out of my way!*" Wes bellowed at Bryson. There was a lethal hatred in his eyes. I knew he intended to kill us all.

"Make me," Bryson said, in the coldest tone I'd ever heard from him. I shivered, watching in petrified silence.

"With pleasure, old friend," Wes grinned sickeningly. He stepped closer to Bryson. "You might like it up the ass too. Just like that bitch over there will. Just like Elaine did before she went to Corbin... Just like your daughter did with me... Just like Corbin's son will, too."

***

I watched the muscles in Bryson's shoulders and upper back bunch with tension. I knew the violent venom in Wes's words must be nearly putting Bryson over the edge of his sanity. I could only pray that he knew how to handle himself in physical combat, before he lost control of his rage.

Wes took a step toward us.

"Bryson, do you have any idea what you took from me all of those years ago, when you butted in on my scene?" he asked. I knew instinctively he was referring to the child pornography circuit. "I was getting so much fresh, tasty, baby skin to just play with and devour..." he seemed to lose himself briefly in the memory.

I swallowed down a rise of bile.

"...I diddled so many little pussies and penetrated so many tight little assholes..."

"*You sick, fuck!*" I raged. My whole being was encompassed with a desire to relieve this world of the burden named Wes Ryan.

Bryson reached a hand behind his back, again signaling me to back off. It was a sharp wave, a warning to get a grip. I knew at that moment that Bryson had the upper hand here.

Again Wes moved forward, tauntingly. Like a schoolyard bully, he seemed to think he had sufficiently cowed his two adversaries. I inwardly begged to differ. The next step Wes took brought him within an arm's distance of Bryson.

That was where he went wrong.

A wickedly quick jab of Bryson's fist connected with Wes's nose, driving a deathly pressure up into his brain. It was a calculated punch, and it took Wes down instantly. Bryson flung himself upon the fallen man and assailed him mercilessly with skin splitting punches.

But he needn't have bothered. Wes was no longer a threat.

***

"Bryson!" I yelped in a high–pitched squeak, my state of mind having passed hysteria some time ago.

He stilled, kneeling in a straddle over Wes' body. Bryson's shoulders were squared and his fists bunched in tension as he stared at the man who had betrayed him in every aspect conceivable. Then he rose to his feet and stepped away.

***

Bryson turned to me.

As if his worst adversary was not lying on the floor behind him, in the final twitching spasms of death. As if blood was not seeping from the side of Wes' head and through his ears, nose and mouth. As if the final synapse of nerve fibers and brain tissue, no longer capable of sustaining Wes' life, were not kicking their last electrical impulses, Bryson came toward me.

He picked up his discarded robe and wrapped it around me as he guided me toward the booth.

"You're bleeding," he said in a hoarse, empty voice.

"No, I'm fine," I denied. I somehow seemed to think that he couldn't see my exposed breasts and pubis, not completely covered by either my open silk pajama top or his robe. I guess I thought the streaks of blood on my inner thighs were invisible, too, as was the burning pain within my most private place that adrenaline no longer concealed.

"He hurt you," Bryson said.

"No."

I couldn't let him help me.

CHAPTER THIRTY–NINE
Survivors

"What about Dean?" I asked after a moment.

"I hope he slept through–" Bryson stopped mid–sentence. "Oh God, Moira!" he spun on his heel and scrambled over the bloody mess that now framed Wes' body.

I panted in fear. *Oh God, please don't let her get to him!*

In my gut, I knew the nightmare wasn't yet over.

***

"Dean!" I could hear the anguish in Bryson's voice. *"Moira! No!"*

BANG!

A gun shot. Upstairs.

BANG!

Silence.

***

I grabbed the boning knife and headed toward the front staircase. I had no idea who had fired the gun, or who was still alive. My hand shook so badly I could barely clasp my fingers around the knife's handle.

I crept up the stairs as quickly and quietly as I dared, then made my way down the hall to Dean's wing. Light from his bedroom flooded into the hallway through the open door.

I heard sobs. Deep, grieving sobs.

***

"Dean! Bryson!" I bawled out, so totally petrified of what I'd find.

"It's over, Amy," Bryson called out in a broken, drained voice. "Call the police."

***

"Father saved me," Dean told me when I asked him what had happened in his bedroom. That explained it, by golly.

Apparently Moira had held a gun to Dean's head, telling him to say goodnight. It was right at that moment that Bryson barreled into her from behind, knocking her and the gun away from Dean. They struggled for control of the weapon and it went off with Moira in its sights.

In spite of the gruesome scene, Dean was calm. He seemed to be relieved.

CHAPTER FORTY
Aftermath

We reenacted the entire nightmare for the police. After six hours of taking our statements, and searching for and locating the point of entry for both Wes and Moira, the police concluded that no charges would be made against any of us. They were convinced we had acted in self–defense. The coroner's wagon took the bodies away.

A policewoman took me aside and strongly urged me to go to a rape treatment center as soon as possible. I saw little need, since Wes hadn't ejaculated inside me. And besides, he was dead. I didn't have to prove I'd been raped. She reminded me of sexually transmittable diseases being a possibility. I told her I'd get tested for them soon. Finally, she suggested that I might benefit from some crisis counseling.

I told her she was probably right.

***

Bryson took my hand with his free one and led me as he carried Dean upstairs. We went into the master bedroom. I stood beside the large bed while he lay his exhausted child down. Then he went over to his bureau and removed socks, jeans, and a sweater. He came back to me, extending them toward me.

"Here, put these on," he said, handing them to me. "Do you want to bathe?"

I nodded dumbly, suddenly feeling a total blankness in my mind. I followed him into the bathroom. He ran the shower for me and got a towel and washcloth for me. Then he left me alone.

I showered. My body was starting to ache from the beating I'd taken. I put on his clothes. We wore the same size jeans. How nice. The sweater was that blue cotton one from the trip to San Francisco. I went back into the bedroom and found him lying on the bed, next to Dean. He motioned for me to lay down on his other side. He was still bare–chested.

I walked over to the far side of the bed and lay down. He covered us all with a fluffy down comforter. I felt a gentle pressure from his hand on my upper arm, squeezing briefly, as he whispered to me that we'd all be okay now. We just needed some time.

I closed my eyes.

***

I opened my eyes.

He had moved closer to me in his sleep. One of his legs was resting against one of mine.

In the movies, in the aftermath of terror, when the bad guy has been taken down, the star characters always come together. Love prevails. All will be fine.

In real life, every moment that I stayed in proximity to Bryson and Dean prolonged the unbearable reality of what I'd experienced. I had to get away. I couldn't breathe. It was right about then that I absolutely lost it.

***

I remember that I stumbled and fell in my haste to flee down the side porch steps. It probably had something to do with my untied sneakers tripping me. At some point, in my frenzy to bolt from Bryson's bed, his house, and his life, I had put the shoes on.

I was sobbing; out of control, blinded by my tears. *What a fool I've been! It was all so clear now. I'd let it happen again. I'd found another mess. Look what I'd walked right into in my cowardly effort to escape the brutality of my former life!*

I'd been raped!

I'd watched my rapist die!

A child I'd come to love had witnessed multiple violent deaths!

I'd let myself fall for a man who had been unable to trust me, almost to the end.

***

I flashed briefly back into reality and realized I was on my hands and knees at the foot of the stairs. The ground was frozen in the early morning chill. I sat back on my heels and remained crouching as I glared up at the sky. There were swirling, ominous clouds overhead. A rainstorm was due to hit at any time. I wasn't prepared to drive in the heavy rain, the mere thought of it intimidated me to an alarming degree. I had no plan, no rational perspective of what I should do now. My common sense and instinct to flee were engaged in a bloody battle in the foreground of my conscious reasoning.

What in the fuck should I do?

I squeezed my eyes shut, forcing the images from the blood bath away; things I would forget to remember, things I would possibly never face...The searing pain of *Mega*–Wes inside me...My nude, battered body exposed to Bryson's view...Wes, dying on the floor. The way I had next moved upstairs to see how calmly Dean had witnessed the death of the woman who had participated in the destruction of his family.

Hot scalding tears quickly turned cold, stinging my cheeks. I looked at my bundles, my two duffle bags having been flung aside as I fell, now wet from sitting in an icy puddle. My favorite knapsack and its contents strewn across the ground in front of me, mocking me, giving further renewal to my disorientation. I stood up slowly and hoisted the two duffle bags. Trying desperately to stem my hysteria, I carried them with difficulty down the side drive to the front of the house where my car was still parked. I opened the hatch back and bent to grab the bags.

A set of pale hands sprinkled with dark hairs was already grabbing one of the bags. Bryson looked up at me from his stooped position. I avoided his eyes, ashamed that he was seeing me like this, and unable to gain control of the intimate images of the two of us in the pool that ran through my mind; the one's that Wes had watched attentively. Now on the defensive, the last thing I wanted to give Bryson was the knowledge that he had the power to hurt me, that I was so vulnerable. Neither of us said anything.

***

I wondered why he had even bothered to come out to help me. I watched while Bryson easily tossed both bags into the cargo area of my little car, then I turned and walked back to where my knapsack still lay on the ground. I gathered the various necessities that I always carried in the knapsack– cassettes, candy, tampons, hair gel, spare earrings, basically a lot of shit.

When I stood up, I again found that Bryson was beside me, observing me. He held out his hand, seemingly for the backpack, but I ignored him and went back inside. He followed me silently, and when I grabbed my compact stereo, he took the box with my CD's. Those were loaded into the car in silence. I had one more box of crap to get from my quarters. I reentered the house to retrieve it, hoping Bryson's sense of propriety would have been relieved so that he would retreat back upstairs. But he was behind me again, only this time he began to disconnect the computer. I looked at him dully.

"What are you doing?" I asked, wishing he'd just disappear. My face was burning with humiliation, and the chafing from the wind on tear streaked cheeks.

Bryson answered in a low voice, not looking at me. "I want you to have this," he said, referring to the computer.

"No, thank you," I said in a dead voice. "I have no use for it."

"Of course you do," Bryson said stubbornly.

"No, I won't," I said in a voice devoid of any warmth, "I don't want your computer, Bryson."

I left him in the room and went to deposit the last box in the car. I got in behind the wheel and started the engine. Large salty tears of guilt and misery splashed down my cheeks again as I thought of the terrible pain that I would be causing Dean. I knew from my own childhood losses that I could do little to alleviate his feelings of abandonment.

Gritting my teeth and moaning in despair, I jammed the car into gear and sped away, the tires squealing wildly in my haste. I gave into the immeasurable pain that was consuming me, my submission in the form of a devastated wail. I bellowed loudly at fate. I cursed the Universe for delivering me this anguish and misery. Then I realized that all of my worst fears had been realized.

The *fear factor* was deflated now.

I forced myself to breathe regularly as I drove, not paying any attention to the direction in which I was heading.

***

It was there, sitting sadly on the side of the road.

The black dog was alone.

I drove by, glaring pure hatred at him. Then I stopped the car. Not clearly certain as to why I did so, I got out and walked slowly back to Blackie. He whined softly and hung his head in despair. I burst into fresh tears and collapsed on my knees in front of him.

"Don't cry for that bastard, Blackie," I told him between sobs of my own. "He was never worth it."

I felt the warmth of his tongue on my face and looked up into his sad eyes. I realized that he had been an unwilling participant in this whole drama, as I had perceived myself to be. "Come on, boy," I said, rising to my feet and slapping my thigh. He followed me to the car and got in.

***

I drove on.

"It's so loud! I can't get it out of my memory!" I could remember Bryson saying that.

Damned straight.

Wes Ryan's loathsome words came back to me again and again. I couldn't quiet them either as they screamed through my brain.

... *"You might like it up the ass too. Just like that bitch over there will. Just like Elaine did before she went to Corbin... Just like your daughter did with me... Just like Corbin's son will, too."*

The cuts and fissures, caused by his enormous organ, ached and stung between my legs in a horrifying reminder of his evil. The thought of what he'd done with his penis to innocent, small children... If he could hurt a grown woman as he'd hurt me, what kind of damage had he done to them? I squirmed in revulsion, causing the car to swerve enough that I almost lost control.

How symbolic.

***

After about thirty minutes of aimless driving, it dawned on me that I'd not even turned on some music. My numbed fingers reached over and pushed the stereo controls. The volume was still adjusted to high, from the last time I'd been driving with Dean. Our mutually favorite artist sang those ever–meaningful lyrics into my ringing ears once again.

...I've been trying to get down... to the heart of the matter...

"Me too, Don, me too," I sobbed quietly as the song played through, mentally making every possible association with the lyrics to Bryson and me, and then to Dean and me. I realized the heart of my matter was that there was just too much shit in the house of the Wildes. Too much even for the most altruistic, romantic soul to overcome. That really sucked. Now I couldn't even fantasize my way through this one.

...Even if, even if, you don't love me anymore....

The black dog licked my hand and whimpered.

EPILOGUE
<u>*Broken Silence*</u>

"Our greatest enemy was silence." -Amy Stuart Wilde

***

I've thought back on numerous occasions during the past eighteen months, recalling how little faith I'd had in my own instincts during the year that had lead up to, and throughout my time on Wilde Lane. Not anymore. Now my gut is my guide, for every occasion. And truthfully, I'm a much happier person. How simple. How ironically simple it is that in order to be happy as an individual, one only needs to honor that voice inside that tells her what she really wants.

No more bullshit. This is my new life.

***

And it was working for me. I'd written my make-or-break novel, and sold it. I was working on the sequel now. It's amazing how much creativity flows out of a person when she stops allowing herself to be deterred by outside distractions. Now, instead of asking *why is this happening?* I was asking *what can I do next?* A minor cognitive adjustment that was completely transforming my life.

I was finally a credible author in my own right. Well, I still liked to write romance, but now I knew how to get right to the good stuff!

***

Saturday morning.

I woke late, nine o'clock, and dressed for a brisk walk and headed out into the cool balmy May air. Blackie usually followed diligently along, but today I sought to avoid the way he inadvertently reminded me of a time that still haunted me. Now safely settled in La Crescenta, California, I kept mostly to myself. Violence no longer followed me, and a sense of calm was gradually encompassing most of my life. I still nursed a broken heart, and had a reluctant fear of sex these days, but I had a feeling I was going to be okay.

I thought about Bryson, and Dean, as I walked, and still missed them enough to get misty-eyed. In healthier circumstances, we would have made a good family unit...

***

"Excuse me, miss..." a familiar, mildly accented voice called to me from the street.

Jesus! What kind of Karma is that!

I stopped short, feeling my face contort into a frown of disbelief as I looked over my shoulder at the silver Jaguar idling quietly beside me. It was Bryson. My heart began to pound wildly.

Oh shit.

What was he doing in La Crescenta?

Bryson leaned over into the passenger area and peered out of the window at me. His face was relaxed and open, although he was obviously hesitant about approaching me. "May I offer you a lift?" he asked tentatively.

Oh my God.

"To where?" I responded dumbly, numbly.

"To Two–Strikes Park, right around the corner from here," he said.

"Why to the park?"

"To watch an important baseball game," Bryson surprised me by saying.

Excuse me?

"Whose?" I asked, feeling as if I was in some sort of parallel universe, where normal things actually happen.

"Dean's. It's the last game for the championship. I'm coaching. Well, actually, I'm assistant coaching, and I really should be there now." Bryson said, unlatching the passenger door to let me in.

I stood debating whether or not to go with him. Was I ready to do this? I absolutely yearned to see Dean, but still was uncertain that any of us were ready to reunite. And I wasn't prepared to start protecting my heart and ego from Bryson again.

"Please?" Bryson was pleading with me, breaking into my reverie. "It's only a ballgame." He truly seemed to be sensitive to my indecision, and for the moment, I felt reassured.

So, I got into the car beside him and turned to look at him head on. "How did you find me?"

Bryson slid his sunglasses on, his eyes now partially shielded from me. A stray lock of hair was falling attractively over his forehead. This was the most appealing I'd ever seen him look. "I hired another private investigator," he said.

"You're serious?" I asked, unable to believe he was willing to trust anyone with such a title. "When did you find out I was here?"

"About three months ago," he said, turning toward me briefly. "I wasn't ready to do this until then."

Do this?

"Define 'ready,'" I requested. My hands were shaking, so I tucked them into my lap, but kept my gaze on his face.

Bryson glanced at the road as he drove, but then looked back at me. "I'm ready to be a real friend," he told me. "I'm no longer shutting the world out."

Oh.

"How long have you been in the area?" I wanted to know.

"Not long," Bryson smiled as he spoke. "Dean doesn't realize how close we're living to you. I'm renting a small house in La Cañada, about a half mile away."

"You gave up your beautiful home in Trinity?" I demanded.

"We tried to stay, but..." he looked at me again, his eyes meeting mine now. He let me see so much. There was much to see. His eyes were pleading with me to give him a chance, I think.

***

Bryson parked the car in the lot that over-looked the park that lay nestled in the hillside. In the distance, I could see a team of young boys warming up for the next inning. I got out slowly, my heart absolutely racing in reaction to seeing Bryson again, and now at the prospect of seeing Dean. Sentimental tears rose in my eyes when I spotted him out on the field, playing shortstop, just as he had once admitted to me that he'd dreamt of playing. Bryson reached for my hand, which shocked the hell out of me with its intimacy. We began to descend the stairs toward the field.

"He doesn't know you'll be here," Bryson told me. "Do you want to watch him play and wait until after the game to say hello?" He squinted over at the scoreboard. "It's nearly over now."

"That's probably a good idea," I said, thinking I'd need to compose myself for this. I stepped away from Bryson and walked at a slower pace while he jogged on ahead and rejoined the game. He looked good. He was wearing light gray sweat pants that were thin from much use and now tended to cling to the taught lines of his legs and butt. His worn T-shirt hung loosely from his broad shoulders, emphasizing the hardness of his chest and upper arms.

Hubba hubba.

Keeping my eyes on my former employer, I headed for the bleachers and found a seat. I watched as two of Dean's teammates went up to bat. Each one hit struck out. Then Dean went up to the plate. Even from this distance, I could see that he was a different child. He'd be eleven now, and looked it. I couldn't believe how much older he seemed.

Bryson was coaching third base. Dean swung at the first pitch and missed. He seemed unaffected and confident as he took a couple of practice swings. The pitcher sent another that went way outside, but Dean swung anyway and hit a foul tip. Two strikes. He shrugged his shoulders defensively, as if he felt no pressure. *That* was reminiscent of the Dean I knew.

I sat biting my tongue, quivering with the urge to call out encouragement to him. Raw emotion surged up into my chest. I could barely breathe with the power of the joy I was feeling.

"Wait for your pitch, son," Bryson called out to Dean. Dean nodded and waited. I half choked on a cough of surprise. Were uncle and nephew actually experiencing a bond, here?

The next pitch was outside again. This time Dean did not swing.

"Good eye!"

Oops!

I forgot to wait until after the game to draw attention to myself. Well, I couldn't help it. I was damned if these two were going to share a moment without me. I'd brought them together, for Christ's sake.

Dean faltered for a second then he broke into a grin as he recognized my voice. But he did not look around for me. I sneaked a look at Bryson and found him smiling at me and shaking his head. My breath caught again in my throat at the unexpected feeling of partnership I felt with him right then. It felt like family.

Uh oh.

***

The next pitch came. It was perfect. Dean swung with all of his might and smacked it way out into the outfield. His teammates screamed at him to run and then cheered him as he made a complete circle of the diamond, bringing in the winning run. It was one of those miraculous moments that a kid never forgets, and I was right here, watching him experience it.

Bryson trotted over to Dean and swung him into the air. He put Dean down then pulled him into an embrace, very much the proud dad. They stayed like that as all of the other players rushed up and joined arms around the two figures, jumping and cheering and crushing into a group hug.

Okay. So they'd done some work on themselves.

I guess I'm getting called to the plate myself.

Both teams thanked each other for the game then broke up to go home. That was when Dean finally came racing over to me. He threw himself at me, nearly knocking me off balance. He wrapped his arms tightly around my back and pressed his face into my sweatshirt, and I knew instinctively that he was crying. The realization made me cry, too, as I stroked his head and back. He was several inches taller and more filled out now. Life had changed for the better for this kid. All at once, I felt both a thrill of happiness and a sense of loss, realizing how much of his development I'd missed.

Looking up, I kept one hand on Dean while I used the other to wipe my eyes. Bryson was talking to a circle of fathers, his voice animated. It was so odd to see him in this setting, without the tension and distance that I remembered so well.

He turned to look at me and his face became serious. He walked toward Dean and me, glancing down proudly at the boy before his eyes returned to mine. There was a longing in his gaze that made me feel momentarily close to swooning. No one had *ever* looked at me like that before!

I still loved him. And for the first time in a long while, I felt secure about such a deep feeling.

When he reached us, he put a hand on Dean's shoulder and then slid his free hand behind my neck and drew ever so gently forward to place a kiss on my lips.

My eyes drooped closed as I was swept away in a brief moment of sensual wonder. It was electrifying. We pulled apart, but Bryson continued to gaze into my eyes while his thumb tenderly caressed my cheek.

"Spend today with us," he requested, his eyes still not leaving mine. Dean pulled back and looked up at us, his face flushed and wet. Bryson realized he had been crying and hugged Dean protectively against his side as he looked at me inquiringly.

I took a calming breath. "I'd love that."

"The only thing you'll need," Bryson continued with a half smile, "is a bathing suit for later. We're having a celebration barbecue at my house that will no doubt end up with the adults in the Jacuzzi and the kids in the pool."

I couldn't believe my ears. *"You're* having a casual party? With children? And splashing water and screaming?"

Bryson grinned at me as he put his free arm around my shoulders. "Now, Amy, you know I like to play in the swimming pool," he said warmly as we walked. I got a gut–clenching spurt of arousal.

Yikes!

It had been ages since I'd last felt one of those.

***

He drove the short distance back to my minute house and pulled his car into the driveway. I lead them inside and showed them around, letting Dean greet Blackie out in the back yard while I searched for my bikini, sunscreen, and towel. Bryson came in from watching Dean and the dog play and entered my bedroom as I was throwing the things into my knapsack.

"I can't believe you kept his dog," Bryson said in a low voice.

I looked up at him, wondering what he was thinking. I was remembering that mad scramble to get as far away from him and his troubled life as possible. I shuddered from a sudden chill. My life had been rather troubled, as well. "I can imagine it seems a pretty sick thing to have done." I admitted. "But there he was, waiting for me on the road when I left Trinity. He's been keeping me safe ever since."

***

I looked up at him. He was walking further into the room, approaching me slowly. When he was in front of me he leaned close to me. "I want to start over with you," he whispered into my hair, and kissed my cheek. Then he looked at me. I made no effort to hide my trepidation. "I'm sorry," he said earnestly.

***

Dean entered the room and saw us touching. He stopped and stared, amusement turning the corners of his lips upward. "I like Blackie a lot now," he said, not needing to explain his reference to the past. "Can we take him along?"

Bryson shrugged, "It's fine with me if Amy doesn't mind."

"This is definitely going to take some getting used to," I commented, trying to shake away the giddiness before I became incoherent.

"What?" Bryson asked. *As if he didn't know!*

"This easy going guy that you've become," I shook my head. Then I remembered Dean's request and winked at him. "Let's take Blackie, but if he's a pain, we'll have to bring him back."

"Yes!" Dean cheered, then ran back to the yard to get the dog.

***

Despite my offer to drive Blackie and me in my own car to spare Bryson's car the mess from the dog, Bryson was more than happy to drive us all. He told me he had no intention of letting me out of his sight.

We arrived at Bryson's house less than two minutes later.

"Bryson, didn't you tell me that you were renting a *small* house?" I asked with sweet sarcasm.

"Ah, that sharp tongue of yours!" he said brightly. "I'm not sure I should admit that I've missed it."

"And I've missed your arrogance," I said graciously. Then I took in the sight of the large wooden structure before me. It had to have at least five bedrooms. "This is not a small place," I insisted.

Bryson shrugged. "It's smaller than the Trinity house," he said innocently.

Oh please.

We got out of the car and went inside. From the entrance hall, I could see directly out into the backyard through a gorgeous bay window. The yard was beautifully landscaped with a tropical flair of ferns and palm plants. The huge pool had lovely turquoise tiles around its perimeters; the water was blue and inviting. I turned to find both Dean and Bryson watching me make my assessment. I gave them an approving look. "This is cozy," I said as if it were some quaint little compartment.

Dean ran off to change his clothes, taking the dog with him. Bryson led me into the airy living room and sat me down on the white couch. He pulled a footrest in front of me and sat on it. He kept my hands in his and stared into my eyes. "I want to make amends for the past, Amy. I want to face what happened between us, and how I hurt you because I was so closed off."

I spoke softly when I answered him. "I want that too," I told him. "It's not all your fault. I've understood why you withheld like you did. It was survival. Besides, I managed to complicate things because I withheld from you as well. So much of it all was beyond our control."

We were silent for a time. But then Bryson cupped his hands over my knees and looked at me with a directness that demanded my total honesty. "You were raped, sweetheart," he whispered. "What has that done to you?"

I sighed. How could I explain? It wasn't the physical trauma so much as the emotional dynamics at the time. A great deal of resolution had come immediately following the ordeal, as I'd watched my assailant die. And the fact that Bryson had been the one to rescue me had helped a lot, too.

But I had set some new rules for myself that he'd need to know.

"I've sworn never to have sex again," I told him.

I could see the remorse, and disappointment in his eyes. "One couldn't blame you," he said sympathetically. Then he smiled ruefully, saying, "It would serve me right, for the way I treated you."

"You'll have to be very patient," I said, "while I work on reversing that." I put my arms around his neck and kissed him with all of the longing I'd been feeling for him. "I love you," I said. It felt right.

In perfect timing, Dean ran by with the dog and went racing out into the yard. "Hey turkey," Bryson called in a broken voice. It sounded good to hear him use my pet name for Dean. "Wait until we're out there to get into the pool."

"Yes sir!" Dean called back.

Bryson returned his attention to me. "I love you, Miss Stuart. Please do me the honor of being my wife."

I flopped back against the cushions and stared at him.

He gave me a sheepish smile. "Will you?"

I laughed in delight. "If anyone had told me, back on that fateful September day, that we'd be having this conversation today, I'd have run for my life."

He just gazed back at me with a devilish gleam.

Then I saw Dean sitting patiently near the pool with Blackie. "Let's put on our suits."

Bryson embraced me again as we stood. We changed clothes then went out to Dean. The shame I'd been feeling over the rape was already easing slightly with the very open emotion and caring that Bryson was directing at me.

This could be good.

***

We linked arms as we made our way out into the yard, where we remained until long after the guests were gone. I spent a lot of time talking with Dean about his new school and friends. He missed Silverside Elementary, but felt happier here than he could ever remember feeling. After the story had circulated about Wes Ryan, the townspeople had urged their kids to accept Dean. In some ways, things had gotten better for him, but he had agreed with his father that they had needed to move. He'd had Bill and

Todd, and even Albert Campbell come and visit him over the past year. And he whispered to me to forget about all of that homo stuff he'd said in the past, because he'd changed his mind. He had a big crush on a girl in his class.

Every now and then, he would swim up to me and hug me tightly, as if he was afraid I'd leave again.

Not this time, babe.

Bryson's hands were on me quite a bit too, but always in non-threatening places – my arms, waist, and face. He kissed me often and stood behind me with his arms wrapped round me, and his chin on my shoulder.

I loved that.

I hadn't answered his proposal, but I knew I'd marry him. I figured I'd tell him later, after Dean was asleep, and when I was finally tired of holding back my absolute glee.

About the Author:
D.S. Kirchen lives in Los Angeles, California, and gets inspiration for her stories from life's many ironies and lessons.

www.ingramcontent.com/pod-product-compliance
Lightning Source LLC
Chambersburg PA
CBHW020613310726
48979CB00008B/1463/J

* 9 7 8 0 5 7 8 0 8 6 3 8 5 *